The Frayer

Also by Patricia Watts:

Watchdogs

The Frayer

A Novel

by

Patricia Watts

Golden Antelope Press
715 E. McPherson
Kirksville, Missouri 63501
2017

ISBN   978-1-936135-46-2 (1-936135-46-9)

Library of Congress Control Number: 2017963450

Published by:
Golden Antelope Press
715 E. McPherson
Kirksville, Missouri 63501

Available at:
Golden Antelope Press
715 E. McPherson
Kirksville, Missouri, 63501
Phone: (660) 665-0273
http://www.goldenantelope.com
Email: ndelmoni@gmail.com

Acknowledgements

I am grateful to my fellow Alaska writers of the Spenard Literary Society, formerly known as the Chugach Writers Group, who read the first drafts of *The Frayer*. Without your generous praise and criticism, encouragement and skepticism, a crazy idea would not have become a finished novel.

To the peculiar-ugly-beautiful buildings of downtown Fairbanks, I thank you for your inspiration.

Before

Big Blue. That's what folks have called me since the old-timers were sprouts.

I've stood on First Avenue and Noble Street in Fairbanks, Alaska, for more than sixty years. Despite the occasional scrubbing or repainting, I've stayed dark blue with mustard-gold window frames that show up nicely in tourist photos. I'm not as popular as the Masonic Temple or the railroad depot. You can find me listed under "other points of interest" in the brochures at the Visitors Center cabin, two pages over from the historic sites on the downtown walking tour.

History has stomped down the hallways outside my sixty rooms. In the fifties, affluent adventurers checked in and out. Whores and rowdies traded sex, money, and blows in the seventies. In the nineties, apartment dwellers unpacked to stay.

By 2013, I thought I had seen it, heard it, and felt it all pass through my twelve stories. But that summer something rotten sneaked in. I watched it drive up in that fancy car and walk right through my front entrance, leaving its sticky markings on the door handle, and glide down the hallway on a current of smoky music. It acknowledged me with a sly smile and a crooked eyebrow.

He called himself Angelo Fallon, but no one could figure out exactly what he was. The smooth skin on his face and neck belonged to a man in his thirties, but there was a dark knowledge

1

in his look that came from a much older person. He had the full lips and bronze skin of a black man, the gray-blue eyes and red-gold hair of a white man, the prominent cheekbones of a Native American.

He was a handsome—dare I say—devil, because he wasn't exactly that either. Angelo was like a rich dessert you knew would make you miserably ill, but you couldn't resist letting it slide over your lips and tongue, relishing every delicious morsel even while your intestines started to twist.

When he moved into 706 to take care of the affairs of the late tenant, his great-aunt, the other residents were almost glad Liza Beechwood had passed peacefully away at the age of eighty-eight and left him the plot of land that made up the rest of my block.

June twenty-first, a week later, I felt the first change. Everyone was looking forward to the annual rooftop party on the longest day of the year.

Corrine Easter, my owner and landlady, was pulling trays of seasoned mushrooms out of an oven and slicing fresh limes for drinks. Lonnie Jackson was carrying his keyboard in the elevator up to the party site. Jasmina Jones was slithering into a red, chiffon, belly-dancing costume for part of the evening's entertainment.

On the roof, above the bugs, where gulls nested and cool air drifted, a crowd of fifty tenants and friends gathered. Words and laughter overlapped, creating an expectant buzz. Anything could happen on such an excessive day without night.

I felt a shudder along the top of the front door's frame. It moved upward, making a weak, scratching sound, through the floors and ceilings until it exited through a hairline crack in the concrete edge around the roof.

Sure, I could have warned Corrine and the others that something terrible had invaded our world, but I couldn't say what or why. Besides, that feverish solstice was not a day of caution, and they wouldn't have listened to me, if walls could talk.

Chapter One

Corrine, in an airy, periwinkle dress that matched her eyes and flowed to her ankles, wove among her guests, drink in hand. With her long legs and short torso she carried herself like a tall woman, although she was barely five-five. At fifty-nine, her shoulder-length tresses were platinum without a hint of the brunette she had been when she first came into my life.

When her gambler husband died in '89, so did the prostitution and other shady businesses he secretly ran out of my rooms. It was Corrine's brilliant idea to convert me from a hotel-turned-flop house to an apartment building. She restored my respectability as well as my walls, walls that had been contaminated by thievery and the musty smells of low-price sex.

"Did you try the fish tacos? How about the mushrooms? You need a refill on that gin and tonic? How about a mimosa?" she sang out across the rooftop, insistent that all the partiers sample the food and atmosphere she had lovingly prepared.

The day was a scorcher by Fairbanks standards—eighty-six degrees at nine p.m., the hottest solstice on record. The locals were dazed and euphoric with the heat, sweltering in shock after a bone-chilling winter that had hung on until late May.

Downtown, canoeists and rafters drifted down the Chena River as young women, holding their hair above their damp necks, watched enviously from the Cushman Street Bridge, contemplating jumping from the railing into the cool water, even the ones who couldn't swim.

From Riverview to Hamilton Acres the smell of charred pork and beef and reindeer sausage drifted up from backyard grills as cooks abandoned stifling kitchens. At the south-side strip clubs, dancers rubbed their bodies down with ice and lingered in the open back doorways during their smoke breaks.

Behind restaurants, ravens mobbed dumpsters, attacking the steamy, ripe garbage. Hordes of mosquitoes assaulted exposed human flesh and tender canine noses with impunity, as though they knew there was no protection to be found on store shelves emptied of repellant.

Corrine moved to where Jasmina stood in her flimsy, sequined, belly-dance costume, a simulated ruby in her navel. The Turkish beauty and owner of Istanbul Coffee sometimes taught dance classes in a room off her first-floor shop. Six years ago, she had transformed the space which had once housed the seedy Petey's Card Room and a string of fly-by-night businesses.

"Jasmina, you look gorgeous in that outfit," Corrine said. "Do you have your CD set up? Did Brad come with you?"

"We broke up last week," Jasmina said into Corrine's ear over the noise of the partiers.

"But I thought things were getting serious."

"Exactly. Who needs serious? I'm too young for that."

"Well, when you start hearing that biological clock ticking ...."

"Okay, 'Mom.' But I'm too busy having fun and trying to make my first million," Jasmina said with a musical laugh as she twirled around with her arms above her head. "And that guy with the saxophone, he looks like a million."

Jasmina looked past Corrine to the handsome newcomer in a white linen suit who stood tall above the crowd on the other side of the roof. Angelo's Panama hat was cocked toward his left ear which was adorned with a black pearl stud. At that moment, he caught her gaze, cracked a smile, and the dimples at each side of his mouth deepened. He slid his hand along the bend of his horn, the way a man would stroke the curve of a woman's neck.

Jasmina's thighs quivered beneath the red chiffon.

"We're looking forward to your dance," Corrine said to Jasmina, and turned to walk back through the crowd, not realizing her friend wasn't listening.

More than just fun, Jasmina thought. A blue spark glowed in Angelo's eye as he and Jasmina stared at each other. The spark jumped out onto a soft ribbon of air traveling above the crowd directly toward her.

She stood transfixed with that same lingering, moist-mouth look that all the women in the building—and some of the men, too—threw Angelo's way. That look said they were ready to give up what was between their legs if he were to express an interest.

Corrine changed her zig zag direction and broke free of the crowd. As she crossed the open space at the center of the roof, she unwittingly interrupted the path of the blue spark, which landed behind her left ear and stuck.

"Hey, Lonnie, didn't you promise some live music? Didn't I hear that you tickled some ivories sometime in the past sixty-five years?" Corrine yelled to her longtime friend who stood near Angelo.

Lonnie rarely indulged in his music. Lately, he indulged more often in the sight of summer's bare-chested, young men who stocked up on beer from his store. Lonnie had started out as a seventeen-year-old stock boy at Big Dipper Liquor on my street level back in 1965. He had taken over as owner ten years later, back when there were no other black business owners downtown.

"Me and my man Angelo about to get it started," Lonnie called back. Dressed in a Hawaiian shirt and baggy pants, he plugged in the keyboard that stood on collapsible legs. Black, horn-rimmed glasses dominated his dark brown face. His wiry, salt-and-pepper hair was cropped within a half-inch of his scalp. As he positioned his stocky frame in front of the instrument, he wiggled his fingers and rolled his neck like a boxer getting ready to enter the ring.

The spot above Corrine's left ear burned. Angelo licked his lips and wet the reed of his saxophone. Corrine kicked off her sandals.

She threw back her head and laughed for no particular reason.

Lonnie signaled Angelo with an upraised finger and shouted, "You know what we got to do, man!"

"Let's do it!" Angelo shouted back.

Lonnie picked out the first notes of "Up on the Roof." Angelo followed with a stream of sweetness from his sax. Then the two musicians joined sounds, lighting a fuse that started the crowd hopping and swaying.

The saxophone's melody pulled Corrine forward through the sultry air to the center of the roof as she floated on the current of the rum buzz in her head. She started dancing in slow, sensuous gyrations, like the music had flipped an internal switch.

I had seen Corrine two-step a couple of times and sway to and fro while she cooked and an Aretha Franklin song played in the background. Her many skills included baking coconut cake and replacing light fixtures and shower heads, taking care of her tenants and me, but not dancing like Salome.

As Corrine moved, the appreciative and curious crowd parted to give her the stage. She danced as though possessed, her lithe figure, toned by her fierce dedication to power yoga, turned and dipped, while sweat streamed down her face and throat.

Jasmina warily watched Corrine, fascinated and frightened that her friend was not acting like her maternal, down-to-earth self. I could see annoyance simmer in her thoughts, too. Corrine's dance performance was delaying hers, and Jasmina was used to being the one who turned heads.

The coffee shop owner was a small-framed woman in her twenties with large breasts that, combined with her glossy mane of black hair and olive skin, made her look exotic. Men felt heat radiate off her as she passed without being able to identify the sudden sensation. She never wore perfume, yet every part of her smelled good. Out of her sensuous, red mouth flowed the insincere words of affection that young men took as true, and sometimes the raw language of a North Slope oilfield worker.

Lonnie's head bobbed with the music, and rivulets of sweat

glistened on the sides of his dark face. Angelo blew notes higher and smoother and longer, and each one infused him with more musical passion. He moved around Lonnie in wider and wider arcs as Lonnie's hands became part of his keyboard. I tried to discover what the sax-playing showman was up to, but I saw only something dark and slithering in his thoughts.

Corrine danced and followed Angelo with her eyes as he elevated himself in one swift motion to plant his feet on the concrete lip that ran around the rooftop. The crowd gasped. Corrine moved toward the roof edge where Angelo squatted, facing her. He weaved his instrument back and forth like a snake charmer with a pipe, drawing Corrine to him like a mesmerized cobra.

When Corrine slid ungracefully up on the edge beside Angelo, Jasmina held her breath. Corrine stood up unsteadily on the border of the roof that was only a foot and a half wide. It was clear to at least Jasmina and me that the older woman was tipsy from the sips of drinks she had taken while she played hostess. Most of the crowd tittered as they watched Corrine, but I, like Jasmina, saw her behavior as more risky than funny twelve stories up from the street.

Angelo stood up and swiveled his hips as he played while Corrine swayed in front of him with the sax in between them like a shiny, brass phallus. With Lonnie's accompaniment in the background, the smooth melody repeated and the notes unfurled, thick and silky. Corrine lost her balance for a second and teetered with one foot over my outside edge. Jasmina bit her lower lip, and I could feel her heart pound. The crowd hooted and clapped at the spectacle. I isolated the vibrations of music rippling across the rooftop so that the concrete quaked slightly under Jasmina's feet to urge her to action.

"Stop the goddamn music!" Jasmina shouted at Lonnie as she waved at him frantically, trying to get Corrine out of Angelo's spell and back on solid ground. Lonnie gazed up at Jasmina from the keyboard with an oblivious smile, like he was in the middle of sex with the partner of his dreams. I wished I could shut off the power and that keyboard, the way I used to in the seventies when an unsavory guest needed some urging to move out. Since Corrine had the wiring updated, that wasn't so easy. Anyway, when Lonnie was into his music, it was like he had his own power source.

Jasmina rushed to the roof edge, intent on grabbing one of Corrine's swaying arms to pull her down. As her young Turkish tenant reached out, Corrine wobbled, tried to reposition her bare feet against the cement curb—and her front foot caught in the hem of her dress. Jasmina's fingertips were sweaty with fear. She stepped forward to grab Corrine's legs, but stepped back again, afraid that she would knock her friend backward into open space.

Corrine braced her back heel against the hard surface to free her other foot. A chunk of concrete gave way. It plummeted, unseen by Corrine or the other solstice partiers, headed for the sidewalk a hundred feet below. Harper Fornette, the mayor's son, staggered down the byway after an earlier than usual visit to the Mecca Bar. The masonry missile hurtled into the back of his skull and split it open like a ripe honeydew. I didn't waste more than a moment of attention on the disaster that was always waiting to happen to the young Fornette, but the brief distraction erased any chance for me to stop what happened next.

Throwing herself forward as a counterbalance, Corrine tumbled sideways and down. Jasmina was unable to break her fall as Corrine knocked her aside with a flailing elbow. The older woman fell awkwardly onto the roof, twisted her left leg under her, and snapped the bone just below the knee. A shriek of pain tore out of her throat and bounced off the helpless inside walls of the roof edge.

In the crowd, Corrine's scream startled Mrs. Graystone of 302 and she whirled around, martini in hand, striking Billy Johnson of 203 in the face. Her glass opened a gash across his cheekbone.

As Billy's hand flew up to his injured face, he stepped back and knocked over Miss Lily of 601, who was precariously propped on her cane. The cane fell with the elderly woman, almost tripping upstairs neighbor Cal Taylor. Cal sidestepped the crutch, but in doing so, elbowed Misty Hernandez in the side and caused her to cry out.

Misty's husband, Roland, who was well intoxicated, defended his pregnant wife by charging Cal. He rammed his head into the other man's chest. Cal punched Roland back, and the fight was on.

Others around the two brawling men jostled and yelled and tried to pull them apart. A police car's siren wailed up from the street as it advanced toward the spot where the battered body of Harper Fornette lay on the bloodied pavement. The commotion carried through Minnie Goddard's open window on the tenth floor and jerked her out of her sleep, and sent her fragile heart flip-flopping before it stopped beating.

The fight broke up and the agitated crowd drew into a circle toward Corrine. Angelo urged the spent revelers back and toward the downstairs exit to make way for the ambulance crew that had been called for Corrine.

The midnight sun gleamed off Angelo's sax, still strapped to a wide leather band across his shoulder and chest. He stood aside, like a director looking over a scene that he had set. I tried to read his purpose, but inside his mind an ominous wall of black water rose and forced me back outside.

Lonnie bent over Corrine and cradled her head in his lap. Jasmina held her fingers against the older woman's wrist, afraid to break the connection to a pulse. Corrine stared, dazed, up at the sky from the empty gray square of roof. They huddled together, but we were already falling apart.

Chapter Two

Lonnie's Jeep crept behind the procession that carried Harper Fornette's body from the Chapel of Chimes funeral home to the church on Airport Way a few days later as he drove Corrine home from the hospital. Jasmina kept him company in the front seat.

"You don't know how lucky you are until you see someone worse off than you," Corrine said from her half-prone position in the back seat. "I'll be up and around in no time, but the Fornettes will never get their child back."

"As long as you don't push your luck," Lonnie responded, glancing at Corrine's image in the rear-view mirror and veering off from the line of black cars. He continued to my parking lot and pulled in next to Angelo's baby-blue Cadillac with the Louisiana plates. Ripples of heat rose off the Caddy's hood from the recently running engine.

"Remember what the doctor said," Lonnie warned. "You'll be in that cast for six weeks. You need to take your painkillers when necessary and chill out on the couch like a lady of leisure for a while. No cooking, no cleaning, no running around trying to take care of other people's problems."

"We'll see," Corrine said.

"I'm serious. You know I leave on my fishing trip tomorrow, and I won't be here to keep you out of trouble."

"I hear you, Lonnie," she said. But when she leaned against him as they walked into the elevator while Jasmina followed with her overnight bag, she looked up at the dim light overhead. She planned to replace the light bulb later that day. On the way up to her penthouse she visualized the Little Mermaid birthday cake she had promised to decorate the next day for the little girl in 202. As Jasmina helped situate her on a melon-green couch, her leg propped on a plump, lavender pillow with magazines and a pitcher of cold water within reach, she plotted to satisfy an urge for homemade spaghetti.

As soon as Lonnie and Jasmina were out the door, Corrine hopped up from an invalid's pose. Balanced on crutches, she hobbled to the kitchen. With a series of hops from side to side and with the use of one hand, an elbow, and the crook of her arm as a carrying device, she managed to line up on the counter the ingredients for a meatless pasta sauce.

With slow, deliberate movements she operated the can opener and handled the chef's knife. Then, as she smiled to herself, rather proud of her awkwardly achieved success with dinner, pain shot up her leg. Determined to ignore it, she scooped up chopped vegetables and transferred them into a pool of butter that sizzled in a skillet on the stove. Waves of nausea and dizziness hit her.

She teetered on the crutches and knocked the skillet and its contents to the floor. As she jumped back to avoid the flying droplets of hot butter, she fell backward against the counter, reached out a hand to catch herself, and swiped the cans of tomato sauce and whole tomatoes. Red juices splashed across her feet and onto the tile floor. Cleanup was impossible. She couldn't safely bend to the floor with a wet cloth, nor competently move a broom or mop. Tomato pulp squished between her toes.

She gimped back to the center of the living room and lowered herself onto the plush white carpet. Her head hung down between her outstretched legs, one whole and normal, the other a burdensome weight sheathed in plaster. A watery red spot spread under the toes at the end of her casted leg. She was on the verge of tears.

I usually didn't search through Corrine's thoughts. Her feelings were as pure and simple as clean, white curtains floating on a breeze through one of my windows. I've always known what to expect from Corrine, except for that dance on the roof, except for the lump of sobs that was rising in her throat.

"Oh, Blue," she lamented. "What was I thinking to get myself into this fix?"

I gently shook the chandelier above her, making the suspended glass birds tinkle a soft song.

"Thanks for the sympathy," she said as she drew her eyes upward, "although I'm not sure if what I really need is a good kick in the butt." I shook the glass birds with a little more vigor. "Yeah, right, that would hurt." She laughed while the tears wet her cheeks.

Her newly prescribed bottle of Percocet sat on a table nearby, but Corrine disdained prescription medication and even over-the-counter painkillers. When she had a double root canal a few years back, she blunted the pain with a couple of joints. She still had a small stash in her bedroom, but it seemed too much of an effort to lift herself and maneuver into another room. Besides, smoking weed made her incredibly hungry, and she had just failed at making a meal.

I waited for her to reach for the cell phone to call Lonnie or Jasmina. Lonnie would drop what he was doing and come running if Corrine ever asked him. Jasmina still had the self-centeredness of youth and beauty but when push came to shove, she would be there for Corrine, too.

But then the unlocked front door swung open and there stood Angelo, holding a couple of grocery bags, wearing ivory slacks, a white sweater, and a rakish smile, like a dark-skinned Gatsby. Corrine looked up as the air wafted from the open door. She took a deep breath and pushed herself back, embarrassed to be seen in such a defeated position.

"Angelo, I didn't expect to see you," she stammered.

"I sensed a damsel in distress," he said with a laugh as he stepped in. He set the bags on the shelf below the mirror that hung next to the door and reflected a framed poster of Lauren

Bacall and Humphrey Bogart on the adjoining wall.

"Distress? I wouldn't exactly say—"

"Aren't Lonnie and Jasmina here to help you?" he interrupted, looking around as though he expected both of them to walk out of another room.

"Oh, Lonnie's getting ready to go fishing, and Jasmina has a business to run."

"But at a time like this, when you're seriously injured—well, never mind them. I've come to the rescue." He strode toward her with purpose.

"Rescue? Well, I don't know that I—" Angelo bent down, then lifted her up effortlessly, and carried her to the couch even as she protested. "What are you—you don't need to—I could have gotten up myself." She pictured how that would have looked, her crawling to the couch and humiliatingly clawing her way up on the cushions and grimacing in pain while he watched. "You must think I'm an idiot," she said, avoiding his gaze.

"Now, why would I ever think that?"

"Dancing on the roof like that and acting—well, I don't know what got into me. I just all of a sudden felt like letting go." Her face reddened as she realized she was even more self-conscious while she recounted the fateful party scene. "I'm a responsible person," she declared with passion. "I take good care of my building and my tenants. Everybody can rely on me. They—"

"You keep things up very well here. I'm sure the tenants trust you completely to take care of all their needs. But, it was a party, after all. And I thought it was a perfectly wonderful dance," he said as he squatted down to level his eyes at her pained face, then said with a gentle smile, "Except for that part where you took a dive and tried to do the splits." They both burst into relieving laughter.

"That was a mess," she said, her voice relaxing. "And I've made quite a mess of things since. You should see what I did to the kitchen. No, wait, you shouldn't. Whatever you do, you'd best stay out of there."

"No way," he said. He stood up and walked toward the door to retrieve his bags. "That's exactly where I'm headed, to make you a batch of my famous seafood gumbo."

"You don't need to go to all that trouble." She planted her palms and tried to push herself up but retreated in pain. "I was thinking about maybe putting together a little sandwich later, so you—"

"So you want me to take my fresh shrimp and tender scallops and succulent king crab and carefully selected peppers and green onions and my hand-blended spices and go?" He drew out the words like a long-handled wooden spoon stirring a steamy, aromatic sauce.

"Seafood gumbo does sound good," she said as her stomach rumbled.

"And it looks like you could use some of Mama Tatum's Good-For-What-Ails-Ya Tea and Potion."

"Tea and potion?" Corrine shifted her hips to ease her discomfort.

"It's something I got from a little shop off an alley in the French Quarter. It'll take that pain right away." Angelo headed to the kitchen.

Corrine hurt too much to give any more warnings about the disorder that awaited him there. She shut her eyes and let her head fall against a cushion.

She was unaware of how much time had drifted by when a smell that was sweet and at the same time sour teased her nose and drew her eyelids open. A steaming cup of dark green liquid floated in front of her, offered between Angelo's large palms.

"Take it in sips," he said, "but don't set it down until it's all gone."

Corrine molded her hands around the warm cup and tasted the brew, which was not unpleasant, though the plant-based flavor was different from any she'd ever sampled. Within minutes the pain ebbed out of her body as the warmth of the exotic tea diffused inside her. The color returned to her pale cheeks and the dark crescents under her eyes lightened. Angelo perched on an olive-and-white, pinstriped ottoman across from her like a watchful guardian.

I had witnessed Corrine's fierce efforts at self-reliance from the time she came to Alaska. Piecing together her conversations with her late and much older husband, I knew she fled from the Lower 48 in the mid-1970s, on the run from death, but whose she never said, to work as a cook in a pipeline camp.

On a trip to town, she'd met Jack Easter. Even though Jack was a hot-cold gambler who didn't have the business sense God gave a monkey, he had lucked into owning me by the grace of his father's death. I lucked into knowing Corrine because she was looking for a man who could give her a home. Her insistence that Jack make her my co-owner was lucky for both of us.

As she finished the last sip of tea, I realized this was the first time she had allowed a man to give her any attention since Jack died, and, truth be told, he never gave her enough. She deserved better than the first man who provided a place for her to land for fifteen years. I'd seen it before, women who sell themselves short for a few crumbs dipped in honey.

"Don't you have better things to do than to fuss over me, Mr. Fallon?" she asked with the hint of clumsy flirtation, before she recovered and asked in a more serious tone, "Shouldn't you be taking care of Miss Liza's matters and the land you inherited? That's why you came up here."

"I've inventoried her belongings and I'm almost through all the financial and real property paperwork. The rest can wait while I take care of another wonderful lady," Angelo said as he slid the ottoman closer to Corrine. He reached out and brushed a stray strand of hair back from her cheek, letting his middle finger linger at her temple.

Her face flushed with the unexpected gesture and the memory of someone who had touched her hair and face in exactly that way a long time ago, before Jack.

She smiled uncomfortably and shifted attention to him. "Tell me about you and your Aunt Liza. Were you close?"

"When I was a boy," Angelo said as a pleasant memory filled his gray eyes, "my mama would often deposit me at Aunt Liza's house while she was out socializing. Mama had an unquenchable thirst for peach brandy and men. Daddy wasn't around much, couldn't be bothered with a child. Work was his priority. I was at Aunt Liza's sometimes for days.

"I wasn't a robust child, rather the opposite, probably the result of being raised by aunties and sisters and girl cousins. I spent a lot of time indoors at Aunt Liza's though she had some sizable acreage. She would read to me for hours on end: Dickens, Thackeray, the Brontes, Thomas Hardy. I was enthralled by those stories."

Angelo's pleasant expression hardened. "But when I was eleven she ran off to Alaska with some silver-tongued dreamer."

He was talking about Harold Beechwood, Miss Liza's late husband and the business partner of Ernest Easter, Jack's father. Though Ernest Easter had built and owned me in 1953, he and Harold, under the name Eastwood, had both owned the land under me and to the south, down to Third Avenue. In 1958, Harold reluctantly allowed Ernest to sell his half of the underlying land to the city, while Harold hung on to the land adjacent to my parking lot, and Ernest hung on to me. Corrine knew this odd history, too, from Jack. Her late spouse had complained, while puffing on an expensive cigar when he was flush with rare winnings, that his father got the short end of the land deal.

"Miss Liza lived her own dreams up here from the stories she told me," Corrine said as her face lit up with the same fervor she had seen in Miss Liza's when she recounted her adventures with Mr. Beechwood. "She and Harold climbed Denali, canoed the Yukon River, hunted for bear and moose, pulled salmon out of the Kenai and the Copper. They had a full life and, thanks to Eastwood, he left her comfortable. Did you stay in touch with her?"

With a sudden smile, Angelo nodded his head with enthusiasm. "After she was widowed, I talked to her on the phone at least once a week." His smile disappeared as quickly as it came. "We could've been together again if she had chosen to come back down south. She said she loved her friends and neighbors here. They were like family, she said." He banged his fist against the side of the ottoman.

"But you must have enjoyed talking with her from so far away," Corrine offered as she tried to lift his mood.

"Yes, of course." Angelo's smile returned. "It was like reliving the days I spent with her when I was a boy, only in reverse. *I* was reading to *her*. We started out with the classics, but then I discovered that she was thrilled by Agatha Christie. We had made it through all the novels and had started on the short stories when she died."

Corrine, relaxed and comfortable, enjoyed the smooth, drawn-out cadence of Angelo's voice. "Somewhere along the way you picked up the saxophone," she said.

"I have Aunt Liza, or at least her leaving, to thank for that. When she deserted me for Alaska, I wanted no more to do with women caregivers. I started hanging out with older guys, drinkers, musicians, gamblers. Since I wasn't good at cards, I figured I had to know how to play something to fit in. I picked up a saxophone at a pawn shop and taught myself," he said with no brag in his voice, which got the desired effect.

Corrine's eyes widened, she was impressed. Although people called her an artist when she baked bread or created a wedding cake, she didn't consider that real art. "Is that how you make your living, as a musician?" she asked.

"Sometimes. I'm also involved in the family business and that takes up a lot of my time. We're in demolition and reclamation," he said with a sly smile.

I went behind that smile and encountered the waves of a black, undulating curtain.

"Like urban renewal?" Corrine responded.

"Something like that. The business goes way back to my great-great-grandpappy's time. We've had our booms and busts, but there always seems to be a need."

"I know what you mean. I've certainly been through ups and downs with Big Blue."

"Well, my hat's off to you. I admire a woman with a brain for business."

She laughed with a hint of self-deprecation. "I don't do anything but collect rent and keep things working. You don't have to be a business genius to do that. If you want to know someone who's used her smarts and a lot of hard work to turn nothing and a dream to success, you should talk to Jasmina."

"Well, you are the lady in the penthouse with the emerald ring."

Corrine looked down at the precious jewel in a gold setting that circled her left ring finger above a newer, plain gold band that was almost invisible next to the brilliance of the other. "This ring is a treasure, given to me a long time ago." She concealed the ring with her other hand and hid a private smile with a turn of her head. "And my place, well, it's just the top floor of an old building."

"I'd say more like an heirloom."

I thought he referred to the ring, but Corrine took his comment a different way. "Not an official landmark but valuable to me."

"How much would you say this building is worth?" He slid the question into the conversation like butter along a hot ear of corn. "Four million?"

"Goodness, I don't know about that. The site would probably be worth more if it was torn down, God forbid, because of the value of the land under it."

"Or if you were to expand, if you had control of the adjacent lot, too."

"I guess so, but I've never been interested in expanding. I'm content with Big Blue. "

I let in a gust of air through a partially open back window, pushing it across the main room to let her know I appreciated her loyalty.

"How much would you say the land under this building is worth?" he went on.

"I have no idea. I'm not interested in buying it and the city has no reason to sell it. Big Blue isn't an investment to me. I saved Blue from my late husband's mistakes, and, it saved me. Blue gave me a home, a place to set down the past and pick up the future, just like it has for Lonnie and Jasmina and Miss Liza and so many more."

"Like who?"

"Cal Taylor. He got himself sober since he's been renting here. He used alcohol to dull all the aches and pains he had from his boxing career. Now, he teaches kids boxing at the Boys and Girls Club. Mrs. Graystone had tried taking her own life after Mr. Graystone passed away, but then she found a new friend, Billy Johnson, in the apartment below her. They play cards twice a week, go to wine tastings, and who knows what else. Misty and Roland Hernandez were kicked out of their last apartment for disturbing the other tenants with their fighting. Now they're having a baby, and the only complaint I get from their neighbors is that their lovemaking is too loud."

I sent a stronger gush of air Corrine's way, and she gently nodded her head.

"I should close that window. It's getting a bit drafty in here," Angelo complained.

"It feels good to me," she said with a smile.

"You're doing an excellent job keeping the place up," Angelo said. "It must be difficult sometimes. People don't always understand that the landlord-tenant relationship is about business. Somebody's always wanting a favor, an adjustment."

"I don't mind doing a favor here and there. For years, I've let homeless families stay in 202 until they could get back on their feet. A young, single woman is living there now with her two little kids. She's got an interview next week for a clerical job with the city. Good turns always pay off in one way or another eventually."

"No harm in long-term investments, but as a businesswoman I understand you have to be smart enough to make your immediate profits from your most reliable sources."

"My most reliable sources?"

"Like Lonnie."

"Lonnie has been around for a while."

"That's not exactly what I meant. Maybe he shouldn't have told me, but for some reason, people just have an easy time talking to me about sensitive matters."

"What sensitive matters?"

"You know, like I said, maybe he shouldn't have told me. I don't want to start any trouble. But, he seems to be a little—how do I put this—bitter that the rent for his store is twice what Jasmina pays even though the space is the same size."

Corrine's eyebrows lifted. "Lonnie's rent is lower and it's been the same for more than fifteen years. He's getting a deal on his apartment, too. You must have misunderstood him. A lemon wouldn't come out of Lonnie's mouth bitter."

"I think he used the word 'gouging,' but perhaps, like you say, I misunderstood."

The air was suddenly swimming with the aroma of Cajun spices and fresh seafood. Angelo stood up and inhaled deeply. "Ah, I think that our meal is ready."

Corrine pushed herself forward and prepared to stand up, as if she expected to be propelled by the delicious smells from the kitchen.

"Don't you get up," Angelo commanded. "Allow me the privilege of serving you with the finest gumbo on either side of the Mississippi."

Moments later he returned with two bowls that brimmed with a concoction of seafood in a thick, red broth poured over a bed of rice. Corrine relished Angelo's creation, punctuating each mouthful with a moan of appreciation as he chuckled softly and dug into his generous portion.

I tried to conjure up the conversation Angelo said he had with

Lonnie about his rent, but Angelo was always talking with someone or absorbing their words, and I hadn't always paid attention.

When Corrine finished eating, she exhaled a satisfied sigh. "My stars, I can't remember the last time someone took care of me instead of the other way around. We hardly know each other and you've gone to all this trouble. I'm really going to have to pay you back with a special dinner when I get back on my feet."

"You don't owe me a thing, darlin'." Angelo took Corrine's empty bowl from her lap and stacked it inside his. "And I'm not done yet," he said with a wink as he proceeded to the kitchen. When he returned he carried a footed sherbet glass filled with something fluffy and cream colored.

"Homemade, bourbon and praline ice cream, my dear," he said, presenting it with a bow.

"I've died and gone to heaven," she said with a breathy sigh. She took the chilly glass from Angelo as he extracted the spoon and held onto it. "How am I supposed to eat without a spoon?" she protested.

"I'm going to show you the best way to eat this." He sat down beside her, took the spoon, and scooped up a generous amount of the ice cream from her dish. "Open," he said. She hesitated for a second, then self-consciously separated her lips so that he could slip the spoon between them. The creamy dessert rich with the flavors of liquor and buttery sugar and nuts filled her mouth.

He didn't have to coax her to open her mouth for the second bite. She hungrily awaited the next spoonful. He let the spoon linger on her tongue and she licked it, at first gently, then with more vigor, brushing his finger wrapped around the spoon with the tip of her tongue.

After a couple of more bites of ice cream she grabbed the spoon and licked it like a lollipop, then his fingers, too, massaging them with her tongue as he traced her lips with his thumb. I could feel the pleasure course through her.

Her head felt like it was filled with air, like she could float upward off the couch. She watched the room undulate with waves of yellow light and she dropped her hands to her sides, unable to hold her arms up any longer.

"All of a sudden, I feel so sleepy," she said breathlessly, unable to keep her eyelids open.

"That's the second effect of Mama Tatum's tea," she heard Angelo's voice say from far away. "You'll be out in about twenty seconds and you'll sleep like a baby until morning."

Corrine's body went limp, her cheek rested against the arm of the couch. Her mouth relaxed into the hint of a smile. A pale glow of evening light reached through the window and caressed her face.

"Sweet dreams, sugar," he said, pleased with his handiwork.

I knew she was dreaming about him, and he knew it, too.

Chapter Three

A BLM firefighter picked up two dozen Yummy Good doughnuts from Jasmina, who greeted him at Istanbul Coffee's front counter. "I have something else for you," she said with a teasing smile. She held up her hand and unfurled a silver chain and medallion that swung like a pendulum. "I found it under my bed this morning."

"My St. Christopher medal," the firefighter said as he grabbed it out of her hand. "Thanks, sweetheart. I might need this today." He tucked the pastry boxes under his arm and went out to join his buddies waiting in a truck. The doughnut run was a brief, morning stopover before the crew headed out to tackle two fires, one northeast and one northwest of town, a fierce start to fire season helped along by the persistent hot, dry weather.

The twin fires had already gobbled up hundreds of acres of spruce, birch, aspen, and cottonwood and threatened to converge into one super-sized blaze. Trails of smoke stretched out from the ominous cloud that hovered over Chena Hot Springs Road to the north and hung in the air over the city, irritating nostrils, burning eyes, and turning the sun a bloody red-orange.

All of the coffee shop's saffron-colored chairs and tables covered in purple paisley were occupied. Some of the crowd sought respite from the smoky air while tenants and other locals didn't want to miss out on the shipment of special doughnuts from the Lower 48 that Jasmina received on the first Friday of every month.

Jasmina delivered an order to Dora and Millie, two women in their seventies who were her neighbors on the fourth floor, and she heard a fragment of their conversation.

"Don't you think he's just the sexiest thing?" Dora said in a mischievous half-whisper.

"He's all that and a bag of chips," Millie answered with a giggle.

Jasmina continued to eavesdrop on her neighbors as she took orders from nearby tables. "I've heard he's moved in with Corrine," Dora said.

"You don't say," Millie answered, "I've been trying to get in touch with Corrine for days. There are some cracks along one of my bedroom walls that need to be fixed. Maybe from the earthquake we had in May? But I just noticed them."

"How strange. Some cracks in my bathroom floor just appeared overnight. I was going up to let Corrine know when I passed you-know-who in the hall." Dora leaned toward Millie like she was about to divulge a juicy secret. "He winked at me."

"Winked at you?" Millie clucked her tongue against the back of her teeth. "Are you sure you weren't imagining things?"

"Well, tell you what, I'll be imagining some things with my vibrator tonight." Both women tittered, then put their hands to their mouths like self-conscious school girls as Angelo walked in.

Jasmina, with her curvaceous body poured into a black dress, glided up to the table where Angelo took a seat with his back against the wall and took his order for a cup of dark roast.

Until now, Angelo had been a regular at Junie's Diner on Cushman Street. He walked down there or parked his Caddy most mornings, likely rubbing shoulders with Alaska Railroad retirees, old-time miners, and Mayor Henry Fornette.

"Anything else?" Jasmina purred as she ran the tip of her tongue along her upper lip. When I looked into Jasmina's mind it was like a walk through the smoldering remains of a forest where at any moment a hot spot might flare up.

Angelo's eyes traveled leisurely up her body. She waited for his pupils to dilate into lustful, black saucers. Instead, he looked coolly over her shoulder at Dora and Millie and others in the room who looked his way and luxuriantly inhaled a roomful of desire.

"Just some of your coffee I've heard so much about," he said as he flung her a casual glance. "I don't like to leave Corrine alone for too long." He leaned back in the chair, laced his fingers behind his head, and brushed his knuckles against the pale gold wall.

When Jasmina delivered the steaming cup to Angelo, sparks of desire prickled along her tawny skin. She conjured up the image of Angelo balancing on the ledge and playing his sax, but she was the one dancing in front of him, not Corrine.

"You don't need to worry about Corrine," Jasmina said. "Nothing gets her down for long. She won't put up with people making a big deal over her."

"Oh, I don't see helping out a friend as a big deal."

"Well, it's nice of you to set aside your business to spend a little bit of time with her. I've been meaning to check on her myself. She doesn't answer her phone."

"I'm sure she would like to know you're thinking about her."

"Of course, I'm thinking about her," Jasmina said, annoyed at Angelo's familiar tone when he talked about her friend of six years. But steamy thoughts of Angelo soon pushed the irritability out of her mind.

A flurry of customer demands interrupted Jasmina's erotic daydreams as she passed through the crowded shop. "Can we get our check, dear?" Millie called out.

"Certainly."

"Have you seen Corrine, dear?" Dora asked. "We have some repairs—"

"I'll tell her if I see her." She caught the eye of a broad-shouldered gentleman with thick, silver hair and a handlebar mustache seated across the room. "Your espresso is coming right up," she called to him.

"I can't get a hold of Corrine either," said another fourth-floor tenant who tapped his hand against Jasmina's wrist as she walked by.

"Okay, Okay."

"Can you tell her my kitchen faucet—" the tenant continued before Jasmina cut him off.

"If I see her."

"Do you know why she isn't answering my calls? It's not like Corrine to—"

"No, I don't. No, it's not. I have something to take care of in the kitchen."

It wasn't like Corrine. Our landlady always gave immediate attention to any of my parts that needed repair. She was adept with a plumber's wrench, a hammer, and most power tools. The only thing she couldn't or wouldn't operate was a car.

Breathing heavily, Jasmina escaped to the kitchen. She leaned against the butcher block table in the center of the room, pulled up her dress, and vigorously stroked her sex as she imagined licking the icing from a strawberry-raspberry Yummy Good off Angelo's erect shaft. As Jasmina's pleasure peaked, she curled her tongue around a sugar cube she had popped in her mouth so that she wouldn't cry out and give herself away to the shop full of customers.

When Jasmina walked back into the shop, Angelo was gone. She retrieved his crisp five-dollar bill from the table, pressed her crotch against the edge of the back of a chair, faced the wall, and held herself there. I thought she was bringing herself off again, until I realized she was studying the wall that was recently Angelo's backdrop.

A pencil-line, vertical crack ran three feet through the gold paint, marring the palatial ambience of the room. Was it possible that the crack wasn't there just a few minutes ago? Probably I just hadn't noticed it until it caught Jasmina's attention. After all, it was nothing more than a tiny zigzag of a scratch in the context of my twelve floors of surfaces and spaces.

Finally, Jasmina remembered to deliver the espresso to the silver-haired gentleman. "Did you save me a Yummy Good?" he asked with a wide grin, with no complaint about the delay in service.

"A chocolate cinnamon coming right up," she said with a sweet smile. "I'm beginning to think you fly up to Alaska just for those doughnuts."

"They always taste better with your coffee than they do down south where you can get them all the time. I hear CEO William Good has a cabin somewhere in Alaska where he visits during the summer. If he would just open one of his stores in Alaska, maybe I would never leave."

"Anthony, you're such a bull-shitter," Jasmina said with a wink.

A muscular woman in a tank top and running shorts, her hair braided into a long rope that hung over one shoulder, sat down at the table vacated by Angelo.

"Good morning, Jan," Jasmina greeted her. "How's the farmer's market going?"

"Good, if the fires don't get any worse," the woman answered. "We sure would've liked to see you out there this summer."

"I have the shop to take care of. Maybe next year. But, I'm planning to have a booth at the state fair. Your usual this morning?"

"Yep."

"Tall soy latte coming right up."

Before Jasmina turned to go back to the kitchen, she glanced at the fissure in the wall again. The flaw already looked longer and wider than it had at first sight.

Broken leg or not, Corrine will want to get that fixed, she thought. *She can't just close herself up in the penthouse for days and let Angelo take care of her. Has he really moved in with her? She would never allow herself to be pampered like that, would she?*

"She's always giving me advice about men. Now I'm going to give her some advice," Jasmina muttered to herself after she delivered the doughnut and the soy latte to her customers. She headed out of Istanbul Coffee into the hall between her shop and Big Dipper Liquor. In the elevator she pushed the button for the twelfth floor.

"I'm a coffee shop owner. She's the freakin' building manager. She should be taking care of things," she said to the numbers above her head as they lit up in progression. "Why can't everybody act like they're supposed to?" Anthony, cinnamon chocolate. Jan, soy latte. Flip the switch, the lights go on. Set the thermostat, the shop warms up. Push a button, the elevator goes up. Everything normal, right, Blue?

I made one of the elevator buttons flare in agreement.

Jasmina's thoughts leapt to a different level. Maybe Corrine was worse off than she thought. She should have checked on her friend sooner. Then Corrine wouldn't need to depend on someone who was practically a stranger. Oh, but such a good-looking stranger. Jasmina snapped her thoughts back before they rolled into another fantasy.

The elevator ended the trip to the top floor inside an alcove with a double door that opened directly into Corrine's spacious quarters. Jasmina didn't press the ornate brass button connected to the door chime. The door was already open a couple of inches. She cautiously pushed the door open wider and stepped over the threshold. She expected to see the fresh green and white and lavender landscape of Corrine's living room with its curvy couches, gauzy drapes, and gleaming fixtures, everything impeccably in place.

Jasmina froze. The snowy carpet was littered with wads of shed clothing and splayed-open books and magazines. Overturned glasses lay atop food-encrusted plates. A globe of black jade that doubled as a sculpture of Buddha and cigarette lighter had rolled partway under the couch. The Bacall-Bogart poster hung askew. A sheer black stocking was suspended from the chandelier's spirals of tiny glass birds. The acrid smell of marijuana and the heady scent of lavender invaded Jasmina's nasal passages.

Fearing that she'd entered the ransacked aftermath of a burglary, Jasmina's heart pounded and the roots of her hair prickled. She was about to call out to her friend when she heard loud, throaty moans coming from the bedroom. Jasmina recognized the woman's voice and the sounds as the unmistakable exclamations of passion. The purr of a male drawl responded to and encouraged the moans.

Jasmina stepped back out the doorway like she'd been slapped in the face. Corrine didn't need a friend to worry about her. She obviously had other things to do that took priority over fixing cracks in walls or answering phone calls.

But what had gotten into Corrine? Jasmina thought. She had never seen her friend with a man other than in a friendly conversation. And now this? With a man maybe half her age? And what was Angelo's game? He wasn't taking Jasmina's bait but he was getting it on with a woman old enough to be her mother?

She needed to talk to Lonnie. He had known Corrine for a lot longer. Maybe she had gone off the deep end before. Or maybe Angelo had her under a magical spell. Either way, Jasmina figured Corrine was bound to be hurt in a way that couldn't be mended with surgery and plaster.

She stepped back into the elevator and jabbed at the first-floor button with her fist. "Is this what Americans call a SNAFU?" I blinked the overhead light. "This situation is definitely all fucked up."

Chapter Four

Corrine let the last drop of tea, that magical brew that Angelo fixed for her every day, slide soothingly down her throat as she sat on the couch, her casted leg stretched out on the table in front of her. Angelo perched on the table facing her, with her pink, satin robe the only thing between him and her naked body.

"You know what I would really love right now?" she asked.

"What's that, sugar?" He leaned forward with anticipation.

"A real bath." Angelo drew back at the unexpected request. "I haven't had one since I've had this darn thing on." She slapped her palm against the side of her cast. "But how is a one-legged woman going to manage that?" she asked with a defeated sigh.

"I'll help you into the tub," Angelo suggested.

"But how? I'll have to take my clothes off."

"And would that be so terrible?"

"I know you've—we've explored each other with our hands, but we weren't, you know, naked."

"And that's not something you want?"

"I don't think I'm ready for that just yet, Angelo. It's been a while and I don't know if I can—"

"Don't know if you can what, sugar babe?"

"I just don't know if I can," she said, holding her arms close to her sides, paralyzed with discomfort and wishing she had never brought up the subject of a bath.

She had accepted that Jack hadn't looked at her naked body for

33

the last five years of their marriage, and that with his inattention she had grown increasingly embarrassed at the thought of him studying her aging form. Of course, if he had been the right kind of man, he would have made her feel beautiful no matter what skin she lived in.

After his death, as the years went by without any sexual encounter, Corrine had become more and more reluctant to face her unclothed image. The sexual part of life, she had decided, was over.

"The last thing in the world I want is to push you into something you're not ready for," Angelo responded, sitting down on the table and stroking her bare leg above the cast, where her robe and reluctance fell slightly aside.

"Now you're going to have that bath. It'll take some maneuvering, but I can be a perfect gentleman when the occasion calls for it. I'll run the water, then you come in, clothed of course, and I'll lower you in with your leg propped on the side of the tub. Then, while you sink in, I'll pull the robe away and leave the room. When you're ready to get out, call me, and I'll come running with a big, fluffy towel."

"But, how am I going to get out?"

"We'll cross that bridge when we come to it, darlin'."

Corrine started to slide toward the edge of the couch and Angelo offered his shoulder for her to lean on as she stood. "Perfect gentleman, right?" she asked with a wary glance up at him.

"Yes, ma'am."

She stood in the bathroom, clutching her robe closed at her chest, about to call out to Angelo to come in. The soothing aroma of lavender bath oils filled her head and floated through the penthouse into the elevator shaft, displacing the smoky smell on the top floors. She looked at the mirrored wall in front of her, hesitated, wondered. She slipped out of the robe, let it fall to the floor, and stared at her uninhibited reflection.

I was as surprised as she was, looking at the nude image in front of her. As she had avoided mirrors, I had avoided noticing the changes. Clearly, a twenty-five-year-old wasn't staring back at her, but her breasts were still firm, her waist trim, the belly that had never been stretched by pregnancy still nearly flat. Her hips rounded into her muscled thighs with only a little extra padding. Her knees were sagging a bit, the skin on her upper arms was creping, and the once-dark bush between her legs had become a sparse, silver triangle. Still, she was a good-looking woman even if "for her age" had to be added to the description.

Corrine's breath caught at the top of her throat as she spied Angelo behind her, taking in a front and rear view and smiling appreciatively. But she didn't hasten to pick her robe up off the floor. She just stood there. Without either saying a word, he lifted her up into his arms, then lowered her into the steamy, aromatic water.

As he placed a pillow under her leg propped on the side of the tub, a kaleidoscope of turning colors and patterns overtook the clear crystals of her mind. Her other leg was bent at the knee, her thighs spread apart. She closed her eyes with delicious anticipation of what would happen next. She felt the heat emanating from Angelo's body, felt his hands on either side of her neck as he knelt behind her on the tiled floor.

A stream of sunshine from the skylight, which I remember Corrine had to beg Jack to put in, turned her skin golden. Angelo's hands moved down to her bare breasts, giving each of her nipples equal attention. Those large, brown hands worked their way down to her belly and then in between her legs. She let her thighs go slack, prepared to enjoy those adept fingers stroking, stroking, stroking. She muffled her moans into his neck as he draped his head over her shoulder.

For a while she felt young again, until the water began to turn cold and she looked down at the wrinkles that suddenly seemed to stand out along her upper arms and cleavage. A mature voice of reason, tinged with embarrassment, nudged her. She heard the faint buzz of her cell phone from the living room.

"This is so irresponsible," she whispered to her caregiver-turned-lover.

"Me pleasing you?" Angelo asked while softly kissing her temple.

"Not that," she answered breathlessly. "I absolutely love every moment. But they keep calling me and I really should get that."

"Not now, darlin'. Just indulge."

The insistent phone buzzed again.

"While I've been indulging, I haven't been taking care of my building and the tenants. I've promised to fix some problems they're having, plus there's the usual maintenance."

"But, darlin', what could be more important than this?" he whispered in her ear, increasing the pressure of his fingers massaging her swollen clitoris.

"The windows," she forced the words out between gasps of pleasure. They've never stayed plastered with grit and grime for this long. I always hire Jimmy Gomez and his crew to clean the outside windows this time of year. I looked out at Golden Heart Park yesterday and could barely see the tourists posing with the First Family statue. There are things I have to do."

"But not right now." Angelo slipped two fingers inside Corrine's juicy opening.

"As ... soon ... as ... we're ... finished," Corrine gasped out, overcome with waves of passion. The kaleidoscope in her mind was silently exploding.

"I'll call Mr. Gomez tomorrow, baby doll, and take care of anything else that needs doing."

Corrine slid back against the side of the tub, pulling her torso upright. "No, today. Get me out of this tub. Please."

"Your wish is my command." He lifted her carefully out of the tub and wrapped her in a body-size towel while she clung to his shoulder and balanced on her uninjured leg. "But no business until you have one more cup of tea. I don't want you to get a chill."

She nodded and shivered as he carried her to the living room and deposited her gingerly on the green couch.

"I don't know what's in that stuff, but it works like a charm. I haven't slept so well in years," she said with a laugh as he turned up the thermostat. "Hand me my phone, please, so I can get you Jimmy's number."

He swiped the phone off a side table and held it tight to his chest like a prize he refused to share. "Tea first." He bent over her and kissed her forehead. "Are you comfortable? Do you need anything else?"

"I think you've done quite enough for me, if you know what I mean," she said as he turned to go to the kitchen.

"Anything for my Corey," he said as he gently touched her up-turned face.

Corrine bolted to a sitting position like Angelo had shocked her rather than caressed her cheek with his palm. "He called me that name, but you're not ... " She shook her head in confusion and licked a sweet memory off her lips. "Are you ... ?"

He sat down next to her, touched her face again, and then noticed her jaw tighten as she narrowed her eyes—as if she was studying his face for the first time. "Just a nickname that came to mind, sweetheart," he said, patting her hand. "We do that in the South. Where I'm from it would be natural for you to be Corey, maybe with another name attached, like Corey Ann, Corey Sue. Corey Mae?"

Her eyes widened like a frightened animal's. Inside Corrine's head was a series of filmy veils that hid something in a back room that I wasn't sure I wanted to discover. Angelo's invasion of privacy was even deeper than me watching the sex scene in the bathroom. It angered me that this stranger might have intimate knowledge about Corrine that I didn't possess.

"Where did you hear that name? Who told you about Corey Mae?"

"No one did, darlin'. I was just playing," he said, coating his tone with an extra layer of balm. "Aunt Liza had a nickname for me, too."

Corrine relaxed a little and hinted a smile. "She had nicknames for about everybody in the building. I suppose, like you said, old Southern habits. "

"That's right, sugar pie. Come to think of it, there were three names she had come up with for people in this building that she mentioned more than once to me."

"Oh, three?" Corrine looked mischievously amused.

"Yes. Sunny, Bear, and Lil' Bit." Angelo narrowed his eyes and Corrine didn't notice the absence of lightheartedness in his tone.

"She told you that?" Corrine covered her mouth and giggled. "Miss Liza called me Sunny because she said I always brightened her day. Bear was Lonnie. According to Miss Liza, he gave the best hugs ever, just like a big, old Teddy bear. Lil' Bit was what she called Jasmina. Miss Liza saw her as a sweet, little girl she wanted to take under her wing. Jasmina wasn't having it. She was determined to be recognized as a strong, independent woman. But, Miss Liza called all three of us her kids. She said she would rather have us as her family than what she called the 'whiny brats' she took care of when she was younger, whose own parents could hardly stand them."

Angelo's face flushed. His left ear lobe appeared to swell and throb around the black pearl stud. He squeezed the phone he still held and it made a cracking sound. "Whiny brats like me?" He threw the phone across the room and it bounced off the back of a chair, landing on the seat cushion.

Corrine jumped at his outburst. "Oh, no, no. She didn't mean you, Angelo. You and Miss Liza had a close relationship. You read—"

"Did she ever mention me or our close relationship?"

"Well, no, I mean, not that I recall, I—"

"Can you guess what her pet name was for me?" His face changed from thunder clouds to rainbows in a blink.

"Oh, it's got to be something sweet and very Southern. Sugar muffin? Honey drop?" She said with a mocking drawl as she giggled, nervously this time. "I don't have a clue."

"She called me Jello." Corrine threw him a puzzled look. "An-

Jello, get it? And because I could always wiggle my way out of any situation, she said." His face grew tense, his opalescent eyes almost watering. "Seriously, Corrine, you must know I'd never say or do anything to hurt you. You do believe that, don't you?"

Her eyes told how much she wanted to trust him. I made the pipes in the baseboard heating ping and gurgle to warn her or at least distract her. But to my disappointment, she said, "Yes, of course I do."

"Close your eyes and rest, dear. I'll get you that tea, and you can tell me all of the things you want me to take care of in this building."

I didn't like the way he spit the word "building" out like a bad taste, but Corrine didn't notice. She sank her head pleasantly onto the arm of the sofa.

As Angelo walked toward the kitchen I saw a shadow move across his face, although there was no light coming through the windows. I felt the cracks on my fourth floor spread wider, and a wet sensation two floors below that, following the direction of his footsteps.

Chapter Five

Lonnie danced across the floor of his liquor store. "Happy Feelin's in the air," he sang along with the tune by Frankie Beverly and Maze. He always had an extra spring in his step after he came back from his annual fishing trip. Every Fourth of July he closed up Big Dipper Liquor, packed his fishing gear and a cooler of beer into his Jeep, and headed east on the Richardson Highway toward Paxson Lake. A week later he returned full of vim and vigor with a smile on his face but never any fish.

Lonnie had the best music in the place. Miss Dickinson in 605 played Sinatra every now and then and Mr. Holbrook in 804 had a date with Etta James and a glass of Scotch every Sunday night, but you could never go wrong with Lonnie. He had jazz from the fifties, soul from the sixties, and funk from the seventies.

The music masked the dripping sounds toward the back of the store. I almost didn't hear them myself but was alerted by the accompanying pale stain that had slowly spread across the ceiling in the same area. It took me back to 1973 when a red puddle from the second floor under a lifeless body slashed by a knife had seeped through the same spot. Lonnie continued his hip sway, his ankle slide, a grin on his face as he restocked a shelf with Jack Daniels.

A three-foot chunk of ceiling crashed down, narrowly missing Lonnie's shoulder but dusting him with chalky debris and knocking half a dozen bottles to the floor. The Tennessee sipping whiskey spilled out in a pungent, amber puddle.

"Lonnie, what the hell?" Jasmina rushed into the store, a silver-nibbed pen in her hand, having heard the crash in the hall as she lettered a new store-hours sign on her shop door.

The liquor store owner was calmly picking up the debris. He glanced at Jasmina's worry-creased face and the ancient-style implement in her hand. "Brought a weapon with you just in case, huh?"

"Oh, this," she said looking at the pen. "I'm teaching myself calligraphy and I was practicing on a sign. Are you all right?"

"No harm done," he answered her. "At least it's not the Hennessey," he said with a chuckle. "Big Blue wouldn't let that happen, would you?" He glanced up at the ceiling.

The cognac was the only liquor I had ever seen Lonnie imbibe. So mellow, he said to himself with an inner smile when he took a sip, for a mellow fellow. Reading his thoughts was like taking a long, smooth drink, without ice or anything else with hard edges.

Every night after work he sat stripped down to his boxers in a deep leather chair, propped up his feet, raised his glass, and drank a toast to himself. The self-toast, I learned long ago, was the celebration of, in his words, "another day without doing anyone any harm."

That was his transition between his work day and his trivia hobby. He spent hours on his computer researching answers to things that had piqued his curiosity during the day. He knew lots of useless facts, like Steve McQueen was arrested for DUI in Anchorage in the seventies, and "Another Night with the Boys" was the flip side of "Up on the Roof."

"Can you grab that roll of paper towels from behind the register, sweetie?" he asked Jasmina as he moved some debris off a shelf. "I'll get the broom and dustpan from the back room."

As Lonnie gathered the larger chunks of glass and pieces of ceiling from the floor and dropped them into a tall, plastic trash can that he'd dragged to the damage site, Jasmina retrieved the paper towels and angrily mopped up the whiskey spill.

Lonnie studied the young woman's movements for a second.

"You having a bad day, honey?"

"It's this shit, Lonnie," she responded, gesturing at the mess on the floor. "Things are falling apart around here, and Corrine ... She's not acting right, I tell you. She's smoking weed and her place is a disaster area and—"

"You know Corrine. She doesn't mess with any drug-store painkillers, and a broken leg has to hurt," Lonnie interrupted, brushing off Jasmina's beginning rant with a dismissive wave.

"And she's fucking that guy from Louisiana. What the hell do you think of that?"

"Whoa, wait. Corrine has a boyfriend?"

"Oh, Lonnie," Jasmina said, rolling her eyes. "You're such a goddamn romantic. You're missing my point. What do we know about this guy? What if he's setting her up? Don't you see how bad this is?"

"Setting her up for what? Ain't nothin' bad about feelin' good," Lonnie responded. "Happy, happy, happy feelin', " he sang along with the next line of the music and dusted off his hands along with Jasmina's urgent tone. "Thanks for helping me clean up."

He pulled the trash can under the hole in the ceiling to catch the water that was still slowly dripping from above. "Is Corrine upstairs? I want to let her know about this leak, and we should get someone in here to check this out right away."

"Jesus Christ on a stick, Lonnie, that's what I've been trying to tell you." Jasmina balled up her fists and shook her head with exasperation. "Corrine is involved with that sweet-talking Southerner. She's not acting like Corrine. She's not paying attention to things like your ceiling falling down and my walls coming apart."

"Your walls? What's going on with your walls?"

"Big, ugly cracks."

"I'll take a look after I finish here. Maybe I can just slap on a little plaster and paint."

"Thanks, Lonnie. I guess that's better than nothing."

Marvin Gaye followed Frankie Beverly, and Lonnie's voice

joined in with a slower rhythm. " 'If the spirit moves you, let me groove you ...' Wow, how about that Corrine? You better watch out, Jasmina. She might steal some of your guys, too." Lonnie chuckled as Jasmina stomped out of the store, mumbling something about talking to a wall.

"Want something done, do it yourself," Jasmina muttered on her way up to the seventh floor and the former apartment of Liza Beechwood, Angelo's late great-aunt and his home base in Fairbanks.

As Jasmina stepped off the elevator she spied Angelo opening the door of 706. She was stopped in her mission by his sudden, unexpected presence, the bronze-sculpture angles of his profile, and the definition of his forearm that clutched a filled grocery bag. She leaned back against the elevator door.

She pictured herself calling to him down the hallway while she closed the distance between them. "Angelo! We have to talk right now," she said in her imagination, which took off at full speed.

Angelo turned nonchalantly with a lazy raise of his left eyebrow. "Oh, about what?" She detected his subtle, musky scent and the slight sheen of moisture on his lower lip. She gritted her teeth to help herself focus on the task at hand. "There are things going on in the building that Corrine has to take care of. You have to stop monopolizing all of her time."

"Why would I do that?" he asked. "We're becoming such good friends. She needs someone right now."

"You're more than friends," Jasmina said.

Angelo's face changed. His light eyes burned like dark coals. He paused and stared at her until she squirmed. "Do you wish I was fucking you?"

"Wh-what?" Her golden complexion flushed red.

"Every time I see you I get a massive hard-on. I think about running my hands over your ass, your breasts. I want to fuck you right now, right here."

"But you and Corrine—"

"Shut up. Back up against the wall. Lift up your dress." She followed his orders and revealed to him her body naked from the waist down, her thick, black pubic hair already damp.

"So this is how you came to confront me, with no panties on, a warrior princess, yet so vulnerable." Angelo smiled with obvious pleasure. "Put your arms above your head and spread your legs."

Again she obeyed his commands. He unzipped his pants, released his engorged penis, letting it slap between her legs before pushing it inside her with one aggressive motion. She let out a low, guttural moan, and her head rocked back against the wall.

While Angelo banged her buttocks against the wall, the door of the apartment next to what had been Miss Liza's place opened and an elderly female resident looked out. As the shock of the scene before her registered, she stammered, "Mr. Fallon, what's going on?"

Angelo glared at the woman and said, "Go back inside. Can't you see we're fucking?" Then his mouth curled into a mean sneer. "Unless you want to watch."

The woman retreated like a turtle into its shell with a gasp and a quick slam of her door.

Jasmina's orgasm built as a scream in her throat, but Angelo put his hand over her mouth to muffle the noise before it escaped as he released violently inside of her, then pulled back to let the warm, thick liquid run down the insides of her thighs.

As she struggled to control her breathing, he grasped both sides of her jaw hard between his fingers and thumb, making her eyes fly open to meet his. "Any time I want, understand?" She nodded.

Would that be the way it would happen? Jasmina thought as she shut her eyes, still leaning back against the elevator door.

Calling her mind back to why she came up to the seventh floor, Jasmina opened her mouth to call out to Angelo at the door of his aunt's apartment, but during her fantasy he had disappeared inside. She heard the faint notes of a saxophone and her mouth burned, thirsting for his.

Chapter Six

The penthouse windows were clean and clear again, although Corrine, not Angelo, had finally called Jimmy Gomez; but when Corrine looked out, her view of the town and the skies beyond was ruined by a smoky haze. "Fire forces Two Rivers families to flee," she read the headline from the top copy of a pile of newspapers that had collected outside her door during the last month.

She felt like an astronaut on the first day back on the home planet after an extended mission, catching up on what was going on outside the capsule of Angelo's care and attention. He had moved back to his late aunt's apartment. Sitting on her couch and reading, she learned that two candidates were opposing Henry Fornette for the October mayoral election. A Connecticut-based corporation was eyeing land around town to put up a new hotel. And a wildfire was advancing toward Fairbanks, forcing residents in an outlying community to evacuate their homes and scatter into school gyms and cheap motels in Fairbanks.

"We can do better for those people, Blue," Corrine announced. She grabbed her crutches and her cell phone and moved urgently out her front door to the elevator. She was thinking of a big, empty space that would accommodate at least twenty-five sleeping bags and air mattresses and several displaced families.

The ballroom, which ran the entire length of the eastern side of the ground floor, was the venue for lavish parties in the 1950s. Jeweled women in satin gowns and men in dapper suits floated across the oak floor while white-jacketed musicians with flowers in their lapels played the top dance tunes of the day. A giant gold North Star was painted in the center of the floor with its points reaching out to within three feet of the room's perimeter. The sunshine that flooded in through the floor-to-ceiling windows on the back wall had faded the gold-and-maroon wallpaper, but the room's centerpiece testified to opulence.

A chandelier descended from the center of the ceiling, spanning six feet across, suspended from a tripod of gold chains, with three tiers of light globes, sixty altogether, to set off the dazzling reflections of four hundred crystal teardrops. Half of the lights were burnt out and cobwebs and dust dulled the sparkle of the crystal, but the sight of the luxurious fixture could still inspire awe, just like when it was my crown jewel.

When Corrine ambled awkwardly into Istanbul Coffee, Jasmina looked up from her coffee-making machinery, surprised to see the older woman. Memories of her unnoticed foray into the penthouse and her lustful imaginings about Angelo made her uneasy under Corrine's gaze. Could the other woman read her thoughts?

Her friend's face looked different, like a younger version of Corrine. Jasmina dismissed that strange thought as a trick of memory since they hadn't seen each other in a while. "Corrine, I'm so glad you're up and around. I wanted to talk to you about a couple of things."

Corrine walked up to her friend and hugged her as hard as she could manage while balancing on crutches. "We can talk about that later. We've got a lot of work to do."

"Yes, my wall. Lonnie tried to fix it but it didn't stick, and the other apartments on my floor—"

"We've got to turn the ballroom into an evacuation center. I've already notified the TV stations that I'm offering the space. We need sleeping bags, lots of them. You know all those fellows at Big Ray's who pant over you? I'm sure they'll donate to the cause if you ask them. Just bat those beautiful Turkish eyelashes at them."

"Wait, Corrine, what are you talking about?"

"The fire is pushing people out of their homes. They'll need a place to stay for a few days. There's a TV with a rolling stand somewhere and a DVD player. I'll get Lonnie to track that down. And we'll get some movies for the kids. I'm sure there'll be kids. Mrs. Jefferson in 201, she's the one with the big movie collection for her grandchildren, right? I'll go talk to her."

"She's gone, Corrine. She moved out last week."

"What? Her lease isn't up for another three months and she's been here for years."

"The water damage. She said she couldn't put up with the mold. It was making her sick. She moved to her daughter's on Tenth Avenue."

"There's no mold problem in Big Blue. Mrs. Jefferson always makes a mountain out of a molehill."

"Actually, Corrine, it's not just Mrs. Jefferson." Jasmina gently grasped Corrine's arms, trying to get her to focus on what she was saying. "The Wilsons and Danny Maverick on the second floor have moved, too."

Corrine shook Jasmina's hands off. "What are you talking about? People are just leaving and not letting me know? Why didn't Lonnie say anything? He lives right down the hall from them."

"I guess you were kind of indisposed and since Angelo has been taking up so much of your time—"

"Angelo? Did he mention something to me about the tenants? The last few days are such a fog." She waved her hand as though the fog was right in front of her.

"Is Angelo living with you, Corrine?"

Corrine laughed nervously. "What? Well, he did stay over for a while, but he's living in Miss Liza's apartment as you very well know. How the gossip travels in this building. Next you'll have us engaged."

"But you are fu-, you are lovers. That's why we never see you anymore."

A sheen of perspiration spread across Corrine's brow and throat. She laughed again, a high-pitched unnatural tinkling. "Well, I guess I can't deny it. You're just too smart to keep any secrets from." A shaky chuckle escaped from her throat.

Jasmina frowned and Corrine felt obliged to explain her situation further. "It just sort of happened. Angelo was there when I needed someone because of my leg, and one thing led to another." Corrine shrugged her shoulders to emphasize the almost accidental nature of the turn of events.

Jasmina huffed and crossed her arms. "Well, if he hadn't gotten your leg broken in the first place ..."

"Oh, dear, you're upset. At Angelo? At me? Ah, I know what this is about. I'm sorry, Jasmina, we've been friends for years, and I've been neglecting you. You said you wanted to talk to me about a couple of things. What's on your mind?"

Jasmina took a breath and wondered if she could trust this younger-looking Corrine. "Maybe, with people leaving, you want to rethink giving me an extension on the August rent?"

"What? Oh, for that fair thing. You'll need to hire people to watch the shop, pay for the booth. That's not a problem. I said I would help you out."

"Thanks, Corrine. Now, about the repairs—"

"We'll catch up on that later. I absolutely promise, Jasmina. But these families need help now. Please ask about the sleeping bags, won't you, dear? I'm going to ask Lonnie for some help getting that room cleaned up."

Corrine planted her healthy leg, swung her crutches out in front of her, propelled herself through the coffee shop exit into the hallway, and headed for the liquor store on the other side. She saw the shiny, hair-thin spot on the back of Lonnie's head as he moved from side to side, interacting with a customer whose face was blocked from her view.

Before she reached the doorway's motion sensor that would "ding-ding" the presence of a visitor when she crossed the threshold, she ran into the wall of Angelo's body moving toward her from the side.

"What are you doing down here, darlin'?" he asked, his eyes wide in disbelief as he held her steady by gripping her upper arms. "I don't want you wandering around, getting dizzy and falling, and ending up back in the hospital."

Jasmina watched from just inside the doorway of her shop, her first sighting of the new lovers together.

"Angelo, I can't stay cooped up like an invalid. I'm well enough to manage on my own. I told you that you could move back to your aunt's apartment. There's work to be done. I've got to get the ballroom ready for guests."

"You're planning a ball? Gracious, sweetheart, are you running a fever?" Angelo placed a palm across Corrine's forehead. "I think I may have abandoned you too soon. I can easily move back in tonight." He bent toward her and nuzzled her ear. Jasmina rolled her eyes and walked back behind her counter.

Corrine burst into laughter that shook her balance, and she steadied herself against the glass case of the fire extinguisher protruding from a nearby wall. "Oh, silly," she sputtered. "Let me explain. And you're not keeping me from what needs to be done with any more of your chivalrous acts." She laid out her plan for the evacuees as Angelo listened with lukewarm interest, but Corrine was too inspired to notice his lack of support.

"I only wish you had talked to me first," he said with a gentle smile. "If you have a relapse, it'll take you that much longer to get strong and healthy again. And that would ruin our plans, if you know what I mean."

Corrine's thoughts raced ahead to when she would be out of her cast in three weeks, their plans to make love completely, instead of just him satisfying her with his skilled hands. Her plaster accessory had conveniently put off a rush to the big moment, but it was almost here. She imagined the warmness of flesh touching flesh, the tingles and burning like tiny eruptions.

When she looked in the mirror lately, she saw a rosy glow to her skin. She had developed a habit of tossing her hair, which seemed fuller and glossier than it had a few weeks ago. Her laugh was full of pleasure, like a response to dark chocolate melting on her tongue. But sensual feelings aside, what about the mechanics? Would she freeze, unable to remember what to do, or would it all come back automatically, like riding a bicycle, after being parked for twenty-five years?

Angelo leaned into her ear again and whispered, "I'm a patient man, but how about going upstairs for a sneak preview?"

"You're a caring man, too, so you'll understand that my priority right now is getting ready for these displaced people. You can help Lonnie sweep and mop the ballroom." Corrine walked around Angelo and into the liquor store. "Hey, Lonnie, I've got an important project for you."

Angelo clenched and unclenched his fists, apparently unconvinced of the important assignment of using a broom or mop.

***

The TV crews descended shortly after the eight families, including fourteen children, moved into the ballroom the next day. Cameras captured Jasmina in halter top and short shorts and two young men in T-shirts with bursting biceps laying out sleeping bags and double-sized air mattresses.

Reporters camped out overnight, one crew recording Angelo telling children stories of dark, dripping worlds populated with frogs and alligators and other slippery creatures that slithered around Louisiana swamps while Corrine assured the younger listeners that there were no snakes in Alaska. A TV crew from the rival station sent live feeds of Lonnie entertaining a hand-clapping, foot-tapping audience on his keyboard and harmonica and coaxing the roomful of temporary refugees into a rousing sing-a-long of "Puff the Magic Dragon."

In the morning, community news queen Hattie McGee from the *Daily News-Miner* and other print journalists gabbed with moms and dads, and photographers framed shots of Corrine carrying in pans of flaky biscuits, platters of crisp bacon, and pitchers of icy orange juice mixed with ginger ale. Jasmina served coffee and passed out toothbrushes and miniature toiletries donated by downtown hotels.

I hadn't received this much public attention since the gala days of the fifties. The media referred to me as "a grand oasis in the midst of disaster," and to Corrine as "the Florence Nightingale of Fairbanks." I graciously accepted the slight hyperbole. Maybe all the good press would even move me up in significance in the next Visitors Center brochure. Corrine was more humble, crediting a supportive community whenever a microphone or camera was aimed her way.

Jasmina happily watched Corrine bustling about, even on crutches back to her take-charge old self again, the love-struck girlishness faded from her face. The peeling wallpaper on the fifth-floor hallway, the loose light fixtures that yawned from the ceiling on the ninth floor, the damp carpets on the second, and the epidemic of cracks on every level seemed like minor inconveniences that would soon be resolved now that Corrine was back in control.

The news crews hung out for days, competing with each other to wring every human interest story from the physical and emotional mass surrounding them. Angelo fended off attempted interviews and stayed on the outer edges of the room perfecting something between sulking and plotting until the last night of the media presence. Just before lights out, he walked to the center of the room with his saxophone. All faces lifted toward him as he serenaded the crowd with haunting blues. The notes floated upward and crawled around loose and unmanageable inside the ceiling. The final sustained blast from his horn pulled everyone's eyes up to the vibrating chandelier. Six windows on the east side of the eighth floor shattered, unheard by Angelo's captive audience below.

Chapter Seven

By late July, the fire crews had contained the blaze north of town, but the Two Rivers residents were still not allowed to return to their homes; the enemy was surrounded but far from beaten down. The air over Fairbanks was even thicker with smoke, prompting daily health warnings for the young, the old, and those with respiratory conditions.

Corrine was still playing the brave social director for the displaced families, especially the shut-in children, with her latest plan to turn the ballroom floor into a soccer field. She was in Big Dipper Liquor talking Lonnie into picking up collapsible nets and indoor-size balls from Play It Again Sports when Henry Fornette entered the front door, unwillingly steered inside by Angelo.

Mayor Fornette had canceled outdoor events and games, including the Golden Days parade, because of the smoke. For sixty-two years, the event had highlighted the festival that celebrates the 1902 discovery of gold and founding of Fairbanks. The parade wound past me every year and the residents hung out their windows cheering the antique car club, high school bands, Jasmina's belly-dance students, and the other local groups.

Festival organizers and citizens raised an outcry over Fornette's excessive caution. Letters to the editor and callers on radio talk shows slammed the mayor's overbearing safety campaign, which had begun shortly after the death of his son. The mayor had introduced a flurry of city ordinances, including ones to mandate helmets for skateboarders and roller skiers, and even the riders on the Golden Days floats if the parade had taken place.

The smell of smoke seeped into every one of my corners and clung in every crevice except for inside the walk-in refrigerator in the back of Lonnie's liquor store. Smoke alarms blasting their unbearable warning sounds at all hours of the day and night prompted many residents to pull out the batteries. Inside my walls, like every place else, heads ached, eyes burned, and tempers grew short.

Lonnie's usual light-hearted banter with his customers turned to a surly, impatient wit. "Why don't you try getting in touch with reality and wear your glasses?" he snarled to a squinting patron as the man fumbled to punch his code into the debit card scanner while half a dozen people waited in line.

Jasmina remained cordial with her clientele but several times a day she retreated to the kitchen screaming epithets in English and Turkish over a slight spill or chipped cup. When her lovers visited her apartment, she was sullen and irritable, and they didn't stay the night, even with the hope of more sex with their morning coffee.

"I thought we were meeting at Junie's," Henry said, red-faced and angry as he shook off Angelo's grip. "I don't want to set foot in this goddamn place. It took my boy."

Fornette had commissioned a bronze plaque inscribed with his only offspring's name and dates of birth and death installed in the sidewalk where Harper met his demise. Just about once a week, the mayor visited the site, did a combination of crying and praying over the metal rectangle, then raised his eyes to my roof and shook his fist while spewing profanity-laden threats about taking me apart piece by piece.

I was on this corner becoming a Fairbanks tradition before Henry Fornette was a twinkle in his daddy's eye. I wasn't afraid of him. He needed some serious backup to take me on, but his standing in the community was on the wane.

His ordinances had managed to rile up business owners on

First and Second avenues, and folks in general resented his latest grand plan to impose a three a.m. curfew for people on the downtown streets "without a legitimate purpose." The last thing that the citizens of smoky Fairbanks wanted was more restrictions while confined behind shut doors and protective masks and rolled-up car windows.

"Settle down, Henry," Angelo said as he patted the mayor on the back, keeping his hand there to urge him forward toward Istanbul Coffee. "Let's just have a cup of coffee and talk. No need for you to be scared of this building."

Henry whirled around to face Angelo and squared his shoulders. "Scared? I ain't no more scared of this building than a cottonmouth is scared of a frog."

"Now you're talking." Angelo slapped Henry's shoulder and ushered his buddy into the coffee shop and to the table in front of the cracked wall.

"Wonder what happened there," Henry said, jerking his head toward the split on the wall behind him, which had become more prominent since the day Jasmina discovered it.

"This building has some problems. It's not exactly in its heyday anymore."

"You don't say."

"I do say, and maybe I could help things along so that both of us would benefit from that."

"Do tell."

"What can I get you, gentlemen?" Jasmina interrupted the conversation with a throaty voice made raw by inhaling smoky air. Tiny red capillaries webbed through her irritated eyes. Henry only noticed how her breasts and hips filled out her flame-colored dress.

"Two French roasts, with sugar," Angelo said, drawing out the last word. She eyed Henry's familiar face, partially hidden under a baseball cap, recognizing him as the mayor.

"You two look like old friends, Mr. Fornette. How did you and Angelo meet?"

"It's Henry, miss. Me and Angelo are from the same neck of the woods. Down in Louisiana, I—"

"We're in kind of a hurry, sweetheart," Angelo cut in as he smiled up at Jasmina with commanding charm.

"Sure, coming right up," Jasmina responded curtly, miffed at being so smoothly dismissed.

As she walked away, Henry studied the sway of her butt. "Would sure like to order me some of that," he said, licking his lips.

"Another married man admitting to lusting in his heart." Angelo grinned and raised an eyebrow. "I can tell you she's as ready as she looks."

"You mean you've ..."

"No, not yet anyway. But let's get back to the building and those benefits. You know I'm interested in that Sheraton Hotel deal. They're looking at downtown and a plot that's about twice the size of my land. I could offer them the perfect location except for one obstacle standing in the way."

"This building."

"Right. But if the city were to knock that obstacle down."

"You mean condemn it?"

Angelo put his forefinger to his lips as Jasmina set down two mugs of strong, steaming coffee with an abrupt, "Enjoy," as she walked away.

"Condemn it," Angelo said. "That's what they do to killers, right? Wouldn't you like to even the score for your son's death?"

"Damn right. The times I've thought of—but one crack on a wall isn't going to get a building condemned. It has to be uninhabitable, no heat, plumbing issues, safety issues. It's a process and the Sheraton people are trying to seal the deal well before spring, otherwise they're on to some other location. Alaska is not the only place they're looking."

Angelo banged the table with his fist, making both coffees spill over the edges of their cups. Customers across the room turned their heads toward the sound, and Jasmina glanced over from the front of the shop. Angelo smiled at her and turned back to Henry.

"Well, it's not just one crack. I guarantee this building will be ready to come down on time. What you're going to do, Henry, is make sure nothing stops that hotel from going up right here." He banged the table again with less force this time. "That's my price."

"You can make this building uninhabitable in less than six months?" Henry chuckled bitterly and slurped his coffee. A dribble on the outside of the mug trickled down the side of his hand to his wrist. "That would be some trick. And you'd have to think about the people who live here. Where would they go? It would be hard times for some of these folks. You can bet some of them will be marching on the sidewalk outside City Hall. There's a secretary in my office who lives in this building. How do you think that's going to play in the press, single mom, two kids, working for the mayor, out on the street?"

"This is business. Hard times are everywhere, Henry. I reckon you had some of your own while you were coming up. What part of Louisiana are you from again?"

"Carroll Parish, little bump in the road called Tall Cane, near the Arkansas state line," the mayor said with a boyish grin.

"You ever heard of a certain clan in those parts who can do certain things out of the ordinary? You know what I mean, the kind of folks you'd rather cuddle up to a water moccasin than be on the wrong side of?"

Henry's eyes flitted from side to side and his grin disappeared. His jaw fell open and his hands went slack on the table. "You mean ..." Angelo's lips spread into a sly grin. "You're one of them?"

Angelo stared coolly and sipped his coffee.

"A Frayer," Henry finished in a reverent, trembling whisper.

I was about to shake the floor hard enough to knock him and Angelo sideways in their chairs and show them it was going to take more than some blowhards shooting off their mouths to harm me. But the mayor's tone sent a shiver through my walls like a cold bolt of lightning.

The resignation in Henry's eyes showed the bargain he walked into was set and there was no way to back out. Behind him, he heard a creak and turned his head. I felt it before he saw the crack on the wall widen by a quarter of an inch. I didn't know what a Frayer was, but I knew it was something that could do that. So Henry had his serious backup, and I was in a fight for my life.

Chapter Eight

Laughter, cheers, rubber soles scuffing against hard wood, and the grunts of children expending energy poured out of my ballroom and into the hallway between Istanbul Coffee and Big Dipper Liquor. Two teams of refugee children were racing after a soccer ball while parents lined up against the walls urging the young athletes on.

"Listen to those sounds. Oh, to be a child." Angelo's cheerful Southern drawl caused Jasmina to turn from the still unrepaired damage on her wall to where he stood, beaming, in the doorway of her shop. In crisp khaki slacks and a peach-colored shirt, he looked as fresh and attractive as the day he arrived in Alaska. She flexed her thigh muscles but couldn't stop the quivering even as she hardened her will to attempt again to snare his interest.

"Well, Mr. Fallon," she greeted him. "It looks like the smoke isn't getting you down like the rest of us. Did you come in for coffee? Or something else?" Vivacious in a strapless, lime-colored sheath, and apparently having forgotten or forgiven his insulting lack of interest in the past, she flashed her dazzling smile and cocked her hip.

"Coffee and some company, which is hard to find these days," he said as he jerked his head in the direction of the ballroom.

"Oh, I guess Corrine's been busy with the displaced people," she said with mock sympathy. "That's what Corrine's all about, helping anyone who needs it, in case you haven't figured that out yet. Not a selfish bone in her body, unlike me."

Angelo smiled and his eyes nonchalantly appreciated some of her selfish bones.

Jasmina looked around the shop where only three customers sat. One sipped tea while reading a newspaper, another licked whipped cream from the top of a mug, the other stirred his coffee while staring at a laptop. "I can keep you company for a few minutes," she said. "Caramel lattes are the special today."

"I think I'll stick with plain French roast with lots of sugar," he said with a slow smile, and noticed the man with the cream-topped drink slide his gaze over the rear view of Jasmina's body.

Angelo chose a seat against the wall and watched the young man's eyes follow Jasmina as she brought two steaming mugs to the table and joined him.

"Ms. Jones," he said, stirring spoonfuls of sugar into his drink. "Not a very Turkish name."

"What's in a name? A rose by any other name would smell as sweet. But Jones is better for an American businesswoman and I'm going to be one of those immigrant success stories."

"Rags to riches?"

"Lowliness is young ambition's ladder."

"Do you always talk in Shakespeare?"

"Oh, no." Jasmina laughed. "I'm reading all of Shakespeare's plays. It's my latest project."

"You're a woman of surprising interests as well as being quite the entrepreneur, from what I've heard from Corrine."

"Corrine has really encouraged me. She made a success of Big Blue and she convinced me that I could find success here, too. She was right. As soon as I walked in that door, I could feel it, like Big Blue was welcoming me in. In my part of the world, we have many healing places. It was like that."

"Well, despite all that touchy-feely stuff, it's just a start. Have you thought about branching out with shops in other parts of town? There's lots of potential there."

"I'm constantly looking. She who hesitates is lost, right?

There's a vacant space for rent in a strip mall in the College area. I would love to tap that university market, but first I have to get the capital together while I work my plan to get the name 'Istanbul Coffee' out there."

"That, sugar pie, is just a matter of time. Henry Fornette owns that strip mall on University, College Corner, if that's the space you're talking about. I can mention to him that you're looking for prospects. But in the meantime, if you have to use what you've got to help you get that capital, why shouldn't you?"

"What do you mean, use what I've got?"

"Well, honey, it's no secret that you have men buzzing around you like bees to a hive. Is 'whipped cream' the one waiting for you to close up shop tonight?" He motioned his head toward the man with a mustache made from his frothy drink.

She stifled a smile, thinking he was interested, after all. "No, 'chai tea' by the window. He plays the guitar. He has exceptional fingers." The lean man in a leather jacket and jeans glanced at her and winked. "But we were talking about my business. I'm planning to increase my visibility by having a booth at the state fair in August."

"That would help with getting your name out, but not immediate capital. I don't see anything wrong with taking money from men, if they're willing to show their gratitude."

Her eyes widened and her mouth hardened. "You mean like a prostitute?"

"Well, I'm sure that's not what Corrine meant."

"Corrine? She was going to give me a pass on the August rent so that I could rent the booth at the fair and pay someone to run the shop while I'm out. Did she say she's backing out of that deal, and I'd have to find the extra money somewhere else?"

"Well, not exactly. Now, what did she say? Something like 'whores have resources that ladies don't.'"

"She called me a whore? It's not like Corrine to use language like that. But then Corrine hasn't been like herself lately." Jasmina's breath quickened and her eyes grew stormy.

"Now, now, calm down, sugar. She didn't exactly use the word 'whore.' I said 'something like' that and I'm sure I've taken what she said out of context."

"What's the fucking context got to do with calling me a whore?" Jasmina pushed away from the table, rocking her coffee mug and sending a teaspoon clattering to the floor. "Where is she?"

"With the kids in the ballroom, I think, but, wait; you really should calm down first." They stood up together and he put his hands on her upper arms before she could walk away and began stroking her.

She slid under his arms, into his chest. The musky smell of his skin beneath his shirt made her lightheaded. She put out a hand to grasp the edge of a nearby table to steady herself.

She imagined herself leaning over the table with him behind her. He was grabbing her hips with his strong hands, pulling her against his naked body. "I can't wait until we're alone," he would say. "I have to have you now."

In her vision the customers seated in the shop dropped their jaws and their drinks. The clatter of china cups against saucers echoed through the room. Angelo's cock teased between the cheeks of her ass, making her wetter and hotter, the heat radiating up through her belly, along her throat, coming out of her mouth in a low, loud moan. The table rocked under her hands as she gripped its side. The sensation of him pushing into her set off blue sparks dancing behind her eyelids.

I was snatched out of Jasmina's fantasy as I felt my ceiling separating at the center of the ballroom, where some of Angelo's leftover saxophone notes still buzzed like angry hornets. I futilely rattled the tall windows at the back of the room to sound a warning, but the soccer game held the attention of adults and children.

A rush of air, followed by a massive crash, shook the coffee shop floor and jerked Jasmina out of her daydream. The vibrations sent a tingle through her arm where her hand rested on the table and pitched Angelo hard against her as she leaned against his chest.

The wails of frightened children swelled out of the ballroom. Jasmina heard Lonnie's voice shouting, "Oh, Jesus, oh Jesus!" and running footsteps filled the hallway outside the coffee shop. Jasmina broke away from Angelo and ran toward the ballroom and toward Lonnie, who was disappearing into a cloud of dust and floating debris in the entryway to the ballroom.

The soccer game had been transformed to a panicked battlefield. In the center of the expansive floor lay the shattered chandelier, like a bulky, dead animal made of twisted metal and glass, directly under a jagged hole in the ceiling where it had ripped loose.

At the edges of the heap of still shuddering glass, children lay dazed with their limbs at odd angles, crisscrossed with bloody cuts, crying in various pitches. They lifted frightened faces to search for mommies and daddies. Parents rushed to them with stricken looks. One child wasn't moving. Corrine was down on her knees between two of the injured children. A bloody smear ran from her forehead across her cheek.

Lonnie retrieved a first-aid kit from his store, Jasmina grabbed towels from her kitchen. They mopped wounds and offered soothing words until the emergency crews descended on the scene a few minutes later and took over with professional precision and equipment. Police officers questioned distraught witnesses on the perimeter of the room. In one corner an EMT attended to a woman who had fainted.

Media arrived soon after with cameras and video recorders and microphones. A reporter stood outside my main entrance interviewing an eagerly forthcoming Angelo, who appeared to be untouched by the chalky dust that settled on the ballroom floor and on the heads and shoulders of everyone else.

I hadn't seen that coming, the chandelier falling, me losing my grip, like I was coming apart piece by piece. Getting into Jasmina's fantasy about Angelo was a dangerous distraction, a moment's inattention that could have cost the life of a child.

Paramedics carried out on a stretcher a boy who looked about eight. His left ankle was turned at an unnatural angle, his right arm was bound in a sling made from bandages, and blood oozed from a cut on his forehead. Corrine followed the stretcher with shaky steps as she leaned against another paramedic who was leading her to an ambulance.

I heard the paramedic say the words, "possible concussion," and something about hospitalizing Corrine overnight for observation. Most of the paramedic's words were drowned out by the voice of a distraught woman who walked briskly alongside the stretcher, repeating, "I'm here, Danny. I'm right here."

The reporter abruptly ended her interview with Angelo to focus on the injured child being carried out and signaled the camera person to get the shot. Angelo walked to the corner of the parking lot, where the ambulances blocked the eyes of cameras and reporters, to meet a man with a baseball cap pulled down low on his forehead.

The two men sputtered back and forth in low voices. Then I heard Henry Fornette say, "I didn't sign on to hurt kids." He raised a scolding forefinger toward Angelo's face. "You better - - "

"Your kid was killed. Did you forget about that?" Angelo said in a cold, accusing voice.

The mayor's stiffened finger wilted and folded back into his hand. He didn't think to ask how on solstice a chunk of concrete from my roof edge had so easily broken loose just like the chandelier, where saxophone music had recently quivered the air.

Chapter Nine

I didn't like the looks of the two guys when they first came into Big Dipper Liquor about twenty minutes before closing time. The squatty one was jumpy, swiveling his head on a short stump of a neck, his hands shoved down in his jeans pockets like he wouldn't know what to do with his arms if they were free from his sides. The taller one was a bony clothes rack hung with a faded T-shirt, a Carhartt jacket, and sagging jeans. He walked with a swagger like a skeleton pimp. Both of them wore dirty baseball caps with Tesoro logos pulled low over their foreheads.

"Make up your minds, fellas, I don't have all night," Lonnie called out, his newly developed rude attitude showing as the two spent an inordinate amount of time walking the aisles and checking out the wares–only to end up with what seemed a reflex rather than a decision. The tall one pulled three six-packs of Bud out of the side-wall cooler and carted them up to the register.

Lonnie gave him a hard look as he rung up the sale. Lonnie had been in business a while, and had a lot of practice sizing people up. He was distracted though, impatiently glancing at the clock every few minutes, like he had an important rendezvous as soon as he wrapped things up at the store. A Coltrane tune started up on the music system, and that reminded me how Lonnie and Angelo had cleaned up the empty ballroom after the accident and then had a saxophone-keyboard jam session there in the middle of the night.

Lonnie had so thoroughly enjoyed playing with another musician, he had been practically begging Angelo for days to pair up with him again. Angelo had said he would meet Lonnie in the ballroom that night as soon as he closed the store. Lonnie said he might be able to convince Joe Patterson, an old-timer and bass guitarist who sometimes played at the VFW, to show up and make it a trio.

The stragglers were on their way out with their beer and Lonnie was already grinning, feeling the music he would soon be making, when the skeleton whirled around, pulled a pistol out of his jacket, and pointed it at Lonnie's chest.

"All the cash. Now," the robber barked.

Stump Neck regained the use of his arms and produced a canvas bag, motioning for Lonnie to fill it with the contents of the cash drawer. It was a Saturday night and Lonnie's take was around two thousand. He gritted his teeth and his hands didn't shake as he handed over the money, but he was fuming inside. He knew he should have picked up on the bad vibes of those two losers and given himself time to get his own loaded gun out from under the cash drawer.

Through the wide plate-glass window in the front of the store, Lonnie saw a police car cruise by as the last of the cash dropped into the bag. Stump Neck spied the police car, too. "Cop. Let's go, Mitch," he spit out nervously to his partner as the taller man stepped back and grabbed a couple of fifths of vodka while keeping the gun trained on Lonnie.

"Hand over your cell, dude," he ordered the liquor store owner.

"Don't have a cell, man," Lonnie lied. He could see the cruiser pull halfway into a parking space near the corner of the building and stop. It was joined a couple of seconds later by another police car and the drivers rolled down their windows and faced each other. The second vehicle triggered one of the motion lights on the outside wall, sending out a weak beam that pointed to the asphalt alongside the cars. Months ago, I could have made that light flare for a second or redirected the beam a few inches into one of the officer's windshields ... but all I could manage was an unnoticed flicker.

"Check his pockets," Mitch told his crime buddy. The shorter man easily found the cell phone in Lonnie's back pocket, dropped it on the floor, then smashed it with his heel.

"There's two cops now. We've got to get out of here, Mitch," the little guy hissed, obviously panicked.

"We've got to keep this guy from getting their attention before we can get away," the brains of the outfit said. I saw Lonnie's thoughts racing, hoping what the thief said didn't mean he was going to get hit in the head with the pistol. Surely they wouldn't risk firing off a shot. "What's in the back?" he asked Lonnie.

"Just storage," Lonnie answered, keeping his voice fearless. He wanted to say, "My three-hundred-pound ninja partner." After all, these numbskulls hadn't thought to check for any other employees.

"Go," Mitch ordered as he waved the gun, directing the liquor store owner to the back.

When the three reached the back room, Mitch's face twisted into a smile. "A walk-in fridge. Looks like we got ourselves a holding cell." The short man giggled, pushed the handle of the refrigerator down, and swung the heavy steel door open. "Get in," Mitch directed Lonnie.

Lonnie hesitated, his heart pounding. He could have taken one of them or both of them if he had his gun. The short guy pushed him forward into the chilled interior of the fridge. The motion light inside came on. The door shut with a loud, metallic click. He heard something heavy being dragged across the floor on the other side, making a screeching metal sound.

The robbers were blocking the door with an abandoned shelf unit, not knowing that Lonnie hadn't gotten the inside safety release fixed after it came loose three years ago. He was the only one who entered the fridge, and he used a wedge of wood to block it open when he was inside so he never locked himself in. He heard a faint sound of glass breaking close to the other side of the door. The tall robber must have dropped one of the bottles of vodka, but he couldn't hear the men as they escaped.

After only a few minutes the cold crept through Lonnie's short-sleeved cotton shirt and khaki pants and penetrated every bare patch of his flesh. He twisted the thermostat dial up to its highest setting, thirty-eight. He slapped at his arms, hugged himself, and jogged in place, trying to generate some heat. He wondered if the sustained cold would drop his body temperature to a dangerous level before the lack of oxygen in the confined space affected his breathing.

Lonnie pressed his cheek against the frigid door with his mouth close to the sealed edge and shouted, "Help!" He repeated the futile cry fifty times, until he was so hoarse, only a feeble crackle escaped his throat.

He scanned his cell for something to pound against the locked door. Something metal would have been best, but the only metal available was the thin aluminum of beer cans that would burst in his hand if he slammed them against the door.

I heard the wailing notes of a saxophone and Lonnie felt the deep vibrations of a bass guitar traveling through the floor from the ballroom where Angelo and Joe Patterson had started up their session without a keyboard player. Lonnie found the wedge hidden in a shadowy corner, grasped it tightly, and beat it against the door. The light piece of wood produced a hollow tap, a sound too weak to be heard over the live music. The sax and the bass continued into the night, the players oblivious to Lonnie's plight. I had no more heavy light fixtures on the first floor to drop from a ceiling to let someone know that everything was not all right.

A couple of hours later, after the jam session wound down and Joe Patterson left out the back door, I saw Angelo walk into the liquor store. He noticed the absence of the security gate, saw the cash drawer open, and went to the storage area in the back. I'm pretty sure he didn't call Lonnie's name, but Joe's old Ford made a lot of noise when he started it up.

Angelo looked down at the broken vodka bottle, glanced at the walk-in door, rubbed his shoe sole against the glass on the floor, crunching it. He left a trail of wet footprints and glass slivers as he walked out of the store, took the elevator to his seventh-floor apartment, retrieved a fleece jacket, then went back down to the first floor. When he headed out the front door, a rock chip that had appeared days ago on the door's glass panel spread into the shape of a spider web.

He strolled in the shadows down to the river, past the drunks sprawled on the grass near Golden Heart Park. He paused against the railing of the Cushman Street Bridge, lit a cigarette and leisurely smoked, looking out at the slow-moving water.

A one-eyed car crept down Cushman, grazed the curb as it turned onto First. A police car emerged from the Key Bank parking lot at the corner; its siren yelped a couple of times, and the officer inside pulled the car over. Angelo looked over his shoulder at the scene, tossed his spent cigarette into the river, and ambled away in the opposite direction. He headed to Junie's Diner.

Three hours passed before Angelo emerged from the diner, his arm draped around the mayor's shoulder, like the two robbers, partners in crime. The morning sun was peeking up through the layers of smoky air behind my eastern exterior when he walked back through the entrance. A strip of the hall carpet frayed along the path of his foot.

Angelo entered Big Dipper Liquor, retraced his steps past the empty cash drawer, again walked back to the storage room, and pulled the handle on the walk-in refrigerator.

When the door swung open Lonnie, who was scrunched on the floor on the other side, slumped through the opening, falling on his side. Angelo knelt down and took the older, shorter man into his arms, rubbing his back and shoulders to warm him. Lonnie lifted his face and the younger man saw the dazed, disoriented look in his bloodshot eyes.

"Tell her I'm sorry," Lonnie mumbled.

"Sorry for what, man?" Angelo asked, rubbing Lonnie's back harder, stroking his neck with his jaw.

"The robbery."

"What about the robbery, Lonnie?" Angelo coaxed.

"T.J. said he'd tell about me if I didn't help him, said 'you know what they do to faggots on the block.'" Lonnie's voice cracked and his tears made wet splotches on the front of Angelo's shirt. "I was the second guy, the one who got away," Lonnie blubbered.

"You're talking out of your mind, man. It's all right now." Angelo's mouth caressed the older man's temple.

Lonnie pressed his face deeper into the strong chest and felt the warmth filling his body as he was hugged and caressed. He wanted to sink deeper into whomever was making him feel that way. Who held him so tenderly, so lovingly? He'd been very cold for a very long time, but before that . . . Lonnie recognized the musky male scent, stiffened, sat up with a jolt, and pulled out of Angelo's embrace.

"What's going on?" He swiped the back of his hand across his cheeks, surprised to find them wet. "There was a robbery, two of them, they got away. They locked me in the walk-in."

"I know," Angelo said, pulling Lonnie to his feet. "Joe and I were jammin', we thought you'd changed your mind when you didn't show. When we finished up, I went out the back way with Joe. I was hyped from the music, so I took a walk down to Junie's, hung out for a while. When I came back in, I saw your security gate hadn't been pulled down. I came into the store, saw the cash drawer open. I called for you. Then when you didn't answer, I walked back here, saw a broken vodka bottle on the floor, looked like a struggle happened. On a hunch, I tried the refrigerator door. You must have been in there for five, six hours."

"Wow," Lonnie exhaled as he rubbed the feeling back into his face and the back of his head. "Thanks, man." He clapped Angelo's shoulder.

"Anytime," Angelo responded, shedding the fleece-lined jacket and pulling it over Lonnie's still shivering shoulders.

"Is anyone else hurt?" Lonnie asked, glancing toward the hall. "Jasmina? She wasn't in her shop, was she?"

"No. It's locked up tight. Her idea to have a street entrance and to close off the one across from your store looks pretty good in this situation, even if she has a different agenda."

"Jasmina wants to put a door in facing the street? She hasn't said anything to me about that."

"Well, she probably didn't want you to take it the wrong way, with her concern over the kind of traffic you bring in. With a front entrance, her customers would come right into her shop without, how can I put this, rubbing elbows with yours."

"What do you mean the 'kind of traffic?'" Lonnie said with renewed alertness.

"It doesn't mean she thinks that way, of course, but I guess she's noticed a lot of what she calls 'your people' come in your store, and I suppose it makes some of her customers uncomfortable."

"My people? That A-rab girl doesn't want my people dirtying up her place of business? She wants a white and a colored entrance?"

"Come on, man. Don't take it like that. Your emotions are a little raw right now. She was just telling me about some jerk customer, saying what he said. Come to think of it, the door idea might have been a whole separate issue."

Angelo put his arm around Lonnie's shoulders and patted him firmly on the upper arm. "Look, you've been through an ordeal here. We should call the police."

Lonnie nodded. "I keep my distance from the po-po. If you were a black man, you'd understand. They don't come in here much. Maybe some kind of energy in Big Blue keeps them away. But I guess there's no getting around it this time."

Lonnie walked into the store, pulled a bottle of Hennessey off a shelf, twisted off the cap, took a long drink, then another.

Angelo walked up beside him. "You all right, man?"

"All right *now*, man," he said. "But I could have been stone-cold dead if you hadn't saved me."

Chapter Ten

It took less than a week for the rumors about the robbery to permeate every one of my apartments, just as insidiously as the smoke, leaving a nasty residue of fear. The gossip about the crime in the first-floor liquor store rose up to the eleventh floor, gaining momentum as it moved among the residents. The tenants were mostly a level-headed bunch, but lately suspicion was as contagious as a bad flu.

Stories circulated that Lonnie had been seriously hurt, that Jasmina's shop had also been robbed, that the residents who recently moved out had fled because of break-ins. It was rumored that a fifth-floor tenant lost all her jewelry to a burglar, and an elderly tenant on the ninth floor would have been sexually assaulted if not for her dog scaring off the intruder.

People being accosted in the elevator was supposedly a regular occurrence, and several residents walked from floor to floor until another tale of a tenant being chased down the stairs by a shadowy figure made the rounds. Single residents paired up to move around the building.

"Have you heard?" Corrine asked between heavy sighs of exasperation as she plopped down in one of the cup-shaped leather chairs in the coffee shop.

Jasmina, wearing headphones attached to a CD player at her waist, set a large mocha on the table in front of her. "*Bonjour, Madame.*"

"Uh, hello, Jasmina, can you hear me?"

Jasmina pulled the headphones down around her neck. "Oh, sorry, I mean, *excusez-moi.*"

"What?"

"I'm learning to speak French."

"Your latest project?"

"*Oui, madame.*

"I was asking, have you heard?" Corrine didn't wait for Jasmina to answer. "Three more move-outs with no notice before the lease was up. And when I told them I have to charge them for the following month's rent and they don't get their deposit back, they act like I'm the one doing something wrong."

"That's what happens when personal feelings mingle with business. Everyone who lives here is not a friend, Corrine. They are renters. Being the nice guy gets you screwed, in a bad way. You should be more like me, never mix business with pleasure, sex over there, money over here." She waved one hand, then the other to illustrate her point. "Do you know what I mean?"

"Well, Jasmina, I don't think I need your advice. I don't think we were talking about sex. You're doing well with your shop, but I've been in business a lot longer than you," Corrine said, surprised by Jasmina's aggressive tone.

"I hear you've been talking to Angelo about how I do business."

"Well, yes, about how you get what you want."

"I work for what I have."

"That's what I said." Corrine sipped her coffee, letting the steam from the brew float up to her face.

"And you could use some business advice. A lot of the older tenants don't feel safe. People shouldn't be able to walk off the street and have access to the residential areas."

"What do you suggest?"

"You should have some key card readers installed on the elevator and stairwell doors; then only the residents could have access beyond the first floor with their key cards."

"That would be an added expense on top of the downturn in renters, but I'll think about it. Maybe I'll run that idea by Angelo when I see him."

"When you see him. Stop being so coy, Corrine."

"He's only been staying with me instead of in Miss Liza's apartment after that terrible accident in the ballroom because I might have had a concussion. It turned out I didn't have a head injury, but he's been overly cautious, which is actually kind of sweet."

"You're the one who needs to be cautious."

"Jasmina, you certainly are acting strange. What advice do you think I need?"

"You may know how to make a good business decision. But you don't know shit about men."

"Well, you're one to talk. I don't know how you remember all their names."

"It's not their names I'm concerned about. I'm fine with a one- or two-night stand. You, on the other hand, are not cut out for casual sex. You're a happily-ever-after kind of woman. The kind of woman who still wears two rings on her left hand. Really, Corrine, where do you think this is going?"

"Where do I think what is going?"

"Drop it already, Corrine. Everyone in the building knows you and Angelo are going at it like teen-age rabbits."

Corrine laughed girlishly. "Who would have thought . . . at this time in my life? I've found that sexual attraction knows no age or bounds."

"Yes, well, everyone's attracted to Angelo."

"Including you, I assume."

"Like I said, everyone is, but why is he— "

"Attracted to me?"

"Corrine, you know I didn't mean it like that. I mean, he is a lot younger, closer to my age."

"You mean why me instead of you? Because it would be so natural for him to fall under your spell? But he's not interested, and you just can't figure out why."

"What I can't figure out is what his angle is with you. I don't want to see you hurt, Corrine. You hardly know the guy and you're head over heels. That's not like you."

Corrine put the coffee down and stood, planting her palms on the table. She stared at Jasmina. "You're right, Jasmina. I guess that's not like me. I'm the one who's there to comfort you and advise you when one of your one-night stands gives you a black eye. I'm the one who gets Lonnie's Jeep towed when he breaks down on the Richardson Highway and can't find his credit card. God, it feels so great to not always be the supporting actor, to be the one who is taken care of for once in a very long time."

"If you would have asked for help, Lonnie and me - - "

"I didn't have to ask Angelo. He was there. And things just happened."

"Things don't just happen with a man like Angelo."

"Well, they are happening. And, it's like what you always say, it's fun, like riding a merry-go-round."

Jasmina folded her arms across her chest and snorted. "Only a fool rides a merry-go-round with a broken leg, but I guess there's no fool like an old fool."

Corrine winced from the sting of Jasmina's words, shoved her cup angrily away, pulled a five-dollar bill out of her pocket, and threw it on the table. "You're calling me an old fool? Keep the fucking, excuse my French, change."

"That's only a fucking twenty-five-cent tip," Jasmina called after her as Corrine hobbled toward the exit.

Corrine turned her head toward Jasmina and tossed her hair. "It matches the service."

"Hey, Corrine," Lonnie called from the doorway of his store. Corrine did a half waddle to meet him, a move she had almost perfected without crutches, holding her arms out for balance, planting her good leg first, then swinging her casted leg forward. "I need to talk to you."

"Good timing, Lonnie, I need to talk to you, too."

"I wanted to let you know I got some new ceiling tiles because of that leak in the back of the store. I'm still waiting for the ceiling to dry out completely before they can be installed, seems to be taking a while. I'll split the cost with you and subtract it from my next rent payment."

"Which is due in two weeks."

"Yeah, Corrine, I've been paying my rent on the first of the month for how many years now?"

"And I've kept your rent the same for how many years now? You don't have any reason to go around complaining about it."

"Who's complaining? Why are you trippin', Corrine?"

"You may have noticed I've had some setbacks—unexpected repairs, tenants leaving because of things going on in your store."

"Things in my store? Like an armed robbery? Like the ceiling falling down because you're not keeping up with the maintenance? What are you saying, Corrine?"

"I'm saying, Lonnie, that I'm going to have to raise your rent by a hundred dollars like I'm doing with everyone else when your lease comes up for its yearly renewal in October."

"Damn, Corrine, a hundred bucks? Do you think you could give me more notice? I'm still waiting for the insurance check from the robbery. Sales will pick up in November. We've always supported each other as friends, like when that accident happened in the ballroom."

"This is business, Lonnie. I can't make an exception for you just because we're friends. I'm giving you more than a month's notice as it is. I'll draw up the new lease and bring it to you."

Lonnie pursed his lips in a sour expression and crossed his arms. "Is that what you and Jasmina were arguing about?"

Corrine backed into the hallway without answering. A loud stream of flute and drum music poured out of Istanbul Coffee, and Lonnie balled up his fists. The last thing he wanted to hear was a reminder of Jasmina's heritage after hearing Angelo's version of what she thought of his. Lonnie walked behind his counter and cranked up Isaac Hayes, who had been playing in the background. "Nobody wants to hear that foreign shit!" he yelled across the carpeted divide into Jasmina's shop. "This is America!"

Jasmina appeared in her doorway, her eyes blazing, while Corrine stood between them on her way to the elevator. "What the fuck is your problem, Lonnie?"

"My problem is that I was here a lifetime before you learned to speak English or stopped wearing a veil, and I'm not putting up with your racist crap."

"What the hell?" Corrine and Jasmina said at the same time, but Lonnie had no more to say. He stomped back into his shop, turned the volume of his music up even more until the walls pulsed from the bass.

A woman in a long raincoat entered the front door at the other end of the hallway, unheard and unnoticed as she strode toward Corrine until she almost bumped into her. "Corrine Easter?!" the woman yelled over the music.

"Yes?!" Corrine shouted back, looking at the rivulets of water tracking off the woman's shoulders.

The woman grabbed Corrine's hand and slapped a long white envelope into it. "You've been served!" the woman yelled, then turned and ran toward the exit.

"Wait!" Corrine screamed after the woman as she wobble-walked to the front door. She pushed the door open and saw the woman leap into the passenger side of a green pickup as it sped out of the parking lot onto Noble Street.

Corrine stepped forward, out from under the entrance overhang. A wet, cold sensation spread across her scalp and trickled into her eyes. She tore the envelope open and unfolded the papers inside. On the top left of the first page she read:

Plaintiff, Ellen Ridge, on behalf of minor child, Daniel Ridge,

v.

Defendant, Corrine Easter

The long-awaited rain was washing the smoke from the sky, already restoring freshness to the air. I wanted to keep Corrine out there and let the wet relief soak through her until she came to her senses and recognized her friends. But within seconds she stepped back inside, without even noticing the way the front door sagged from a loose hinge, rushing upstairs for help like a fly to a spider.

Chapter Eleven

Lonnie rolled the sump pump into the back of his store. He'd rented it from Ace Hardware on Cushman, even though he knew Corrine kept one that she bought during the heavy rains in 2008 in a storage area off the ballroom. He had chosen to pay the rental fee rather than ask Corrine for help.

He finished setting up the pump and switched on the motor. The loud hum filled the store and sent a low vibration through the bottles on the shelves. The half-inch of water that had crept across the back aisle from the flooded parking lot on my southern side after twelve days of steady rain would soon be suctioned away. Then Lonnie could remove the "Sorry, We're Closed for Repairs" sign taped on the glass of the store's door.

I wouldn't be dealing with this, he thought, if Corrine would have had the lot re-graded years ago so that the asphalt didn't slope down into the side of the building. And she bumps up my rent? Don't that beat all? He hadn't spoken to her since their talk about the rent increase.

The machine's sound faded into the background after a while and Lonnie cleaned up around the store, sweeping, mopping, listening for suspicious sounds. Jumpy since the robbery, sometimes he heard imaginary clicks and sudden shoe scuffs behind him.

He'd moved his loaded gun into the cash drawer and put two more security mirrors near the back of the store. He also counted the people who came into the store, keeping track of where they were from the time they entered until they left. That hadn't been a challenging task as the customers were too occasional lately.

Istanbul Coffee was probably doing a brisk business, he thought. In this weather, people preferred a warm cup delivered to them in contrast to a bottle of mellow liquid that had to be taken home and poured. Also, Jasmina wasn't having any flooding problems on the north side of the building, although Lonnie had heard her apologizing to a grumbling customer about the lack of heat in the shop.

No heat, plumbing issues, safety issues, that's what gets a building condemned, I had heard Henry Fornette tell Angelo. When I felt the zone that brought heat to my northwest side go dead a few days ago, I rushed my energy to the other side, forced an extra stream of warmth through Big Dipper Liquor and through all the higher floors on the south and east sides, defending those unaffected areas until the assault on my system subsided.

Moving toward his doorway, Lonnie spotted through the hall-side window of the coffee shop several patrons in coats hunched over tables. He wanted to ask Jasmina about her heating problem, but she had given him the evil eye the last three times they passed in the hall.

The day before, he had almost said "good morning" out of habit over the last six years, momentarily forgetting that they weren't on friendly terms anymore. "Women," he said to himself, pulling Corrine into his sights for blame, also. "They'd just as soon stab you in the back as look at you."

A tall man in a gray slicker tapped on the glass door. Lonnie's heart raced at the sight of the sinister figure, but as the man pulled down his dripping hood, Lonnie saw it was Angelo. "Hey, man," Lonnie greeted him as he unlocked the door and opened it.

"Nice weather we're having," Angelo said as he stepped in, trailing water.

"Sure is, for ducks," Lonnie said with a deep chuckle as he

straightened a couple of bottles on a front display shelf.

"As long as they're not coming in two by two," Angelo said, returning the laugh and holding his hands away from his side as droplets of water ran off them.

"You got that right, man. But I wish the customers were coming in two by two." Lonnie jerked his head toward the vacant aisles before him.

"Well, maybe if you had some better tunes in here. What is that awful noise?"

"Sump pump. I've got a little flooding issue in the back, had to close down until I get dried out. Don't want to get sued for a slip and fall. What's going on with you?" Lonnie asked, suspecting from Angelo's grin that he'd come in to spill some news.

"I was just down at the Mecca, setting up a gig, Thursday nights for the next three weeks. I don't want my reed to get rusty."

"Yeah? You think you can make enough noise to get that crowd's attention?"

"Sure, along with Joe Patterson on bass and if we had a good keyboard player. What do you say? Ten to two, a hundred and fifty cash for each of us, easy money."

"I don't know." Lonnie rubbed his chin and frowned with exaggerated seriousness. "I'd have to knock off here early."

"You been doin' it big on Thursday nights lately?"

"Naw." Lonnie shook his head and laughed. He put his hand out to grasp Angelo's. "I'm in, man."

Of course, he was in. Lonnie would rather be making music than doing just about anything else. Angelo had his number from the get-go. Angelo suggested they bring the Mecca roof down with some New Orleans jazz and Lonnie threw out the names of songs, all the while shaking with excitement.

In the late hours between Thursday and Friday, after the gig, I spied Lonnie and Angelo on their way back, full of laughter and accomplishment and alcohol after drinking up half their pay. They staggered through my front door around three a.m., arms around each other's shoulders like long-lost Army buddies, singing "The Thrill is Gone," in a way that would make B.B. King cringe.

"I'll walk you home," Angelo said, when they couldn't remember the next line of the song, and they both laughed uproariously.

When they were already in the elevator, they both remembered they had left their instruments in the back of Lonnie's Jeep, but they laughed again, and continued to Lonnie's place on the second floor.

"How about those southern chicks?" Lonnie said, recalling their earlier activity in the bar, as they stumbled into his plainly furnished apartment. "I thought that Lindy Sue was definitely your type. What was that perfume she was wearing? Bayou Mist?"

They collapsed, convulsing with laughter, side by side, onto a gray suede couch. Angelo propped his feet on a narrow, black coffee table. "And Mary Jo?"

"No, Sarah Jo," Lonnie corrected.

"Sarah Mary Jo, she was hitting on you all night. I'm surprised you could keep your mind on your music."

"Do you think they really believed your name was Jim Bob Walton?" Lonnie sputtered out a laugh.

"Oh, man, *I* was starting to believe I was Jim Bob Walton. Just like you were, what was it? Avalon Buchanan Jackson?"

Lonnie scrunched his face up and squared his shoulders in an attempt to be serious. "But I *am* Avalon Buchanan Jackson."

Angelo slapped Lonnie's thigh and renewed laughter burst out of his mouth. "Does anyone know that?"

Lonnie placed a shaky finger across his lips and made a shushing sound. "Don't you tell anyone, Angelo. Don't you tell Corrine or Jasmina."

"Corrine and Jasmina? If anybody is a.k.a., it's those two. That Turkish babe. Jones, are you kidding me? Maybe her ticket to America was a G.I.? We have a base in Turkey. If it's not a married name, she could have come up with something a little more imaginative if she wanted to reinvent herself. Do you know if Alaska was her first stop in the U.S.?"

"No. Seattle, I think, or maybe Spokane? Washington state, for sure. She said when she opened her coffee shop here, there was too much competition there."

"Now Corrine. . . . That one does have a little more mystery about her. Have you ever heard anyone call her Corey Mae?"

"Corey Mae? No way." Lonnie shook his head, then regretted the sudden increment of blurred vision.

"Maybe that's what she was called when she was younger? Somewhere in the South?"

"She did mention once that she lived in Texas." Lonnie squinted like he was trying hard to extract another thought. "That was a long time ago, way before she hooked up with Jack Easter."

"Before Jack, in Texas? You know that's not really the South, that's the Southwest," Angelo said, louder than he needed to, and laughed like he had just told a joke.

Lonnie started to giggle. "That Lindy Sue looked like she wanted to go south on you." Lonnie's laughter bubbled over. "And you, I think your horn was ready."

Angelo reached behind Lonnie and squeezed the back of the older man's neck with his long fingers. Lonnie's giggles dried up like a shut-off tap. Angelo shifted his body so that he stared into Lonnie's puzzled, sobered gaze.

"No, Lonnie, it wasn't." Angelo said in a serious tone. Still holding Lonnie's neck, he used his other hand to stroke Lonnie's thigh. "No one knows how to treat a man's stuff like another man."

His hand moved higher. Lonnie's breath quickened as his erection strained against his fly and he felt Angelo's fingers move to release it. "I know it gets lonely, man. You don't have to make do with that one fishing trip a year, now that . . ." His hand reached Lonnie's hard dick. ". . . I'm here."

Their faces moved toward each other, extinguishing the warm breath between them as their lips crushed softly together. Angelo ran his tongue across his upper lip, then lowered his head to Lonnie's crotch. Lonnie moaned with anticipation even before he felt the first stroke of Angelo's tongue along the head of his cock.

Ten floors above, Corrine looked out the rain-streaked window, down at the parked Jeep, and wondered what was taking Angelo so long to come up to the penthouse.

Chapter Twelve

Jasmina immediately recognized the forty-something, slightly overweight man in a green flannel shirt and jeans seated in front of the cracked wall. The flaw was covered with a tapestry of a tiger lying in front of a palace with a backdrop of an amethyst sky.

She hadn't seen the mayor come in, but he was making good on his promise to visit her shop when he stopped by her booth at the fair. She had been so overwhelmed with customers, she'd barely had time to say hello.

"Nice place you've got here," he said, getting Jasmina's attention as she passed to wipe off a nearby table.

"Thank you, Mr. Fornette," she said, thinking he must have come in when she was in the kitchen for a moment, taking a batch of pastries out of the oven. "What can I get you?"

"It's Henry, remember? Whatever you're cooking back there that smells good and fattening, I'll take one of those. And a regular cup of coffee, with chicory, the Louisiana way, if you've got it."

"I can bring you a bear claw and a regular coffee, but, I'm sorry we don't have—what did you say? Chick-a-REE?"

"That's OK, honey. What you got is fine," the mayor said with a wink.

"You haven't been in here for a while, Mr. Fornette," she said. "You came in that one time with Angelo Fallon."

"Henry. That's right. We didn't have much of a chance to chat then as I recall."

"You and Angelo seemed to have some serious business to talk about." Henry rocked side to side as though his chair had suddenly become uncomfortable. "I'll get that coffee and bear claw for you." She felt him watching her walk away.

She was curious to continue the conversation to draw out more information about the mysterious Mr. Fallon, but a steady stream of customers interrupted for the next hour. When business quieted down again, she noticed that Fornette was still there and brought him a refill. "Have you and Angelo known each other for a long time?"

"Oh, no. We just met since he came up here. But I did know some of his people back down in Louisiana."

"Really? His parents, brothers, sisters?"

"More like cousins."

"And does he have a wife down in Louisiana?"

"Well, not that I know of," Henry said with a laugh and a wink. "No offspring either, legitimate or otherwise, that he admits to anyway."

"Would you say he's a ladies man, a player?"

"I guess I would say that. Now you don't have your eye on him, do you?"

"Is that a warning, Henry? Is Angelo Fallon trouble?" Henry motioned with an open hand for her to sit down. "Well, I guess the owner won't mind," she joked, surveying the nearly empty shop and taking a seat. "We were talking about trouble?"

"It's nothing. I was just being a little silly, Ms. Jones, but I've heard you've had a little trouble here."

"You mean someone has made a complaint? Was it about the heat?" She leaned forward on the table, dropping her hands and widening her eyes.

"Oh, no, no, no, not a complaint about your business. I've heard that there have been some problems with the building, some hazardous situations."

"Well, I don't know that you would call them hazardous. The

heat hasn't been working right for weeks. Not in the apartments either on this side of the building. It seems to be fine in Lonnie's liquor store, but then he's had the flooding and the robbery."

"Flooding and a robbery?"

"Yeah, and the ceiling fell in before that, well, not really the whole ceiling, not like when the chandelier came down on those kids, but I'm sure you know about that."

"Of course, that was tragic. I guess I should have looked into things before it got this far. I've just been so distracted, you know, since Harper ..." Jasmina heard a gurgling sound from deep in his throat.

She put her hands gently on top of his. "I'm sorry for your loss," she said, just like she'd heard it said on TV cop shows.

"It's changed me," the mayor said, looking at her with watery eyes. "I'm re-committed to making this city safer."

"You canceled the parade," Jasmina said, remembering how she had to console her dance class about not participating in the event. "The smoke was terrible, but a lot of people were disappointed."

"Yeah, I'm taking a hit in the election polls over that. But I don't want to see any of our citizens come to any harm. We are planning a big event next month, the weekend after September 11, to honor all our warriors."

"Our warriors?"

"Our firefighters, police officers, and, of course, the brave men and women of our Armed Forces. The city and the military haven't always seen eye to eye, but we've been planning this together for weeks. We'll kick the day off downtown with a 10K run led by our people in uniform to support the Wounded Warriors program."

"I haven't heard about any of this."

"I put a poster up outside your shop door. I was hoping you wouldn't mind."

"Of course I don't mind helping out with a community event."

"I appreciate it. And if I can ever be of any help to you, Miss

Jones, don't hesitate to ask."

"Well, there is something, Henry. It's not that I need help, but I would like to talk to you about a potential business transaction."

"Well, I am intrigued, Miss Jones."

"I'm planning to expand in the future, with Istanbul Coffees all over town, North Pole, too. But I want to start with a second shop near UAF. I hear that you own some vacant real estate on University Avenue."

"That I do. And I'd like to get somebody in there who could really attract some business. I could give you a tour tonight after you close up and we can talk about price."

Jasmina took a slow breath and smiled. "That would be a little premature. I don't have enough to invest yet."

"Well, how do you know? Maybe we could work out some kind of discount."

I forced the smoke alarm above them to send out an ear-splitting bleat. I had used the streak of good luck settled somewhere in the floor to help Jasmina get her business off the ground years ago, but this time I couldn't bridge the distance from ceiling to floor to tap into it. I could only maintain the noisy disruption for seven seconds.

The interruption to Henry's come-on put an angry scowl on his face. Jasmina cast her eyes around the room in distress. "I don't smell any smoke, but I'd better check the kitchen," she said, starting to rise from her seat.

He reached across the table and patted her hand. "No, it's stopped. Sometimes these alarms are overly sensitive. Now, we were talking about a possible discount."

"I'm not looking for any special consideration, Mayor Fornette."

"Henry."

"Mr. Fornette, that's not how I do business. I just wanted you to know that I was interested in some space in the College area. But I certainly will contact you when I'm ready to rent or even buy."

Again, I pushed a deafening bleat from the plastic dome in the ceiling to hurry the end of the conversation and send Henry on his way, but it faded to a quivering beep in less time than the first blast. Jasmina covered her ears and cursed.

"You think it's nothing to worry about?" she asked Henry with imploring eyes.

"A false alarm, I'm sure. Probably you should change the battery if it keeps doing that," he said. "But, I can come back later and check on you if you want me to."

"I don't think that will be necessary. But, I would like to hear some more stories about your days in Louisiana and the people there," she said with a smile as she stood up and glanced with a worried frown up at the alarm.

"I don't know that you'd care much for the people I know. There are some dangerous characters in those backwoods."

"Like Angelo Fallon?"

Henry laughed nervously. "Well, he is a character, I'll say that much."

"But not dangerous?"

"Nothing that you couldn't handle." Henry laughed nervously again. "I can tell you know your way around men."

"But what about someone who doesn't know her way around men? Would he be dangerous to someone like that?"

Henry stood up quickly. "Let me tell you a little story. When I was a boy, I was like most boys, tripping over trouble without thinking where I was stepping. One hot August day I got a notion to strip buck naked and take me a nice float in the river. I was lying on my back in that cool water looking up at the sky like I owned that river. Just about then along come the blackest, most evil-eyed, most jaggedy-toothed alligator, nudging up on me, letting me know whose territory that really was. If I had been a lick slower getting out of that water, that sucker would have had my crown jewels for lunch. When I told my daddy, he said to me, 'You know how to keep a river gator from biting off your business, boy? You stay out of the river.' You know when to stay out of the river, don't you, Ms. Jones?"

Henry pulled a couple of bills from his wallet and tossed them on the table. "Now, if you have any more trouble with this building or anyone in it, you can call me personally." He stood up and puffed out his chest. "If there's anything Henry Fornette knows how to do, it's handle trouble."

"How do you handle trouble down in Louisiana, Henry?" she asked.

"Well, down there, if somebody seriously messes with our grits, we go looking for a Frayer."

"What's a Frayer? One of those dangerous characters you were talking about?"

"Did I say Frayer? Well, that's a ... that's kind of ... that's a whole bunch of trouble that'll unravel everything you hold dear quicker than you can say 'blueberry pie.' Good night, Miss Jones, and when you're ready to set up that second shop, you come see me, and we'll work something out."

He exited through the main entry and spit a glob of hate at the front step. I considered sending a small chunk of concrete from my roof his way, just to shake him up a bit. But he walked quickly to the sidewalk with a toothy smile, like an alligator.

Chapter Thirteen

Corrine sat wrapped in an old quilt in her lavender chair as Angelo turned on the CD player across the room and the insistent funk-jazz sounds of Grover Washington Jr.' s "Mister Magic" made the air quiver. "Want to stretch those legs a little?" he asked as he danced toward her, rocking his hips and snapping his fingers. He offered his hand with an exaggerated bow.

She pulled her legs from under the quilt and stretched them out like a diving board in front of her. The cast was gone and the calf muscle of the leg it had shielded hung slack compared to its toned twin.

"I'm trying to think, Angelo. I have to figure out how I'm going to come up with seven hundred thousand dollars."

"You can think and dance at the same time, and anyway, it might only be six."

"Wow, big difference," she said, rolling her eyes as she let Angelo pull her up. He guided her slowly around the room as she moved hesitantly in bare feet, wearing only an oversized sweatshirt that fell to the middle of her thighs.

Her attorney had advised quickly settling the lawsuit alleging that Corrine's negligence as a building owner had caused the chandelier to fall. The Ridges knew they would never get a million dollars, no matter how the medical expenses added up and how much pain, suffering, and emotional distress they had forecast for the rest of young Danny's life. Her lawyer had said this while

Corrine had him on speaker phone so that Angelo could hear, too. The lawyer had said, "They're asking for seven hundred thousand dollars. We'll counter with six."

Angelo twirled Corrine in slow motion, watching her toes so that he wouldn't step on them. "Baby doll, I've already told you I'll loan you the money. You can put up this building as collateral, just as a formality, of course. If you were to find yourself with your back to the wall, I'd be a lot more flexible with the terms than a bank would."

"That's what worries me, having my back to the wall. I wouldn't want to be in that situation with anyone, having to beg for a favor, even from you. I'm not going to borrow against Big Blue."

"I'm willing to take the chance. And, seriously, Corrine, you don't have anything else of value." Corrine huffed out a frustrated breath, unable to come up with a defensive response. "I'll make us some lunch. If you want to think some more, think fast. Whether the Ridges accept the counter or not, you're going to have to come up with the money."

"I've got it!" Corrine shouted at Angelo as he reentered the room and set down a tray of turkey and cucumber sandwiches and two glasses of iced tea. She was so excited, he put out his hands to stop her in case she decided to shed her quilt and jump up on her still weak leg.

"You've got what?"

"My ring." She held up her hand and the light dazzled off the emerald facets, making Angelo blink. "I'll sell my ring. It's worth almost the whole amount."

"But, sweetheart, you can't sell that ring."

"Of course I can. It's my ring."

"But darlin', I can see how much it means to you. He must have promised you everything with that ring."

"How do you know anything about that?"

"Because, Corey Mae, that's what I would have done if I had given you that ring." He reached out to move a strand of hair from over her eye. She pulled back. Her heart was a trapped butterfly beating its wings against the inside of a jar.

"It was a long time ago." She willed the butterfly to fold its wings and rest. She covered the ring with her other hand. "I'm not going to take out a loan and worry about not being able to make the payments and take a chance on losing Big Blue. I appreciate your offer, but this is my decision, not yours."

I made the crystal birds vibrate triumphantly above her. Angelo looked up, his mouth pressed into a thin, annoyed line as one of his fists clenched at his side.

"You really think that would be the wisest thing to do?"

"The ring would let me make a one-time payment. I can't be so sure about my future rent income. Things haven't been so stable since half of my tenants have jumped ship, thanks to Lonnie getting robbed and setting off this panic."

"Hey, sugar babe, you make it sound like it's Lonnie's fault that he got robbed."

Corrine shook her head and huffed out a loud breath. "Well, you don't ever hear of a beauty shop being robbed, do you, or a florist? He has a liquor store. That attracts a certain element."

"Has Lonnie ever been involved in a robbery before?"

"We've never had a robbery since I've been here and Jack never mentioned anything like that happening to Lonnie in the past. Why do you ask?"

"Oh, it's just something he said to me that night I saved him from the freezer. He was out of it, with the hypothermia, so it was probably just gibberish. Something about being sorry for his part in some robbery."

"His part? He did grow up in a rough neighborhood, in Cleveland, but Lonnie would never— "

"Yeah, Lonnie's a good guy. I think he was just talking out of his head. Cleveland, you said?"

"Yes." She picked up a sandwich and nibbled at the corner.

"Just so I know you're not talking out of your head, promise me you'll at least sleep on your decision about the ring." I rattled the crystal birds again, and Angelo jerked his head upward. "I should check the mounting on that thing. We don't need another chandelier falling on someone."

"It's fine. It's sensitive to the movement of air. I'm not changing my mind. I am thinking very clearly."

"I have my doubts about that. But I know how to clear all the fuzzy stuff out of your beautiful head," Angelo said with a mischievous raise of an eyebrow. He finished his sandwich and licked a dribble of mayo from the end of his pinky finger. "I haven't kept my promise to you."

Corrine frowned up at him. "What promise is that?"

"I promised you that when you got your cast off ..."

"It's only been a couple of days."

"A couple of days too many."

"Oh, Angelo," she said, exhaling a puff of air, and waving her hand to dismiss his banter. "Now is not the time."

He swooped down on her and, in one smooth motion, lifted her out of the chair and flung her, still wrapped in the quilt, over his shoulder.

"Angelo, An-ge-lo, put me down. What are you doing?"

He ignored her protests and the weak blows of her fists against his back. He strode to the door at the back of the kitchen that led to the roof, sprung up the stairs, carried her to the middle of the roof, and laid her down with the quilt as a barrier between her back and the hard surface.

The incessant rain was coming down in cold but gentle sprinkles as he stripped off his clothes and straddled her. His already dampened hair clung to his forehead and released wet drops that fell onto her lips. She closed her eyes and caught the wetness with her tongue and then his tongue joined hers, warming her mouth and sharing the raindrops.

Her sweatshirt rode up to the top of her ribs and she felt his stomach hot against her chilled skin. She reached down and grasped his hard cock and guided it between her legs. He eased himself in, an inch at a time, allowing her to feel pulses of pleasure strengthening with each push deeper inside her velvety moist opening. She curled her legs around his back and rocked up against him.

The motion of their entwined bodies grew more furious. Corrine felt all the blood in her body boil up and rush through her, then the heat escaped through her mouth with a loud, feral howl. Angelo's body tensed, he thrust hard into her, lingering there for a few moments before lowering himself gently to cover the length of her body.

Corrine's skin and the quilt under her were soaked. She was shivering even though Angelo's body shielded her while he exposed himself to the chilly rain.

"We should go in," she said in a worried whisper. "You'll be freezing in a few seconds."

"I'm fine," he said, raising up on his arms to look down at her, a slow smile spreading on his face. "See how wonderful things are when you do things my way."

Taking his words as lighthearted, she smiled and answered, "This time, but not always."

"You will," he said, looking down at her without smiling.

She trembled either from the cold or the power in his gaze and watched in wonder as the rain pelted his burnished shoulders. Wherever the rain hit his bare flesh, clouds of steam rose up and then vanished like droplets of water on a hot griddle.

Chapter Fourteen

Eight women bundled in sweaters and fleece jackets, with leotards or shorts or dance costumes underneath, gathered in Jasmina's classroom. When they shed their shoes near the doorway, they sighed thankfully for the room-size Oriental carpet that covered the cold floor. They chattered about their work, their children, the last catch of fish, the most recent camping trip. A couple of military spouses talked about the latest deployment and the homecoming celebrations they had planned. Every few seconds, they put their fingers up to their mouths and warmed them with their exhalations.

Jasmina waited for her students at the front of the room in a purple chiffon skirt slit up each side, revealing the full length of her legs when she moved. A belt embellished with lavender seed beads circled her abdomen just above the top of the skirt. Her purple-sequined bra with turquoise fringe exposed the goose bumps erupting on her chest and arms.

She clapped her hands crisply, then turned up the Middle Eastern music coming from a CD player. "I know it's cold in here, ladies, so let's get warmed up," she directed. Her words came out with puffs of icy breath. "Everyone in position. We're going to work on shimmies today."

For forty-five minutes, Jasmina demonstrated quick, shivering motions with her hips and abdomen, and the students followed with varying degrees of success, occasionally synchronized. Some were clumsy, some were out of shape or inflexible, but Jasmina was not deterred by their varied potential.

"You're really improving," she commented to one. "That's the way to do it," she praised another, and to their classmates, "Loosen up a little more in the hips." "Beautiful." "Move those sexy bodies." At the end of the class, she announced, "Yes, I promise, ladies, I will get the goddamn heat fixed by next class."

The temperature had been dropping in Istanbul Coffee for the past few days. My limited victory was that I managed to keep the heat from being sabotaged throughout most of the apartments. The vicious words and blows from the unsavory activities in the room which once had been Petey's Card Room had stayed, locked inside the walls in spite of Jasmina's elegant gold paint; and that lingering violence had weakened my control of Jasmina's space.

Except for the early mornings, when approaching autumn brought the outside air down into the frosty thirties, it was colder inside Jasmina's shop than it was outside. Sit-down customers gulped their drinks, others felt the chilly air when they entered and either grabbed cups to-go or turned around and walked out. The meager take in the cash register at the end of the day showed that business had chilled along with the air.

Jasmina had noticed that the air in the hallway was normal and, judging by the sight of Lonnie in short sleeves, Big Dipper Liquor was outside the cold zone. She had turned up the thermostat in the shop all the way to no avail. Cold air poured out of the heater vents. After leaving message after message on Corrine's phone, the last two punctuated with expletives, she had shut the vents and ordered a large electric, standalone heater.

After the belly-dance students hurried out, Jasmina put faster, urgent music on her CD player. She lifted her bangled arms above her head, gyrated her hips a few times, then began twirling. Faster and faster, she spun, until she was a blur of purple sparkles and damp with sweat.

"Ma'am! I'm here with your heater, ma'am! " a young male voice called from the coffee shop.

Jasmina was still turning, her cheeks warm and flushed. The broad-shouldered man, in gray coveralls and a cap with a logo that read "Cache Heating and Fireplace," stepped into the doorway of the classroom, apparently having followed the music. His mouth hung open, the saliva collecting just inside his lower lip as he watched in stunned silence the whirling display of beauty before him.

The music ended and Jasmina stood still, breathing hard. She stared at the stranger inside the door. "Your ... heater ... ma'am," he said as though he was also recovering his breath from frenzied activity.

Jasmina smiled. The man stepped back like he'd been hit by an electric shock. "How long will it take you?" she asked.

He inhaled her voice like it was perfume and wiped the sweat from his brow as he melted under her sensuous gaze. "A few minutes, ma'am. It's my last delivery of the day."

"So you don't have to rush off then."

"No, ma'am, if you could show me where you want it."

Jasmina walked up to him, her smoky eyes trained on his, and pulled her flimsy skirt aside. He didn't need any more encouragement to lift her up and wrap her legs around his waist. She crossed her ankles at the small of his back as he shed his pants and entered her.

With his hands under her ass he rocked her up and down, moving slow and deep at first, then building to the furious pulsation of a well-oiled engine. Her orgasm nearly knocked him off his feet and he had to brace against a wall to stay upright as he joined in with his own release. The event took only ten minutes, about the same amount of time it took him to set up the heater in the back of Istanbul Coffee.

"You should read the owner's manual, ma'am, and if you have any questions, just give us a call."

"I'll do that. Come by for a cup of coffee sometime."

"You mean ..."

"I mean coffee, Jake," she said, using the name embroidered

on his coveralls as she signed the delivery receipt and avoided glancing at the renewed bulge in his pants.

After Jake left, Jasmina pulled a chair in front of the ordering counter twenty-five feet from the heater, sat down with her bare legs stretched out in front of her, and let the warmed air wash over her sweat-chilled skin.

A tiny flare of orange winked at her through the vent on the front of the heater. For a couple of seconds, she wondered, is it supposed to do that? She considered reading the owner's manual, or calling Jake back to check it out, but she had been done with him at the first touch. She had imagined Angelo inside of her the whole time. The comforting warmth after the sexual release lulled her to sleep.

I felt the cold escaping to the floors above the shop on the north side of the building. If it went unchecked for another couple of months, when the brutal cold of winter descended, my pipes would burst. Billy Johnson, on the second floor, fiddled with his thermostat, and Mrs. Graystone, above him, put on a heavy sweater, but neither could get warm enough.

Finally, they both went up to the penthouse to pound on Corrine's door to complain, only to be ignored. Corrine slept through the angry summons of fists on her fancy portal. Or her moans of pleasure from Angelo's attention drowned out the sounds, or she was too busy pleasuring him to care.

He called her "Corey" and she didn't mind so much anymore, but when he said it, she rubbed the bareness of her left ring finger above the insignificant gold circle where she used to wear the emerald before she sold it. It wasn't just the ring she missed. It was what she had been when it was given to her, compared to how much less she had been when she received the smaller ring from Jack Easter.

I hated the way Angelo smiled as he lay on his back in her bed with his arms crossed behind his head while she was between his thighs working her mouth on his dick. She enjoyed doing that. For the first time, I realized she wanted to give in to his manipulations. Maybe she had helped along Jack's neglect of her, too.

It rushed through me like a cold, dark wind: She was complicit in what was happening to her, and to me. Was it possible that she cared more about Angelo than she did about either of us?

In the parking lot far below the penthouse, groups of shabby, scary-looking men congregated in the shadows of my corners. They urinated against my increasingly stained and broken exterior, and laughed drunkenly, ridiculing my pathetic state. I rattled all the windows from the first floor to the penthouse, enraged that for a few moments I had let Angelo turn even me against Corrine.

Chapter Fifteen

Corrine attempted to bend herself into pigeon pose on her bedroom floor, lowering her upper body over her angled right leg with the left leg stretched out straight behind her. Only a couple of months ago, before the accident, she could have accomplished the yoga position fluidly. Now her muscles and joints felt like taut cables connected by rusted springs.

"You're going to hurt yourself," Angelo said as he walked into the room, wiping mint green paint from his hands with a white cloth that he then shoved into the back pocket of his jeans. "That's not on your list of exercises. If you're not going to comply with your at-home therapy, you'll have to start going to the clinic."

The admonishment irritated her. The smell of fresh paint from Angelo's skin and the kitchen walls that he'd been redoing was making her slightly nauseous. She had been hurting all over lately, even inside. She was too dry when he entered her, and it hurt. The memory of Angelo pleasuring her for the first time as she lay naked in the bath tub, that feeling of renewed youthful ecstasy, was mocking her.

The tendril of a dark thought snaked into her mind: How much longer can he stay interested in me? How long before he moves on to a younger woman who can keep up with his sexual calisthenics? Just the night before they'd had to stop their love-making because she got a cramp in her right hamstring, and the night before that she'd had to get up and pee when he was about to come.

She bent lower at the waist, feeling the obstruction of belly fat that wasn't there two months ago, and pictured how Angelo must have watched the roll around her middle jiggle and bounce the last time she was naked and moving up and down atop his body. Angelo's burgundy loafers planted themselves in front of her. She felt his eyes looking down at her exasperated, prone form with disapproval.

"You're right," she said, pulling herself up. "What I really need is to get on a walking regimen now that the smoke is gone. I haven't been outside for more than a minute for months. I'll get back in shape." She strode toward the closet. "I can start right now, as soon as I find my shoes," she said as she rummaged through the shoes on the floor and pulled out a pair of pink and silver Nikes.

"Hold on," Angelo said, standing above her again as she sat on the floor and pushed her feet into her walking shoes. "Who says you're out of shape?" For a second she almost believed that he hadn't noticed. He squatted down to her level and interlaced his long fingers with his hands resting casually between his knees. "I don't want you traipsing across town," he said with gentle firmness. "Broken bones take a while to heal. You may think everything's back to normal, but - - "

"Angelo," she cut him off. "You say that every time I want to do a little more. I need to get moving again. I think that's the medicine I need right now." She tied her left shoe and moved on to the right. "All I've been doing these past two months is eating and sleeping and having sex with you."

"Oh, I didn't realize I wasn't pleasing you, I thought—"

She brought her hand up to the side of his wounded-looking face and caressed it. "No, sweetheart, that's not what I meant. You've been—you are—wonderful. It's just that I need—"

He looked away from her. "Sometimes I don't know why I try so hard to make you happy. I was about to make us some

lunch, but I guess it can wait until you get back from your walk."
He turned back to her with a hard stare. "Or I suppose I could
just leave you alone from now on and you could do whatever you
want."

"For Pete's sake, Angelo, it's just a walk," she said, but at the
same time she was slipping off her shoes, pushing them away and
pushing her body toward his.

He stood up, leaving her lurched forward on her knees. "You're
right," he said with a sweet smile. "I'm probably overreacting.
You go ahead and enjoy your walk. I can finish painting the
kitchen while you're gone." He extended his hand for her to grasp
and pulled her up.

"I so appreciate you doing that. I could have done the painting
myself. I'm used to fixing things."

"No, darlin', you're not climbing any ladders while I'm around."
He cradled her face with his hands and kissed her nose.

Her aggravation with him only moments before was already
faded. "I could put off my walk until after lunch."

"Nonsense, go on now. Well, maybe you could just sit down
with me for ten minutes and we could have a cup of tea together
before you go?"

"Sure." She put her arms around him. A few seconds went by
before she felt him hug her back.

Corrine fell asleep with the tea cup dangling from her fingers.
Angelo gently extracted it and set it on the table next to his full
cup. He lowered her onto her back on the couch and covered her
with a quilt. Before leaving the penthouse, he looked in the mirror that hung next to the door and smoothed his hair back with
one hand.

I looked at Corrine's sleeping form, a tamed creature, for the
price of a little green paint and not having to be alone.

As Angelo rode down in the elevator I harnessed a flash of energy, drawing from the remnants of the long-ago joy of a young
couple who brought healthy twin boys into the world on the floor
of that moving cubicle. For a couple of intervals, a few seconds

each, I paused the elevator between the tenth and eleventh floors, then the ninth and tenth, making it shudder each time.

A brief pulse of muscle in Angelo's jaw exposed a hint of surprise. He flexed his biceps and leaned forward like he would with another man who was picking a fight. He was squaring off with me. A minute later he shook off my attempted prowess and stepped with a confident smile into the hallway that led to Istanbul Coffee.

Chapter Sixteen

Jasmina stood with her back to the door in a red, sequin-covered belly-dance costume, rivulets of sweat running down her spine. She had been dancing as entertainment in the shop to increase business. That evening the place was empty of customers, and her perspiration was from the rogue heater that would shut down for hours at a time, then with non-stop output turn the room into an inferno.

She smelled Angelo, the pungent scent of a cracked cumin seed, before she heard his footsteps behind her. She was already light-headed as she whirled around to meet the unexpected image of his smiling face.

"It's warm in here," he said, watching her chest rise and fall with quick breaths and the tops of her breasts glisten with sweat.

"The heater," she said. "It goes crazy."

"I can take a look at the controls," he said glancing at the panel on the front of the heater and a brief flare of orange from inside. "Got a screwdriver?"

"In the kitchen," Jasmina said, then went to search for the tool. A few minutes later, her voice called out from the kitchen, "Still looking!"

He was standing in front of her. She hadn't heard him come in. The room was hot, without enough oxygen for her to take a normal breath. She wasn't going to wait to see what he did next. She had to take his clothes off. "Come here," she heard herself command as she grabbed the waistband of his pants and pulled him toward her, pushing him back against the butcher block table. Her fingers fumbled with the slick, pearly shirt buttons, but she undid all of them, and pushed her hands up under the pale, yellow cloth, along his ribbed undershirt and up to his bare shoulders. The shirt fell to the floor.

The zipper tab of his pants was hot between her fingers. He stood perfectly still as she separated the fly. She braced a palm against the hot flesh of his lower abdomen, ran a finger through the curly red-gold hairs that spread in a downward line, turning darker where they peeked out of the top of his blue silk boxers.

"Why have you been acting like you don't want me?" she threw the words up to him, cold and hard, like shards of glass, "when you know damn well you do."

She grasped the waistbands of his jeans and underwear and felt his hips thrust against her hands. "So the waiting would make you out of control with desire. Isn't that your fantasy?"

She smiled and shook her head in acknowledgment, then dropped to her knees, and with the swift, downward motion of her arms stripped the lower part of his body. His swollen shaft was larger than she had imagined, silky purple-brown, with the tracing of a vein that ran along the side. It waved slightly, invitingly. Below a thicket of reddish black hair, his balls hung heavy, beckoning to be touched.

She had to reach around him and grab his buttocks to pull herself up high enough to reach the head of his penis with her mouth. It jumped against her upper lip as she teased it with the tip of her tongue, felt the little ridge on the underside, tasted its salty flavor. Her lips wrapped around it, inching forward to engulf the entire slippery sword before unsheathing it again and repeating the motion. She pushed down on his hips to raise herself to a standing position, tilting her face upward, presenting her warm mouth.

"Do you have secrets, Angelo?" she whispered as he bent his mouth toward hers. "Are you a Frayer?"

He shoved her backward and, caught off balance, she dropped

to the floor as a loud pop came from the shop, followed by a flash of orange and a roar. Jasmina scrambled on hands and knees out of the kitchen, screaming as she pulled herself upright and ran toward the flames that were shooting out of the heater and blistering the creamy skin of a nearby chair.

She grabbed a tablecloth and rushed to the fire. As she tried to smother the flames with the purple cloth, the fabric erupted with fire. She threw it down as hot needles pierced her face and neck. The hem of her costume shriveled like paper in a fireplace.

The floor slammed into her shoulder and she felt her arms and legs constricted as Angelo rolled her across the floor in another tablecloth. Above her screams, she heard glass breaking in the distance, then the loud whoosh of the contents of a fire extinguisher as Angelo subdued the flames, followed by the sharp slap of the heater cord as he kicked it loose from the outlet. Angelo unwrapped her from the tight fabric and bent over her. She thought he was saying, "You're all right," but she clutched at her cheeks and screamed, "No! My face! How does it look?"

He pulled her up against him and held her face, which was dotted with red marks, against his chest to still her hysteria. "It's not too bad," he said stroking her hair. "In a few months, the scars will be practically invisible." She lifted her cheek from the wet spot her tears had made on his undershirt. "And the one on your breast ..." Jasmina looked down in alarm at her left breast and the red slash across the top that was starting to sting " ... it won't even show most of the time, depending."

"What's going on? I smelled smoke!" Lonnie yelled as he burst into the shop.

"It's under control," Angelo said as he pulled Jasmina to her feet and maneuvered her to a chair. "It was the heater. It malfunctioned. Luckily, I put the fire out before it damaged more than a chair or two."

"What about her?" Lonnie looked past Angelo to where Jasmina sat with a table cloth pulled around her shoulders and up over the lower half of her face. "Jasmina, are you all right?"

Jasmina nodded as she looked down at the floor and mumbled, "It's my fault."

Lonnie walked over to her. "What's your fault?"

"Everything."

"I'll take you up to your place." Lonnie stretched out his hand.

"Why don't you get her some brandy first?" Angelo said, while he backed up toward the heater.

"Yeah," Lonnie said as he looked back and forth between Jasmina and Angelo and the charred, overturned furniture.

"The brandy?" Angelo said impatiently as he stood with his back to the heater and reached behind his hip.

"Your fly's open," said Lonnie as he moved toward the door, with a second's glance at Jasmina. Angelo maintained a cool, unblinking stare.

"Hey, man, I got us another gig next week, classier joint, too," Angelo called after Lonnie as he walked into the hallway. "I'll come by your place tonight so we can talk."

Jasmina lowered the table cloth from her face and glared at Angelo. "You're a dangerous man, Angelo Fallon," she said.

"If you don't want to get wet, stay out of the river, darlin'," he said, crooking his eyebrow and sending a shiver through her.

With the hand behind him Angelo pulled the remnants of a paint-streaked rag from a slot in the heater and shoved it into his back pocket.

Chapter Seventeen

Lonnie spied the eighteen-inch-long, flat, cardboard box sticking out of the dumpster the next day when he hauled out the burnt debris and destroyed chairs from Istanbul Coffee. It was an ordinary piece of trash, but the company name on the side of the box piqued his interest. Next to a symbol of a heart with a ring and "14 units" were the words: "Mama Tatum's Good-For-What-Ails-Ya Tea and Potion."

"Sister Daisy's world," he said, as he walked inside through the back door. I followed his thoughts back to his boyhood home. In his memory he sat with his grandma up from Mississippi for a visit. Sister Daisy, a medicine woman and soothsayer, talked about potions and spells.

"Just crazy tales spun by old ladies from the South, that's all," he said with a chuckle as he entered his apartment. But it occurred to him that he had made his living for forty years in the liquor business from people's belief that "elixirs" would change their moods or even their lives.

Sitting at his computer, he got thirty hits on the Internet for "Mama Tatum," most referring to male-stripper-turned-actor Channing Tatum or others about child star Tatum O'Neal. "Tea and Potion" brought a proliferation of home cures for everything from bunions to impotence. He added "love potions" to the search, surmising from the talk of charms and curses he had heard as a boy that they most often involved matters of the heart.

After a half hour of wrong turns and dead ends and two and a half glasses of Hennessey, well over his usual limit, Lonnie arrived at a site that bore the same heart and ring symbol that he had seen on the box in the dumpster. The Web page was a garish graphic with purple, red, and black letters and images, the most prominent a pair of dark eyes that stared out from under a polka-dotted kerchief. He presumed the hypnotizing orbs belonged to Mama Tatum herself.

Below this image Lonnie read: "Is your lover: Lukewarm? Contrary? Cheating? Mama Tatum has the answer to your troubles! Her special Mama Tatum's Good-For-What-Ails-Ya Tea and Potion will unleash the passion in the one you desire and give you COMPLETE CONTROL! Don't Delay!! Order Mama Tatum's Good-For-What-Ails-Ya Tea and Potion Today!!!" In small letters at the bottom of the page were the words: "Distributed by Frayer-Dumont Industries, Carroll Parish, Louisiana."

Lonnie closed the page and pushed his chair back from the computer. Angelo was from Louisiana. "Complete control?" he repeated, still seeing the purple letters in front of him even though the screen had turned dark. "Corrine?"

He downed the last half glass of brandy. Then he stood up and laughed at himself, a snicker that built to a hearty belly-laugh until tears rolled down his cheeks and his sides hurt. "You old fool," he said to himself. "It's tea! Not a magic potion! Tea!" He picked up the bottle of Hennessey and poured himself one more shot. "I got my tea, too."

Corrine doesn't need me babysitting her, he thought. Give the woman a break. If she wants to delude herself into believing Angelo's spin so that she can grab a little good feeling, why not? You know yourself, Lonnie boy, being lonely ain't no way to live. He drank a last shot, shook his head, and put the glass down. "Tea, humph," he muttered.

He went over to his organ and ran his fingers over the keys from side to side, enjoying the sound and even more the fact that his hands could elicit the sound. He jumped into a Billy Preston song about a story with no moral. Disturbing the neighbors at night was not a worry; the apartments above, below, and beside him were vacant.

"Making music is a communal art." I heard the words in Lonnie's head as he glanced at their source in a faded black-and-white photo on the wall: a weathered, bald guitarist under the smoky sign of the Green Horse Lounge. You told the truth, Curly, Lonnie thought, and Angelo has reminded me. We musicians have to share our rhythms. I can do without Jasmina or even Corrine if I have to, he thought, but not my music.

He sang, "Let the bad guy win every once in a while . . ."

On the seventh floor, Angelo sat in front of a computer in Miss Liza's apartment. The room was dark with only the bright rectangle of the screen visible. A pungent mix of odors, mold and mothballs and rotten wood, permeated the place. On the computer desktop was a collection of folders. Five of them were marked with people's names. He clicked on the ones marked "Sunny," "Bear," and "Lil' Bit." Pages displayed from newspapers in Houston and Cleveland, and from *The Army Times*. The fourth folder, marked "Henry," he left closed.

The fifth one was not named for an individual but I recognized the name "Eastwood." I expected if Angelo opened that folder it would reveal his plans for the parcel of land that Liza Beechwood had left to her dear nephew. But how did his plans involve Corrine, Lonnie, and Jasmina?

In the penthouse, Corrine was glad that Angelo was downstairs for a while getting the last of Miss Liza's things packed up to be moved out tomorrow. She had been having a hard time keeping her thoughts clear when he was around since he had moved back in after the ballroom catastrophe. Maybe she hadn't been getting enough rest. After all, she had been too tired to go for that walk.

One thought that was perfectly clear now as she sat cross-legged in a lavender chair in her living room was that she was angry. She hadn't said anything to Angelo yet and that was what she was thinking on intently. This time he'd done something that couldn't be soothed away with his sweet words or arousing touch or a cup of tea.

The day before, he had smelled of smoke and something else that she couldn't identify. She had been cooking salmon and rice when he came up behind her. She thought he would be displeased that she was cooking. For some time, he had handled all the meals and she was virtually banned from her own kitchen.

But instead of lecturing her, he had caressed her breasts until she moaned, then he picked her up and set her on the kitchen counter facing him. He had kissed her throat while he pulled her panties off and stimulated her with his fingers until she was dripping wet. She started to come before he entered her.

"What do you want, baby?" he said into her ear. She grabbed for his cock and in the tangle of his crotch hair she felt a tiny, slick object.

As she sat in the lavender chair she studied the object poised on the tip of her finger. It was the same color as her anger, a red sequin.

Chapter Eighteen

Angelo held the door of 706 open as two men in blue coveralls exited, rolling a couple of dollies stacked with cardboard boxes. He watched the workers head to the elevator as half a dozen older men and women advanced down the hall toward him. His brief glance their way betrayed that the residents had caught his attention, even as he attempted to duck back inside the apartment.

"Mr. Fallon," called out the woman at the front of the group. She moved awkwardly forward in a bulky pink sweater, fleece pants, and black felt boots.

Angelo turned his annoyed expression away from her, then within a split second, faced her with a sunny smile, "Good evening, ma'am."

"We only wish," she said, then clucked her tongue with a hint of disgust.

"Can I help you in some way?" Angelo asked, raising an eyebrow with a look of concern as he edged a foot forward over the threshold of the apartment.

"We certainly hope so," the woman said as her companions nodded in unison. "We're from the second and third floors. We've been having some problems with our heat."

"Leaks, too," shouted out a short man in the back of the group.

"I can't get my windows shut," added a thin woman with silver hair peeking out from a cable-knit beret.

"Well, I'm not sure what I can do. Shouldn't you be talking to

Corrine?"

"A lot of flippin' good that does," the pink-sweater lady cut in. "We've been complaining for weeks."

"But why are you coming to me? I—"

"You're such a nice, young man, Mr. Fallon," the woman continued, sweetening her tone. "You came all the way up here to take care of Miss Liza's things and we heard how you helped out Lonnie after the robbery and how you came to Jasmina's rescue from that fire."

"Still, I don't see—"

"We want you to sign this petition," a round-faced man blurted out as he shoved a piece of paper and pen toward Angelo.

Angelo took the piece of paper and studied the typed paragraphs at the top and the short list of signatures scrawled underneath. "Hmmm, I hate to get anyone in trouble, seeing as how I'm not really a permanent resident. What do you plan to do with this?"

"We're going to get everyone in the building to sign and then we're going to present it to Corrine, like a show of force," said the woman in pink.

Angelo chuckled. "Oh, is that all. I thought maybe you were going to do something drastic, demand some official action with winter coming and all, and the heat and the health issues, not to mention the electrical hazards."

"Electrical hazards?" the six residents said in unison.

"What do you mean, 'official action?'" the woman with the hat asked.

Angelo smiled with a hint of discomfort. "Well, like I said, I'm not trying to get anyone in trouble, but it seems that taking your petition to the mayor might get the results you want. I've had a cup of coffee with him a time or two—he's a Louisiana man, too, you know–he seems like someone who would listen. And he is running for re-election."

The residents exchanged enlightened glances and the round-faced man grabbed the petition out of Angelo's hands. "That's what we need, someone who will listen," he said to the group. "Thanks, Mr. Fallon."

"I don't know what for," Angelo said, "but good luck with your petition."

He slipped into the apartment while the residents walked toward the elevator talking in animated tones. A man in black coveralls and black cap emerged from the apartment a short while later.

In the parking lot the man in black work clothes climbed into the driver's seat of a white box truck parked facing the street across from the front entrance, where more than thirty cardboard boxes were stacked and lined up. The sky was in between day and night, the flat light that tricked perception.

Corrine stepped off the elevator on the first floor, headed outside where she expected to meet Angelo directing the movement of the last of Miss Liza's things: Alaska memorabilia, books, and art that he was donating to a Fairbanks historical society and to the library.

She had seen only one keepsake that he had brought to the penthouse for himself. When he had carried in the five-by-seven, framed, black-and-white photo, she guessed it was a fond picture of Angelo as a boy with his beloved great-aunt. Later, when he was out of the room, she took a closer look and saw instead the image of a stately, columned mansion with a wide lawn, devoid of human figures.

Outside the penthouse, away from the rooms where she and Angelo made love, she felt lighter. She could think more clearly, organize her thoughts about what she would say to him about his infidelity, how she would be willing to forgive a one-time transgression, but she would not stand for any further disrespect.

She passed Istanbul Coffee. The shop was dark, the door shut, although it was only six-thirty and it normally stayed open until seven. That's odd, she thought. Is Angelo in there with her? How many times have they been together? Has it been going on all along? How big of a fool am I?

Corrine pushed the door handle and the door gave way. The faint sounds of flutes and drums reached her ears and she followed the music on tiptoes to the entry of the side room. Jasmina, in a sheer black skirt and silver bra, gyrated to the music, lost in a memory with her back to the doorway. A gray cap embroidered with "Cache Heating and Fireplace" covered the crown of her dark, swaying hair. Corrine rapped sharply on the open door and Jasmina whirled around. The Turkish dancer's head jerked back in shock from seeing anyone in her shop, especially Corrine, and from seeing Corrine's appearance.

Her once luxurious, platinum mane was pulled back in a limp ponytail, a few wiry strands escaping to stand out comically from the top of her head. Harsh marionette lines were carved in her puffy, pale face from the outside of her nose to the corners of her mouth and down the sides of her chin. Her eyes appeared more dull gray than blue, the upper lids drooping. Baggy, gray sweats, bloused at the knees and with a tomato stain over the outline of a braless left breast had replaced the flattering, flowing outfits that Corrine had often worn.

Through Jasmina's reaction, even I couldn't avoid seeing Corrine's exposed cracks and decay and flaws of age. I thought I had noticed a limp as she walked into the shop. In any case, she moved with less grace, dragging along extra pounds that had settled around her hips and waist. I waited for the lovely lilt of her voice as she opened her mouth, but when she spoke the sound was coarse and dry.

"Expecting someone else?" Corrine squawked.

"I wasn't expecting anyone," Jasmina snapped back, turning off the music. "What do you want?"

"I want you to keep your hands and the rest of what you've got off of Angelo."

"We haven't spoken in over a month and you barge in here to tell me to stop banging some guy?"

"Not some guy, the one I'm in a relationship with."

"Really, Corrine? A relationship?"

"I know that's a foreign concept to you, but I'm in it for love. I'm not just a vagina."

"You think you're so much better than me, Corrine? We're all just parts in the end, male parts, female parts, and I plan to enjoy using mine, without complicating things with love."

Corrine narrowed her eyes and tears squeezed out the sides. "So it's all meaningless sex for you. I'm warning you, Jasmina, leave Angelo alone, or I'll kick you out of this building."

"Yeah? Well, don't do me any favors." Jasmina placed her hands on her hips and tossed her head back defiantly. "Maybe I'll just leave on my own and take the rent money with me."

Corrine's lower lip quivered and she bit down on it to hold back a sob. She remembered a night long ago, gently holding Jasmina's chin, dabbing the blood away from her eye where an abusive boyfriend had planted his fist. "After all I've done for you. After I've looked out for you."

"I don't need you to look out for me." Jasmina's eyes filled with water. "You're not my mother!" The tears flooded down her cheeks as Corrine turned to go. "Get out of my shop, you crazy, old bitch!" Jasmina flung the gray cap toward the older woman and it glanced off the door frame and landed on the floor.

As Corrine hurried out of the coffee shop, she spied Lonnie straightening a sign at the end of an aisle, looking nervously over his shoulder, cocking his head, listening for something. When he looked toward the entrance and their eyes met, he turned away.

"Watch out, ma'am. Got a lot of junk here," a man leaning on a dolly said to Corrine as she moved into the shadowy space in front of the building where the motion lights no longer worked, hiding her tear-streaked face.

"One person's trash is another person's treasure," she said, peering behind the man, looking for Angelo.

"Huh?" the worker responded.

"The library and the historical society will be glad to get this old stuff."

"Library? Lady, we're taking this crap to the dump."

"What? You can't be serious. Some of this is art work, valuable books."

"All I can say, lady, is I have my orders."

"Orders from whom?"

"The dude who's getting rid of it. Fallon."

A pair of taillights flared and an engine growled as the box truck zoomed in reverse toward the group of boxes and to where Corrine was standing. A male voice shouted and she felt someone grip her left upper arm.

She fell backward as the bumper of the truck tapped her left leg. She didn't remember going down but recalled an elongated flash of red light and the smell of vehicle exhaust as she lay on her back against crushed cardboard, the hard corners of boxes digging into the backs of her arms. The side of her left knee was throbbing. She touched the spot where the skin was scraped off, then looked at the blood on her fingers. When she tried to sit up, groaning as her stiff muscles refused to cooperate, Angelo knelt beside her, gently pushing her back down.

"Darlin', you could be seriously hurt. Don't try to move." He pressed his hands firmly against her legs, arms, fingers, spine, asking her if she felt pain. After he inspected her head, he moved his arms under her shoulders and slowly lifted her to a sitting position.

"That truck tried to hit me," she said, looking up at him, dazed.

"No, sweetheart, it was an accident. You're going to be fine. I'll take you upstairs." He helped her to her feet and she discovered that, although she was sore, the fall, cushioned by the boxes, had barely impaired her normal movement. "What were you doing down here standing in the dark anyway?" he asked, almost angry.

"I wanted to talk to you about something," she said, apologetically, as he opened the front door for her.

"What was so important that you needed to talk about it right now?" As they stepped into the elevator, he put his arm around her, but his touch didn't make her feel safe.

"Jasmina."

"How is Jasmina? I haven't seen her around in a couple of weeks."

She was having second thoughts about asking him too much, already deciding to be content with what she had. She looked at him and said in a flat voice, "Those guys said they were taking Miss Liza's stuff to the dump."

Angelo smiled. "Probably their idea of a little joke. You can't believe everything people say, now can you, darlin'?"

He pushed the button for the penthouse and wiped a patch of cardboard dust off the leg of his black coveralls.

Chapter Nineteen

A tall, young man with a scraggly, red beard, wearing a Boston baseball cap, approached the counter at Big Dipper Liquor, carrying no merchandise, and reached into the inside of his jacket. Bullets of sweat erupted along Lonnie's hairline. His heart quickened as he carefully opened the cash drawer and slid his hand inside, feeling the hard, cold pistol and curling his fingers around the grip.

"Hey, Lonnie," the man said, breaking the store owner's concentration, "you got any Moosehead in the cooler?"

"Uh, uh, yeah, right side there," Lonnie said, pointing as the man followed his direction, extracted a vibrating cell phone from his jacket, and walked to the cooler while finishing a phone conversation.

"Two for one, right?" the man asked, looking back at Lonnie, referring to the one-day promotion advertised on a sign in the front window.

"Just the wine," Lonnie said. The man hesitated before he pulled a six-pack out of the cooler, then returned to the counter. "Do I know you?"

"Sure. Mike O'Toole, on the second floor." He pulled at his whiskers and smiled. "I guess I look different with the beard. It's for the Red Sox. Solidarity, man. We're going to the Series this year."

Even though he was not a fan of the game, Lonnie followed

sports enough to know Boston's baseball team had been calling up its mojo by growing beards since spring training. Baseball was too nervous a game for Lonnie. Watching the players with all those tics, adjusting their batting helmets again and again, hitting their shoes with the bat, spitting, scratching, spitting, hitting, scratching–it drove him up the wall.

"Oh, yeah, yeah, Mike, Mike O'Toole. You're right, man, the beard threw me off." Lonnie laughed off his nervousness, continuing to laugh to chase away the tension even after Mike left the store with his beer.

He glanced at the security mirrors like he was in the habit of doing every five minutes now. By his accounting there was no one else in the store. Mike had bought the last six-pack of Moosehead. *Do I have time to go back and get more out of the big fridge?* No, *better not chance it,* he said to himself, in mid-stride from behind the counter. He might not hear the motion alarm at the entrance and someone might come in unnoticed.

Lonnie's growing wariness puzzled him. He expected the fear that afflicted him from the robbery to dissipate as the weeks went by, but it had intensified. Maybe he would never be the same. He no longer toasted himself at the end of the day with his glass of brandy. He swallowed it hard and fast and thought of someone named Miss Leibowitz, imagined the terror in her face just before a guy called T.J. knocked her to the floor, then emptied the cash from the safe, and fled the store. *But it wasn't like I was the one who robbed her,* he told himself.

Lonnie held his hands out in front of him and willed them to stop trembling. *Pull yourself together, man,* he said to himself. *You're out of places to run.*

The motion alarm sounded and Lonnie registered two more customers, both women, one young, one old, with matching noses and cheekbones, maybe mother and daughter. They slowly surveyed the wine aisles. He inhaled deeply, set his jaw, checked the mirrors again, glanced down each aisle left to right, right to left, tapped the cash drawer, on alert, with his own set of tics.

Inside Istanbul Coffee Jasmina studied her reflection in a window that separated her from the darkness outside. She knew the exact location of each of the tiny, worm-like puckers spread across her forehead and chin even though they were nearly invisible. The welt on her right cheek was the only noticeable damage left by the heater fire.

Underneath her red jersey dress, the scar on her breast had faded to a thin, pink line. She still had the looks that had made Michael Jones fall in love with her. The fire had pulled her secret shame back to the front of her mind, like an acrid smoke overlaying the embers of sweet incense.

She wondered if he had found another woman, someone who could look at his face the way it was now and see him for the man he was inside. Maybe he had met a nurse during his stay at the hospital and they had fallen in love and married. Perhaps they had a baby or two.

Probably, Jasmina thought, she had never really loved him. Likely, it was just prolonged desire. His dancing blue eyes, his devilish smile, the way a lock of his sandy hair grazed his eyebrow—had disarmed her. She had been enraptured when she looked up into that face and climbed into the warm wall of his muscled chest and arms. They'd had so much sex, she was constantly aflame.

The coffee shop door sighed as it was opened and chair legs squeaked on the floor behind her. Jasmina turned around to face a young couple. The man with black, curly hair leaned into the red-headed, freckle-nosed woman and nuzzled her neck. She giggled and her cheeks colored pink as she saw Jasmina walking toward them.

"Do you two need a minute?" Jasmina asked with a warm smile.

"No," the man said, straightening up with a grin and a wink for his blushing partner. "We know exactly what we want. The same thing we had three years ago when we met at this same table."

"It was love at first sight," the woman gushed, and her hazel eyes sparkled. "And we've been on our honeymoon ever since."

She displayed the modest-sized diamond on her left hand for Jasmina's admiration.

"Congratulations," Jasmina said. "What can I get you?"

"Two buttered rum grandes," they said in unison, then looked at each other like kids eyeing a double-scoop ice cream cone.

After Jasmina delivered the coffees, she gave them a mischievous grin, then went back into the kitchen. A few minutes later she brought out a chocolate-frosted cupcake, left from a dozen she had baked the day before, topped with a lighted candle.

"Happy anniversary," she said as she set the miniature confection in front of the couple. They gasped and thanked her like she had brought out a six-tiered cake.

"Shall we?" the man said to his wife.

"Yes, let's make a wish," she answered his immediately understood question.

They extinguished the candle with one synchronized breath and then sealed the ritual with a prolonged kiss.

Jasmina had walked away to give the lovebirds some privacy, but before she reached the kitchen, the young woman called after her, "Oh, miss, where's the bathroom?"

Jasmina motioned toward the door and the rear of the hall as the woman stood up. "Out and turn left just before the double doors."

"Be right back, baby," the young woman said to her husband and blew him a kiss.

As his wife left the shop, the man beckoned Jasmina back to the table.

"Do you need something else?" Jasmina took a step closer to the table. He grabbed her hand and pushed it down on his crotch. She felt his dick swell into her palm through his jeans.

He grinned up into her burning face. "I can come back later, alone, if you want to have some fun."

With her free hand, Jasmina swooped the cupcake off the table and smashed it into the man's face. He let go of her other hand and leapt up. "What the fuck?" He swiped a glob of chocolate frosting out of one eye with his finger. "Why'd you do that?"

Jasmina made two fists at her sides and backed away from the table toward the kitchen. "Because people should fall in love and stay in love for more than two minutes. Because we aren't just parts." She walked backward behind the counter and was almost in the kitchen when she shouted, "And because you're a horrible, horrible person and she deserves better!"

As she sat on her kitchen floor, her knees drawn up to her chest, her body shaking, she heard the couple's voices from inside the shop. "What happened?" the female voice said.

"That woman. She just went off on me," the male voice answered. "Let's get out of here."

Jasmina heard the rub of chair legs on the floor, followed by a pause in the conversation. Then the woman again, "You're leaving her a tip? You should be calling the cops. She assaulted you."

"She's just having a bad day," the man said.

"More like a bad life," the indignant spouse said and Jasmina heard a chair slam against the table and footsteps fade toward the door.

"Yes, a bad life," Jasmina echoed to herself.

An ice-blue coolness settled between her legs and spread through her insides. She felt no desire to be with a man ever again. She remembered the crude phrase used by her husband's Army buddies about where their wives should be while they were deployed. That's where Jasmina decided she would go: cold storage.

Chapter Twenty

In the penthouse, Corrine woke in mid-afternoon on the green couch, breathing hard and shaking. Aches and pains in her back and legs lingered after the fall behind the truck and sapped her energy. She had nodded off but rest escaped her. A disturbing memory played and replayed in her brain like a movie as soon as she closed her eyes.

She saw a Mustang zooming in reverse out of a garage and down a driveway and she heard the two sickening thumps. She saw herself kneeling beside Price lying still on the flagstone in his crisply pleated pants, a pool of blood underneath his head and a stray drop of red on his butter-colored tie. His fixed blue eyes accused her as her tears fell on the face of the man she loved.

"It was an accident," her thin voice cried out as sirens and lights surrounded her.

"You need to come with us, Corey Mae," a male voice said. Her emerald ring caught for a second in her lace blouse as an officer pulled her away. The police didn't even have enough respect to call her Mrs. Cunningham.

"I've lost my ring," she said rubbing her finger as she shook off the grogginess of her nap and tried to focus on the man's face that floated in front of her. "It was an accident. Don't be angry."

"Angry? I did tell you not to sell the ring, but I'm not angry."

"It was an accident. I even told them in court ..."

Angelo grabbed Corrine's shoulder and shook her. "Wake up,

darlin', you're talking nonsense. You sold the ring, remember? To settle the lawsuit. You didn't go to court." Corrine's eyes bounced from side to side. "It's Angelo, I'm right here."

"Angelo." She steadied her gaze. "I thought you were—" He let go of her and she sank back on the couch. "I was having a dream." He pushed a pen and some papers toward her. "What's this?" she asked, looking at the documents. Again she rubbed her third finger. "I miss my ring."

"You'll have another ring one day, my sweet." He bent down and kissed her forehead. "This is the power of attorney we talked about so that I can make quick decisions when necessary about fixing up the building and handling the tenants."

"A wedding ring?"

His head jolted up like the unexpected question had popped him under the chin. "You're thinking, you and I?"

Corrine's face deflated like a leftover party balloon. The way he touched her temple when he brushed her hair from her face was just a coincidence, she thought, the nickname he called her just a guess. "Of course not. I mean, I know we're just casual."

Angelo squeezed her unadorned hand. "No, sweetheart." He kissed her fingertips. "But every time there's something between a man and a woman it doesn't end in marriage." He picked up the pen and put it between her fingers.

"It does in my life."

"And how did that work out?"

"They died and left me alone."

"I'm not going to die and leave you alone. Seems like I'm the better investment."

She couldn't help smiling just a little at his logic. As she signed her name, she glanced at the seal stamped on the document, and thought Angelo must have used his influence with someone at City Hall to save her a trip to the notary.

"You'll keep me posted?" she asked. Angelo's brow crinkled with confusion. "About Big Blue."

"Of course, my love. I'll tell you everything you need to know."

In disgust, I pulled up a musty odor from a lower floor and expelled it through an air vent. Angelo wrinkled his nose at the brief, foul smell.

As he walked out the front door, he spied his accomplice in the parking lot, leaning against the front fender of the blue Caddy.

"I have power of attorney, Henry, and that old woman doesn't have a clue. When the time comes, I'll pull the switch." Angelo pumped the mayor's hand.

Henry slapped Angelo's shoulder. "What did you have to do to get that?"

"Something short of marrying her. Hey, I thought we were meeting at Junie's. I thought you didn't like coming here."

"I was in the neighborhood, shaking some hands, showing my appreciation to the downtown business community for support-ing the Run for the Warriors," Henry said with a grin. "Thought I might go in and pick up a good deal on a half-dozen or so bottles from Big Dipper. I see Lonnie's running a sale."

"Yeah, one man's famine is another man's feast. You stocking up for some big election victory party?"

"Not yet. I'm having some guests over to the cabin on Harding Lake this weekend and that, my Frayer friend, should pay off for both of us."

"Keep that word under your breath; you've already shot off your mouth enough to people in this building," Angelo scolded.

"What?" Henry feigned shock. "I don't know what you're talk-ing about."

Angelo crooked his eyebrow with mistrust. "Who are these guests who'll be wetting their whistles with your liquor?"

The mayor beamed like he'd just been elected governor. "The Sheraton people. The ones who have the votes that count. I'm going to give them a real taste of Alaska hospitality."

"Just make sure they leave with the right frame of mind."

"Damn right I will. How are things looking inside?" Henry jerked his thumb toward one of the half-open windows on the second floor. I banged it shut and he jumped back against the car. Angelo didn't twitch a muscle.

"Coming right along. Time for you to get the official process going. Why don't you check things out while you're in there?"

"Yeah, maybe Lonnie's not the only one giving discounts."

"I'm talking about the building, Henry."

"I know, I know."

Inside, Henry noticed with a sly smile the sign in the coffee shop window advertising half-price lattes. I tried to bunch up the hall carpet to make him stumble as he swaggered by the shop, but he had already darkened the door of Big Dipper Liquor.

Chapter Twenty-one

A fierce wind that had persisted for days rattled my windows, knocked over cyclists on fat-tire bikes, and sent debris flying through parking lots. Old-timers ruminated over morning coffee about the rarity of snowless streets and temperatures above thirty-five in October.

On the corner of Cushman and First Avenue, a red-faced man with a snarled, gray beard wore a cardboard sign that proclaimed, "The End is Near." He held onto the railing on the Cushman Street Bridge to keep his balance. A strong gust lifted the sign away from the doomsayer's body and flung it into the Chena River, almost taking him with it. Another blustery blast threw open the front door and catapulted the city building inspector into the first-floor hall.

At first, I mistook him for a repairman dressed in loose jeans and a flannel shirt, armed with carpenter's tools, a flashlight, a video camera, and a laptop. I expected Corrine authorized this visit and would soon come down from the penthouse to give him a list of jobs that would heal my malfunctioning parts. Instead, the recently formed Big Blue Action Committee stepped from the elevator and greeted the visitor.

The six residents who had accosted Angelo with their petition acted as tour guides for the inspector, escorting him to each floor, ushering him into various apartments. He pulled back corners of carpets, photographed moldy floors, and measured cracks on walls and ceilings. He ran faucets, flushed toilets, slid his hands along pipes, and reached into heating vents, periodically stopping to tap notes into his laptop. After riding the elevator up and down eleven floors three times and taking more notes, he headed for the ballroom with the shiny-eyed committee members leading the way.

"This is going to take longer than I thought," he said to the residents, as he stared up at the jagged-edged chasm in the ceiling where the grand chandelier was once suspended. "I'm going to take a short lunch break and we can continue in, say, twenty minutes?"

The intruder set down his equipment, opened a metal tackle box, extracted a thick sandwich, and chomped into it. A shower of bread crumbs and a drop of mustard soiled the finely crafted oak planks of the former dance floor.

Lonnie noticed the activity on the first floor as he opened Big Dipper Liquor. His curiosity brought him out in the hall as he glanced at a patron coming into the store and saw the inspector heading into the ballroom carrying an expandable ladder retrieved from his truck.

"Hey, man, what's going on?" he called out to the stranger when the inspector came out of the ballroom several minutes later with the ladder in tow.

The inspector leaned the ladder against a wall, pushing back a flap of loose wallpaper. He presented a quick smile and his outstretched hand to Lonnie. "Clyde Clinger, city building inspector."

Lonnie shook the man's hand. "Lonnie Jackson. So, what are you doing here, Clyde?"

"Following up on some concerns. Never been in this building before, but I hear you've been here a while. I'll bet you've got some stories," he said with an easy chuckle like they were pals out for drinks.

"Me and Big Blue do go back a ways. So the owner called you in to look over some things that need fixing?"

"Yeah, in fact I'm waiting for the owner to let me in the furnace room."

"I didn't see the owner down here before you went in the ballroom."

"Ballroom? Wow, you don't expect to see that in Fairbanks. I guess, back in the day ... but it's a mess in there now."

"Yeah, I didn't see the owner let you in there."

"I'm allowed access to any areas that can be accessed by others, like the people who live here, the apartments, the elevator, pretty much anywhere, except places that are locked up like the furnace room."

"I'm sure Corrine will be down soon."

"Who?"

"Miss Easter, the owner."

"Naw, I'm waiting for the guy I talked to on the phone. Fallon, I think his name is, got a Southern accent kind of reminds me of the big boss, Mr. Fornette."

Lonnie's confused response stuck in his throat and came out as a cough.

"Hey, Lonnie, want to take my money?" a male voice called out from inside the store.

"Looks like you got a customer, Lonnie," Clyde said with grin. His head jerked toward the sound of the elevator door opening, revealing its passenger, Angelo. Lonnie frowned and reluctantly re-entered his store without setting the inspector straight about Corrine's status.

Over the next couple of hours, through the limited view from his shop, Lonnie watched Angelo and Clyde enter and exit the ballroom, knowing that access to the furnace room was through a door off a back corner of the dance hall. He saw the two laughing and talking, one with an arm thrown casually around the other like buddies.

Lonnie found displays near the door that needed replenishing and streaks on the outside of the shop window that faced the hall. While he rubbed out the offending marks on the glass with a dish towel, his eyes and ears were alert to movements and sounds near Istanbul Coffee, where he saw Angelo exit.

Lonnie was waiting to catch Angelo alone so that he could inquire about his apparent new role of landlord, but when Angelo came out of the coffee shop he was joined by an older man whom Lonnie recognized as the newly re-elected mayor, Henry Fornette. He had seen the mayor's grinning face and raised hands flashing "V's" for victory Richard Nixon-style plastered across the front page of yesterday's paper.

Two weeks before the election, Lonnie recalled, another top-of-the-fold news photo had shown Fornette in lumpy sweats, striding alongside a tall man with prosthetic legs who was wearing running shorts and an Army logo T-shirt. In the picture, the pudgy mayor and the stoic soldier led a crowd of runners. An American flag unfurled behind them, carried by another soldier as they passed cheering spectators on Noble Street. Lonnie didn't like the mayor any more than I did, but he had to give him credit. Henry Fornette had known how to play the patriotic card just in time to make it pay off at the ballot box.

With his ear cocked in Angelo and Henry's direction, Lonnie picked up snatches of phrases as they traded words in a low but forceful tone. It was hard at first for Lonnie to define which words were coming from which man. Although Lonnie had heard the mayor's voice before, he now noticed the pronounced Southern accent following the building inspector's comment.

From Fornette he heard "outrageous," and "you overestimate my influence." Angelo's accent was similar, but his honeyed tone differentiated his voice from the mayor's. Lonnie picked up, "I'm not asking you to sell your soul, just take it down by March" and "you don't want to cross my kind," but the scattered words had no meaning. When the voices stopped, Lonnie polished the glass more vigorously, trying to make himself look even more like a man focused on his work and less like an eavesdropping bystander.

"Hey, Clyde, come look at the damage on this wall," Angelo

called toward the inside of the coffee shop and his footsteps faded in that direction.

Lonnie turned his head to the side, and out of the corner of his eye noticed Henry Fornette still standing outside the coffee shop, muttering to himself. As the mayor turned and walked toward the front exit, he passed Lonnie, and Lonnie heard Fornette's clear and angry utterance, "'Sell my soul,' he says. 'You don't want to cross my kind,' he says. Fucking Frayers."

I gave Fornette some help leaving, forcing the front door to catch him by surprise, slamming it behind him, hard enough to smash his pinky finger right across the middle of the nail. He cursed and grabbed his injured hand with the other one.

Inside, Lonnie wondered, Frayers? What does he mean? Southern slang? Not a compliment, that's for sure. A hint of a memory flicked through his mind, but it was gone before he could grab hold of it. Lonnie felt a firm hand grip his shoulder.

"Hey, man, this is—"

"Clyde, the building inspector," Lonnie finished Angelo's sentence, as Angelo motioned back toward the city employee dragging the ladder behind him. "We've met."

"Good. How about you let Clyde in to take a look at your ceiling?"

"You don't need my permission to do your inspection," Lonnie answered sharply, glaring at Angelo.

"Well, of course, we have to give you notice, Lonnie."

"Be my guest," Lonnie said to Clyde waving his arm to the side in a welcoming motion that the inspector followed by walking inside the liquor store. "Thanks for the heads-up," Lonnie said to Angelo, "since you're passing yourself off as the landlord."

"Passing myself ... Oh, that's the reason for the attitude. I'm not passing myself off as anything. I'm just helping Corrine."

"Corrine knows you're acting as the owner of Big Blue?"

"Well, of course, she's given me power of attorney to take care of some of the problems around here. Corrine wants the building brought up to snuff, to make things better for all of us. Corrine

and I are in harmony on this," Angelo said, smiling sincerely, seductively, "like you and me making music together. Say, when
are we going to get together again?"

"Making music. Uh ..." Lonnie looked like a kid who was about
to confess to breaking a parent's valuable possession. "You know
Mack Telford?"

"Yeah, the trumpeter who sometimes follows our gig. They
call him Mack the Knife, right? That's too much rep, if you ask
me."

"I've been doing some gigs with Mack. I'm playing with him
at The Blue Loon next week."

"Oh." Angelo stepped back from Lonnie, the smile dropping
off his face. "Could you use a third man to make it a trio?"

"Not a sax, Angelo. Two horns is overkill." Lonnie laughed
nervously, studying the redness intensifying on Angelo's face.
"Now if you played the drums ..."

"Well, I don't play the drums," Angelo snarled, "and I don't
play this game either."

"What the hell you talking about, man?"

"Are you going to tell me you're sucking Mack's knife, too, or
is he sucking yours?"

Lonnie shook his head. "There's no reason to go there, man.
We're playing a gig, it's not like you and every goddamn—"

"Like me and every goddamn what?"

"Like you and Jasmina," Lonnie spit out, surprised at the anger
rising inside him.

"What about me and Jasmina?"

"You're cheating with her."

"You think I'm fucking around on you with Jasmina?"

Lonnie breathed out in hard, quick puffs, like a pitcher about
to wind up for the throw, all of a sudden identifying his anger.
"You're cheating on Corrine with Jasmina, and I'm not okay with
that."

Angelo threw his head back and laughed. "I'm cheating on
Corrine with you. Are you okay with that?"

Lonnie staggered back like he'd been sucker punched.

"Got a huge problem in here!" Clyde shouted from inside the liquor store.

Angelo clapped his arm around Lonnie and led him inside the shop. Lonnie felt the heat from Angelo's fingers curled into his shoulder like burning metal, but he absorbed it without protest, like penance.

Clyde peered down from the top of the ladder, his head partially obscured inside an opening in the ceiling. He dropped a chunk of ceiling material to the floor where the impact made a thunk and raised a cloud of chalky dust.

"What's the verdict?" Angelo yelled up at Clyde.

"I want to see Corrine," Lonnie said, his voice quavering. He cleared his throat and said more forcefully. "Corrine and I are friends, and I want to see her."

"What's wrong with you, man?" Angelo responded, again pressing his hand into Lonnie's shoulder. "You can see Corrine anytime you want."

"I see you've tried to patch it up, but you haven't gotten to the root of the problem, just like that heat issue on the other side of the hall," Clyde was saying. Lonnie heard the inspector's words like a whirring in his head. "This whole thing could come down, and if things freeze up on the other side, this whole building is going to be shut down."

I saw the doomsayer's soggy sign floating down the Chena in my direction. "The End is Near."

Chapter Twenty-two

The stiff wind blew loose pages of the day-old newspaper across the parking lot, and they snagged on a crumpled, male body that lay face down on the asphalt. Nothing like this had happened in my shadow since the pipeline days. The police swarmed in, and I expected a story in tomorrow's *Daily News-Miner* about a drug death on my premises, although, technically, the fatality was on city ground.

"Where's the snow?" Corrine spoke her thoughts more to herself than to Angelo who was lighting a fire in the fireplace as she looked out the penthouse window in the opposite direction of the police activity below. "What's the date, Angelo?"

"October the thirteenth."

"It can't be," she weakly protested. "We should have snow." She walked to her front door, opened it a crack, and stooped to retrieve the Sunday paper just on the other side.

Angelo watched her from an arm chair pulled close to the crackling fire as she sat down on the couch, unfolded the newspaper, and read the date at the top, confirming what Angelo had already told her.

The four-column, eight-inch-deep, color photo on the front page, along with the bold, black headline floating above it, grabbed her attention. Corrine read out loud, "Mayor Vows to 'Take Down' Big Blue."

Her heart quickened as she studied the photo of a building

that she didn't immediately recognize. The brown-gold window frames in the monolithic shape looked familiar to her, but dirty streaks had been drawn down the front façade. An inset photo in the corner of the main picture showed a close-up of cracked windows. The caption below claimed that the images belonged to Big Blue. "Wha ...?" Corrine's voice stuck in her throat.

With trembling hands she held the page and read the story beside the suspicious photo. The small print alternately blurred and sharpened as she tried to make sense of the confusing phrases and sentences:

"Building inspector uncovered ... mold creeping across ... hundreds of cracks ... widespread water damage ... lack of heat throughout half of the ... broken windows ... ceilings like bombed-out ... dangerous for human habitation ... two ground-floor businesses in peril ... will be the first step toward condemnation ... Mayor Fornette supports the move ... demolition would follow if ... a deadline of December 3 to present a plan to renovate the sixty-year-old building."

"Why are they saying this?" Corrine screamed as though each word she read was a sharp blade stabbing into her chest. "Who made up these lies? When did a building inspector ..."

She flipped to an inside page where the front-page story had directed her to read on. There, in a large, vertical photo, Jasmina, wearing a form-fitting black dress and a worried look, pointed to a crack three times the length of her arm on the wall of her coffee shop.

"Jasmina! She started all this, over one measly crack on her wall! And those old geezers who are mad because I raised their rent," Corrine continued as she looked at a smaller photo of the Big Blue Action Committee gathering around a splotch of mold as one of the members pulled back a carpet.

"Now, now, don't get yourself all worked up, darlin'." Angelo stood up, motioning both of his palms downward in a patting motion, like he was talking to an excited puppy. "I'll make you some tea to calm you down."

"No! No tea. I'm going to fight this. I can take some photos of my own." Corrine tossed the newspaper aside, rushed into
the bedroom, and started rummaging through drawers and closet
shelves. "Where's my camera? Where is it? Where have you put
my camera?"

"Sugar pie," Angelo cooed from the bedroom doorway. He
picked a thread from his gray, cashmere sweater. "I'll talk to
someone at the newspaper tomorrow. Don't trouble your—"

Corrine spun around, her face red and splotchy, a Nikon camera clutched in her hand with the strap wound around her wrist.
"Angelo, please! You weren't going to say 'pretty, little head,'
were you? Am I stuck in a scene from *Gone With the Wind*?"

Angelo rolled his eyes and Corrine rushed past him, pushing
him aside, headed for the front door. He called after her nonchalantly, "Where are you going, dear?"

"Outside," she said, "and you can't stop me."

"Well, of course I can stop you, silly," he said, taking a casual
step toward her as she jerked open the penthouse door.

Lonnie stood in front of her with one hand reaching out for the
door chime, the other holding a copy of the newspaper, sympathy
in his eyes. "Corrine?" He looked over her shoulder at Angelo's
scowling face. He saw what looked like a tendril of smoke coming from the side of Angelo's neck and blinked hard to shake the
apparent hallucination. "Is everything okay?" he asked, focusing
again on Corrine.

"Yes," she answered without looking back at Angelo, shutting
the door behind her, and marching to the elevator with Lonnie
following.

Corrine was unprepared for the strong wind that slapped her
in the face, peeled her light sweater back from her shoulders, and
drew water from her eyes as she and Lonnie stepped outside. But
she shook off Lonnie's offer of his windbreaker that he'd grabbed
from his store on the way out. She walked backward through the
parking lot to the sidewalk.

Flashing lights atop three parked police cars and an ambulance drew red arcs on the south side of the walls. Corrine glanced at the activity, but trained her eyes, stinging from the wind, on the ground floor, slowly scanning up to the roof's edge above the penthouse, raising the camera to capture an unblemished structure.

But what she saw in the camera frame was the life-size version of what she had seen in the newspaper. "Lonnie," she cried as he came to her side. "How did this happen?"

"You haven't been paying attention, Corrine."

"What about the inside? That, too?"

"There're a lot of problems. You should check them out yourself."

"Serious problems?"

"Yes, but not unfixable."

"Not according to the mayor. He wants to tear my building down."

"The mayor's a nut job."

"What am I going to do, Lonnie? Big Blue is not just a building. It has a heart and a soul."

"Then come up with a plan to save it. And don't put your trust in the wrong people." She searched his eyes, trying to understand.

"You two move along now," a strange voice called out to them. Corrine and Lonnie saw a young, male police officer approaching them. "This is police business, no place for civilians. I need you to vacate the area ASAP."

Corrine's eyes bounced in confusion with the unexpected distraction. She protested, "But, this is my build—"

"Come on, Corrine." Lonnie grabbed her elbow. "Let's get out of this wind."

He escorted her a few steps down the sidewalk away from the parking lot, circling toward the front door without crossing through the area with the police activity. "No, Lonnie. I'm not ready to go home yet. Let's take a walk up the street."

"But you're not dressed for this weather, Corrine."

"Just a short walk. Up to the *News-Miner*."

"Why?" Lonnie asked the question to the back of her head because she was already walking away toward Cushman Street and the newspaper building across the river.

"I have an idea that I want to talk over with Hattie McGee."

"The community news writer?"

"Yes." Corrine picked up her pace and Lonnie had to quickstep to come even with her again. "She's the only old-timer left on the staff and her motto has always been 'Every story is a human-interest story.' And I have the perfect story for her."

Two hours later, Corrine and Lonnie were headed back my way and both were talking animatedly about the conversation with the veteran reporter. Corrine had convinced Ms. McGee and the managing editor that there was another story beyond the screaming headlines about my inevitable date with the wrecking ball. The six- or maybe even eight-part series would take the form of conversations with people in town who had fond memories of living or attending events or visiting their loved ones here.

Ms. McGee even had a story from her own family. A cousin had worked as a housekeeper in the 1950s and polished the hundreds of crystal teardrops on the ballroom chandelier until she was swept off her feet under that same chandelier by a Southeast Asian royal who courted and married her within a week. The editor was most interested in the card-room disputes that sometimes involved drawn guns and the swindling and prostitution that occurred in the dim hallways and bedrooms in the notorious Jack Easter days.

Hattie planned to start soliciting human subjects immediately. She had already convinced Lonnie to grant an interview inside his store. Newspaper staff tossed around plays on words from simple to silly for a series title—"Big Blue Lives, (verb or noun?)" "Blue Horizons," "Tangled Up in Blue." The graphics artist was assigned to work on a logo and the advertising department would announce the series, then preview each Sunday story.

I flattened out the expelling steam from the roof vents, trying to force the stream of vapor into a circle to catch Corrine's attention, to endorse her plan, but she went inside without looking up.

As Corrine and Lonnie walked down the shadowy hall toward the elevator, Corrine glanced up at a burnt-out light and leaned against the wall. "I can't wait to tell Angelo how Hattie's stories are going to ignite the support of this community for Big Blue. Then the mayor will have to rethink his campaign to tear it down."

Lonnie grabbed Corrine by both of her shoulders. "I told you, Corrine, don't put your trust in the wrong people."

Angelo stepped out of a dark corner near the entrance to the coffee shop, making both of them jump. "So, Corrine, you and your old friend Lonnie have figured out a way to save your building?"

Corrine's words spilled out with excited breaths, "The newspaper is going to run a series about Big Blue and—" But before she could finish, Angelo spun Lonnie around to face him and bestowed a long, hard kiss on his lips. Corrine recoiled, her head swimming with confusion. Angelo nudged Lonnie aside and looked at Corrine, his lip curling upward in a smile.

"You thought it was Jasmina coming between us, didn't you darlin'?" He put an arm around her and ushered her into the elevator. "Now, who can you really trust?"

She pressed up against the wall and sobbed. Lonnie watched, dazed, his glasses askew, his lips stinging, as the elevator door shut.

Chapter Twenty-three

A group of do-gooders with a cause had staked out the sidewalk in front of me, three to five people a day, in parkas and moon boots, marching with signs that read "Save Big Blue." Two parts of the Hattie McGee series had appeared in the newspaper, with a logo that showed the stylized version of a rectangular building rendered in blue, white, and black. The series was titled a generic "Remembering Big Blue," which sounded like a eulogy.

But the attention stirred up some good will, just like Corrine predicted. An op-ed piece by an arm-chair historian waxed eloquent about saving old-time Fairbanks, with a call to action answered by the sparse gathering of sidewalk marchers. The leader, by virtue of showing up every day, was an elderly woman who wore yellow, star-shaped earmuffs and carried a house-display-size Alaska flag.

Shots of the "Bluers," as they'd been dubbed by the media, were good for a slow day of news photos, but their quirky campaign hadn't translated into business for Jasmina or Lonnie or attracted more renters.

Jasmina, in the kitchen of Istanbul Coffee, was boxing up dozens of surplus muffins to take to the food bank at the end of another slow business day when she heard the shop door open and shut. "I'm about to close!" she shouted. She hated to turn away even a last-minute customer, but she had already shut down her coffee machines.

She turned a faucet handle to fill a sink with water, but only a gurgle came out. "Damn it!" she cried, stomping her foot. The water had flowed sporadically for the past week and every additional problem with the plumbing or heating found its way into the newspaper days after the Sunday installments of "Remembering Big Blue."

The city was running a counter-campaign with inside information likely passed from Angelo to Henry at their increasingly frequent meetings at Junie's. Statements from the mayor gave credence to rumors. I was a suspected crack house after the single drug death in the parking lot. Then the city announced a zero tolerance for downtown liquor sales to minors. No law-breaking incidents were reported in the media, but Big Dipper Liquor was the most well-known liquor store downtown and the implied target of the new policy, obviously dreamed up by the mayor.

"Work, damn it!" Jasmina futilely exhorted the faulty plumbing. She mused with regret about posing for the news photo with the damage in her shop, thinking it would help get things fixed. She'd even voted in early October to re-elect Henry Fornette, believing his agenda would include supporting the tenants and Lonnie's and her businesses. No fool like a young fool, she thought.

"Henry," she said with irritation as she walked out of the kitchen and saw her late visitor. He had removed his jacket and was hanging it over the back of a chair, making himself at home. "I'm closed."

"You might want to think about opening up for me, if you know what I mean," he said as he casually rubbed his hand against his crotch.

Jasmina recoiled at his gesture. "Henry, you need to get the hell out. I have a dance class in twenty minutes."

"Now, that's no way to talk to someone who has your best interest at heart," he said with a mean smile. "You've got something I want, and I've got something you want."

Jasmina backed up toward the kitchen, thinking that the nearest big, sharp knife was about fifteen feet away. "The only thing I want is for you to leave, now," she hissed.

He closed the space between them, reached around her, and slapped her hard on the butt. "You are a hot little bitch, aren't you? You'll come around when you're out on the street corner begging people to buy your coffee once this building comes down." She raised her arm to bring her hand across his face, but he caught her wrist and shoved her back.

"I could put in a good or not-so-good word for you with the health inspector when and if you ever find another location where you can afford the rent. I have a lot of real estate connections in this town that can work for or against you, depending on how you want to play this. "

Fear rushed through Jasmina's veins as Henry stood firm and she wondered if he was going to become more violent. I was close to releasing the sprinkler in the ceiling to douse him good, to catch him off guard long enough for Jasmina to grab a knife from the kitchen. We would send him scurrying out like a wet cat.

"Hello-o-o, Jasmina!" Fornette and Jasmina turned around to see a slim, fortyish woman with a mop of curly hair, dressed in hot pink spandex with a matching skirt. "I hope you don't mind me coming a little early for class." The woman stopped her approach across the shop as she saw Jasmina's tense face and wide eyes. "You are still having class, aren't you? I heard that the city is trying to shut this building down." The dance student glanced at the mayor without any apparent recognition.

"Oh, yes, yes," Jasmina responded, a smile lighting up her face, "I mean, yes, we're still having class. Come right in, Judy." She gave the woman an unexpected hug. "I'm so glad you came, so glad."

Jasmina turned to the mayor as Judy headed for the dance room. "I guess you'll be going now, Henry?"

Fornette snatched his jacket from the chair and glared at Jasmina. "For now. But you'd better think about being nice to me if you know what's good for you."

"Yeah, Henry, I'll think about that," Jasmina dismissed him.

He accidentally banged his leg against a chair as he stomped toward the door.

I fluttered a loose ceiling tile, making him look up, then sprayed a puff of chalky dust down in his face. He rubbed his irritated eyes as a sprinkler head hissed out a drop that landed on the back of his neck while he exited the shop.

Only two other women showed up for the belly-dance session, but Jasmina hid her disappointment with the exuberance the students had come to expect. Judy lingered after the other students left.

"When a door closes, God opens a window," Judy said. Jasmina responded with a confused frown. "Oh, I guess you don't have that expression in Islam."

"I was raised as a Christian, Judy. All people from the Mideast aren't Muslim." She spoke with a smile to mask her exasperation over an assumption she'd heard many times since coming to America. "What does it mean?"

Judy looked like she would burst from holding in a secret. "It looks like you might not be able to keep your coffee shop in this building much longer, you know, when it's condemned. At least that's what I've read in the papers. A door closes. But, I happen to know that the person who has the coffee kiosk at the PX on Fort Wainwright is losing the lease at the end of the month. All you have to do is apply and, who knows? A window opens. See?"

"A kiosk? But I have a shop."

"Don't turn your nose up at an opportunity, young lady. That little coffee stand does a booming business. You already have all the equipment and supplies. Come by the AAFES office tomorrow. That's where I work. I can even put in a good word for you with the base commander. We're good friends with Leo. He and my husband played high school football together in South Carolina. Southern boys do stick together. "

"The City of Fairbanks wouldn't have any say about it," Jasmina said, thinking out loud. "It's on military land."

She mentally weighed the possibility. A kiosk wasn't a shop

that she had planned and decorated and where she could proudly hang the name Istanbul Coffee. But it would keep her in business until she could again be a shop owner on her own terms, without any extorted payment to Henry Fornette. "I'll be there tomorrow, Judy. Thank you so much." She drew the other woman to her and hugged her again. "I like your windows that open."

Judy laughed. "Glad to do it for such a nice girl and you've done more for me than you know. Since I've been belly dancing for my husband, it's put the zing back in his thing," she said with a wink. "Next, you better find a place where you can keep teaching your dance classes."

***

"I don't want to leave you, Blue," Jasmina said as she returned to work the day after a trip to Fort Wainwright where she had filled out the application to lease the kiosk and visited the post exchange mall to look it over. "You know this is home for me." I dimmed the lights over the counter where she stood, then made them flare.

"Remember when I got these?" she said, kneeling down and studying the collection of black and plum cups and saucers behind the counter. "I picked these so carefully for color, weight, and size. And these and these," she said as she touched the gold teaspoons and tiny cream pitchers. "We made the perfect couple, didn't we? I miss you already."

"Whoever he was, he must be an idiot."

The voice from the man at the counter shook Jasmina out of her reverie. "Sorry, what?" She stood up shakily and steadied herself by placing her palms flat on the surface in front of her.

She looked up at his elegantly sculpted face that showed just a hint of stubble at the chin and jaw. His eyes were deep brown, fringed with thick lashes, and every strand of his dark hair was locked in place. From the crinkles of laugh lines at the corners of his eyes and the furrow between his eyebrows, she guessed his age at mid-forties, but the contours of his chest and arm muscles under a skin-hugging, long-sleeve T-shirt broadcast the body of someone in his twenties. He was around six-and-a-half-feet tall, forcing her to crane her neck back to meet his gaze.

"No, I'm sorry," he said. "I didn't mean to intrude on your thoughts."

"What can I get you?" she asked in the best professional voice she could muster in her flustered state.

She delivered an Italian roast to him a few minutes later where he had chosen to sit at a secluded table against the back wall. A couple of fresh-faced Army troops in camo, on their way out of the shop, suddenly wheeled around and saluted him. "You salute the uniform, not the man, soldiers," he said to the youngsters, pointing to his attire.

They answered in unison with a sheepish, "Yes, sir," and walked out.

Jasmina looked at him quizzically, with a question on the tip of her tongue, but he spoke first. "Great place you've got here." He took a drink of his coffee and shut his eyes for a second, savoring the strong flavor. "And excellent coffee. How long have you been in business?"

"A little over six years," she said with a whimsical lilt, thinking how things can change in a short time. She stepped back to return to the front of the shop.

"This is an old building," he continued, stopping her motion away from him.

"Yes," she said with a smile, half-turning to go.

"Historic."

"Yes," she said, turning back to him.

"It's a little cold in here. Heat not working?"

"There have been some problems. Can I get you anything else? I'm about to close in a few minutes, so ...."

"I read in the paper about the problems with the building." He pushed out the empty chair across the table from him with his shoe and motioned for her to sit down.

"Yeah, I may not be able to stay here much longer," she said as she sat down.

"A few minutes would be fine," he said.

She smiled. "I mean in this location."

"What are your options?"

"I've put in a bid on a coffee station at the PX on Fort Wainwright, but I don't know if that will be approved."

"It will be."

Jasmina's chin jerked up and her eyes widened. "How do you know that?"

"Because I put in a good word for you."

"But you don't know me. Are you somebody ... I mean, those soldiers saluted ...who are you?"

The tall man took another long gulp of coffee. "I know about you, Ms. Jones, and I know a good cup of coffee."

Jasmina frowned and pursed her lips. "And you are?"

"Greg!" a male voice boomed from behind Jasmina. "Good to see you." A flannel shirtsleeve reached across the table to shake the man's hand as Jasmina recognized the mayor's voice. "I'm glad we could join forces on the first annual Run for the Warriors. I'm looking forward to working with you on the event again next year."

"Henry," the man called Greg said, releasing the other man's hand. He noticed Jasmina squirm as the mayor touched her neck, and he saw her press her fingers together to stop them from shaking.

"I'm about to close, Henry," Jasmina said, not looking up at the mayor.

"I know," he said, chuckling.

"What do you want, Henry?" she asked, fear and anger mixed in her voice. Greg stared at the two, drinking his coffee in measured sips.

"I came by to handle that business transaction we talked about earlier," Henry said, bumping against the back of Jasmina's chair, pinning her against the table.

"What business transaction is that?" Greg interjected, surprising Jasmina with the rudeness of the question asked so politely.

"Just a little payment we had discussed taking care of at a convenient time," the mayor said with a sly smile.

"Well, it's not a convenient time, Henry," Greg said, returning the smile.

The mayor stepped back and uttered a nervous laugh. "Excuse me?"

"Ms. Jones and I are in the middle of an important meeting."

"Oh, oh," Henry stammered. "Well, maybe another time? Jasmina?" Henry walked backward toward the door. "Good to see you, colonel."

"Same here," Greg called out to him with a friendly wave. "Say hello to your wife for me," he added as the mayor hurried out the door.

Jasmina suppressed a giggle as she looked up at the man across the table. "What important meeting?"

He flashed a smile. "Gregory Leonides meets Jasmina Jones."

"Colonel Leonides?" she said as her dark eyes widened.

He nodded. "You can call me Leo."

"Base commander Leo?" He looked down at the table and nodded again. "Pleased to meet you," she said smiling and extending her hand.

"The pleasure is mine," he said as he folded his hand around hers. The warmth traveled through the surface of her fingers and palm awakening her inside like ice melting into spring.

"Thanks, colonel, Leo, for everything."

"There is something I want you to do for me," he said with a mischievous smile.

Jasmina didn't blink. She knew what was coming. She tried to picture how he would perform in bed, although she hadn't even thought about being with a man since the cold storage began. He would start slow, but he would grow impatient. He would want to be in control. He would give her orders. He would call her someone else's name. No, he wasn't so easily figured out. How had he so quickly perceived that she was in danger and maneuvered against Henry? He would surprise her. He would whisper what he wanted.

"What do you want, Leo?" she asked, searching his smiling eyes.

"I want you to go out to dinner with me sometime."

"Dinner? You're asking me out?" she said, again caught off guard, unexpectedly giddy.

He laughed. "I think that's what I'm doing. Can I call you here at the shop?"

"Yes, yes." She could feel herself blushing and looked for an excuse to get up. "It is a bit chilly in here. I'm going to turn up the heater."

When she returned to the table, Leo was gone. She turned off the heater as she shut down the shop. Since the fire, she never left the heater on for more than a few minutes when she wasn't in the same room to monitor it. She didn't notice the temperature of the air dropping, on its way to well below zero, as she prepared to lock up the shop and head upstairs to her apartment.

Soon the pipes in the kitchen would freeze, then rupture, and the released water and ice would dampen the inside of the walls. But the only temperature she was aware of was the warmth from Leo's lingering presence, wrapping around her like a beautiful ribbon.

Chapter Twenty-four

Lonnie leaned against the back of the couch in his apartment and downed his second glass of Hennessey. "You know, Blue, when I've pictured leaving you, I've always seen myself being carried feet first to the sweet sounds of a trumpet with friends raising glasses high in a final toast.

"But, the hand-writing is on the wall, at least on the walls that are not already falling down." Lonnie chuckled at his attempt at dark humor. "There's no dignity in leaving when someone else picks the time that you have to go."

The notice to vacate by order of the city had been put up the first week in November for Jasmina's shop and most of the apartments on the northern side of the building, where the heat from the furnace did not reach. The water on that side had been shut off after the pipes froze and busted in Istanbul Coffee and the place had flooded with foul water.

Jasmina's apartment on the fourth floor, which was outside the no-water, no-heat zone, was spared. The bathroom near the ballroom was shut down. The liquor store, with heat and water, was still open but with temporary scaffolding holding up the sagging parts of the ceiling. Lonnie figured it was only a matter of time before the city would order him to abandon his business and home.

He visualized the inside of Big Dipper Liquor and mentally counted the inventory. Four shelf units in the middle of the store, two across the back, two on each side, six hundred bottles of wine, four hundred medium-range whiskey, vodka, gin, bourbon, rum, two hundred more of the upscale stuff. The cooler by the door, more than half stocked with beer: How many six-packs bottles? How many six-packs cans? A scattering of fruity wine coolers, always an uncertain sale item. He thought about how he would clear out the whole kit and caboodle.

"Jasmina will land on her feet, she's young, but Corrine and I? Maybe we'll have to move into some mid-scale apartment. We could be roomies. That would be a hoot. Unless she's planning to stay long-term with you-know-who, but I don't expect that will work out."

He thought about the Bluers, how he had advised them, now that their numbers had swelled to a dozen, to take their cause to the pavement in front of City Hall. They agreed to move next week and put some heat on Mayor Fornette. I made a shudder run up the wall across the room that shook Lonnie's turntable and the James Brown LP skipped.

"Yeah, I did hear the historical society may be moving toward your preservation—there is some currency in pity. But too little, too late, my friend."

I shook the wall more forcefully and made the floor vibrate, too, causing the needle to screech across the record, making the Godfather of Soul get on up to where he didn't mean to go.

"Hey, hey!" Lonnie went to the record player and rescued the album. "That's a classic you've scratched up there. So you still have some fight left. Well, okay, let me think this over. We need to buy some time from the city to regroup and renovate this place."

But what to do about that idiot Henry Fornette and his obsessed agenda to tear you down, Lonnie thought. "Obsessed" was the word for Fornette. Maybe there was something there to use. He remembered the mayor's odd behavior. Why was he hanging out at Istanbul Coffee after the first visit by the building inspector?

"Lord love a duck!" Lonnie exclaimed aloud. "The mayor is

trying to get next to Jasmina." Old Henry wasn't the male model type, he mused, not Jasmina's usual cup of tea.

Tea, tea, tea, the word tapped against the inside of Lonnie's head like a tiny hammer as he dozed on the couch, until it knocked loose a fragment of memory that jerked him wide awake. He remembered Henry Fornette's mysterious words muttered outside Istanbul Coffee, "Fucking Frayers," and where he had seen the word before that. He pictured the Mama Tatum's tea box in the dumpster, the Web page that described the supposedly spell-inducing concoction distributed by Frayer-Dumont Industries, Carroll Parish, Louisiana.

Frayer was a company, but Henry had said Frayers, plural, like it was a group of people, a family, a family company, a Louisiana family company. Lonnie leapt to his feet, shook off the shot of dizziness brought on by the brandy and the sudden movement, and sat down in front of his computer. The floor was shaking under his feet with my anticipation.

Lonnie looked up the biography of the Fairbanks mayor on the city site and read, "... born and raised in Tall Cane, Carroll Parish, Louisiana ..." Then he researched that strange word "Frayer."

The computer offered information on devices that can be used to fry whole turkeys, an essay about the simple life in a monastery, as well as an educational model for teaching vocabulary. He searched sites about Louisiana, discovered the best places to catch redfish, flounder, and speckled trout, checked out hotel prices during Mardi Gras, explored the origins of jazz, learned the ingredients in Doberge cake and the price of New Orleans Saints season tickets.

Lonnie's anticipation hardened into frustration; he mopped the sweat of stress from his forehead with his bare arm, and then he tried French variations of the unfamiliar word, and sites about Louisiana folklore and myths and old wives tales. Then an hour and a half into the search, Lonnie clicked on a red-highlighted Web address embedded in a story about the intertwining of pagan and Catholic traditions in Louisiana. Lonnie homed in on the lighted rectangle of words in front of him, and the room around him glowed red and dropped away as he read:

The Story of the Frayers

The Frayers are an obscure clan that appeared in the backwoods of Louisiana near the Arkansas state line in the decade after the Civil War. The name may be the original family name or a metamorphosis of the French word "defaire," which means "to unravel" knitting or a piece of cloth, and may be additionally related to the fraying of cloth as in unraveling.

They may have begun as an elite group of holy men and women who were ostracized from a small religious sect for misuse of their spiritual powers. Creating their own society, they made their living by using their powers to bring about destruction. People with grudges or who were bent on revenge hired Frayers to "unravel" or "fray" their enemies or those who had done them wrong.

Although they were not considered to be demons, supernatural beings, or minions of the devil, the male members of the clan often took nicknames related to Satan, as a kind of dark joke.

It has been said that Frayers could spontaneously self-combust if they were experiencing extreme or uncontrollable emotion although such an event has never been confirmed. If true, some members of the clan may have met their demise in this manner.

Frayers made their own enemies through their acts of destruction and many Frayers or suspected Frayers fell victim to violence. The intermarriage of Frayers with non-Frayers over generations also diluted their powers.

Although some Frayers found they had greater opportunity to profit from their powers if they lived among regular society, their history of living a remote and secret lifestyle and the many myths and folk tales surrounding them has made them difficult to study. An exception is a brief inclusion in a 1976 study of the subgroups of Louisiana culture, published in The Anthropology Journal of the American South. *At that time it was estimated that only 16 true Frayers, who were members of three different families, existed and two were over 90 years of age.*

Lonnie felt woozy, maybe from the brandy or worry or lack of sleep or the realization that something sinister was on the other side of the door, walking through the halls, riding in the elevator, running its hands along the hundreds of bottles on the shelves downstairs. He was still staring at the Web page about the Frayers as I orchestrated a little power surge, picking out certain numbers in the text, making them flare on the screen, one at a time: 7-0-6.

Grabbing a flashlight, Lonnie headed out of his apartment and to the elevator. He pushed the button for the seventh floor, thinking there must be something incriminating left behind in Miss Liza's old apartment where Angelo had spent his time over the past few months when he wasn't with Corrine.

I accelerated the elevator to hurry Lonnie to his destination and inadvertently threw him off balance. "Guess this thing is on the blink, too," he said as he caught himself with an outstretched palm pressed against the elevator wall.

Standing outside 706, Lonnie jiggled the knob of the locked door in frustration. He hadn't thought about how he would get inside. But I knew this apartment's past and the good energy that had been saved between the door and the wall, where a groom had carried his bride over the threshold. I waited for him to turn the knob hard to the left, and as he did I flexed the mechanism inside that was preventing him from opening the door. He tried the hard turn three more times before our actions were in sync and the lock released.

A lingering smell of mold tickled his nostrils. He turned on the flashlight and scanned the room. The black streaks that had defiled the walls and made the apartment a putrid cave when Angelo stayed here had faded to thin, gray scars. A laptop computer sat in the middle of the floor, a lone, abandoned object. Lonnie squatted down, plugged it in, and hit the power button. In a minute a blue screen came up with a window asking for a password. He stared for a few seconds at the blank area for which he had no answer and punched the power button again, making the screen go dark.

Lonnie moved across the floor boards left swollen by water

that had evaporated, from room to empty room. Even the blinds had been stripped from the windows. Staring down out of a back window, he spied a young black bear rummaging through the overfull dumpster. He wondered, why hasn't the garbage been picked up? Why isn't that bear hibernating? But, he considered, it was still warm as spring with only a dusting of snow on the ground.

Somehow, from seven floors below, he heard a rustling noise as the bear dug his paws into the refuse. Then, he realized the sound was from his shoe nudging a pile of papers stacked in a corner of the vacated bedroom. Lonnie sat down on the dusty floor, pulled the papers into his lap, and examined them under the light from his flashlight.

They were newspaper stories printed from a computer. He scanned through several reports from the Fairbanks newspaper detailing the DUI, assault, and disturbing the peace arrests of Harper Fornette. A lengthy obituary described the mayor's off-spring as "a loving son who enjoyed fishing on the Kenai River and camping along the Denali Highway."

Next in the stack was a story from *The Houston Post*, 1974, about the death of Price Cunningham, the son of a wealthy oil family, in the community of The Woodlands, Texas, and pending homicide charges against his wife, Corey Mae.

Under that was a clipping from *The Army Times*, a photo and caption from 2005 that read "Welcoming a hero home ... Capt. and Mrs. Michael Jones ...." A young Army officer in uniform, with half of his face covered with bandages, stared expressionless into the photographer's lens while a beautiful woman with dark hair leaned against his arm and displayed a painful smile.

"Mrs. Jasmina Jones?" Lonnie whispered the words like a question, but neither of us had any doubt about that striking beauty.

Lonnie's heart rate jumped a notch as he stared at the next news page. It detailed the robbery of a drug store in Cleveland in 1965. The story said the store owner surprised the masked safe cracker who knocked her unconscious with a blow to the face. Police had sought a teen-age store clerk for questioning, but believed the theft of more than nine hundred dollars was the work of a lone man who had hidden in the store after closing time. There were no signs of a break-in.

"How did Cleveland follow me here?" Lonnie looked around as if someone besides me might have heard the fear in his voice. He covered the robbery story with the other news reports, folded the papers into a thick half-roll, and tucked them under his arm.

He was pushing himself up off the floor when he saw what remained of the pile in the corner, not more sheets of printed-out paper but a small stack of photos. He picked up the photos and spread them in a fan across the floor, then let the flashlight beam travel across them. Miss Liza's face at various ages smiled up at Lonnie with her refined features–except that all the eyes had been poked out with something small and sharp. Lonnie gathered up the pictures.

I wanted him to look for more, some hint of a deal brokered with the city to grind me into dust, to profit off the sale of land under me, or what would be built on it after I'm gone. As Lonnie swept the flashlight around a final time, we both saw there was nothing else to discover unless it was locked in the password-protected computer. What Lonnie had found here and on the Internet about the Frayers would have to be enough to confront Corrine, and maybe break Angelo's spell.

The cell phone in Lonnie's back pocket erupted. The call was from eighty-five miles down the Richardson Highway. Half an hour later Lonnie was headed out of town in his Jeep with a hastily packed bag and the items from 706 thrown in the back. The confrontation with Corrine would have to wait. Lonnie was taking a fishing trip.

Chapter Twenty-five

Corrine poured her tea down the kitchen sink as Angelo headed downstairs on his way to Junie's Diner to have a cup of coffee with Henry Fornette. The first morning light was still hours away and the two men had a lot to talk about. City officials were meeting that night to discuss my future. Angelo was making a presentation. I had heard about their plan from Angelo's half of a phone conversation earlier, but all Corrine knew was that Angelo would be out for a while.

On my ground floor, Angelo gritted his teeth in aggravation and tapped his foot impatiently as I delayed the elevator doors from opening for an extra minute while the spirit of a Korean War soldier traveling to the eighth floor for a happy reunion with his brother breathed from the walls.

With Angelo out and without the dose of tea to dull her observations, Corrine planned to explore my rooms and halls to see for herself if what Lonnie and the newspaper had told her about my condition below the penthouse was true. Bundled in a sweater and T-shirt over tattered sweatpants, and carrying a load of keys and a flashlight, she began her inspection on the eleventh floor. Two of the apartments at the southeast corner were still occupied, but she quietly let herself into the four vacant ones that faced west.

The first two interiors were cold enough that her breath lingered in frosty clouds in front of her face, the third was a comfortable temperature, but the last apartment was barely warm. She put her hand over the baseboard, felt the heat pushing out, but also the chilly fingers of air seeping in through a half-inch gap of an open window. The moving air stirred sagging strips of wallpaper. She gripped the cold, metal window crank above the sill, but even leaning into it and pushing with both hands, she couldn't budge it to shut the window.

Powdery, white flakes drifted past the outside of the window, illuminated by a lingering moon. Pressing her nose against the cold glass, she looked down to the ground and saw, under the glow of a nearby streetlight, swatches of asphalt covered with snow. She wanted to stand there and watch the silent snow obscure what was shabby and dirty, but a blast of frigid air reached through the window opening and reminded her that she was on a time-sensitive mission. She ripped away a section of drooping wallpaper, balled it up, and stuffed it in the window's air-leaking crevice.

Where the wallpaper was torn away, she saw a crack running from the bottom of the wall and veering up and sideways where it was hidden under more wallpaper. Corrine tore at the paper, throwing the remnants behind her, searching for the end of the crack. By the time she found it, past a corner at the far edge of the adjoining wall, halted there by a door frame, almost every inch of wallpaper from half the room was heaped in the center of the apartment.

Corrine continued her survey floor by floor. Where carpets covered some floors, her feet squished, and the damp, rotten smell revealed the mold and decay underneath even before she peeled back the rugs. Few of the hallway lights worked and some of the spent bulbs appeared black, like they had burned from the inside.

Along her tour, a few residents invited her inside their homes to present their incessantly dripping faucets, groaning toilets, dangling light fixtures, warped doors, and disintegrating ceilings. She tallied the number of remaining residents. Only sixteen of the sixty apartments were occupied.

When she tried her key in 706, she found the door already un-locked. She warily pushed the bottom of the door inward and held the flashlight out in front of her like a sword as she stepped in. The freshness of the air inside was more shocking than the foul-ness of the areas she had already visited. Someone's love and joy must have filled these rooms in the past, and the spirit lingered, she thought, an antidote to the decay infecting the other apart-ments. She took in several cleansing breaths. The uncovered win-dows gleamed back at her as she swiped them with the flashlight ray, and she blinked hard.

Moving slowly across the even, dry floor, she spied the plugged-in computer, knelt down, and turned it on. When the password box stared back at her from the lit screen, she thought for a minute, then typed in "j-e-l-l-o" and a desktop, blank except for a blue "e" icon, came up. She clicked on the Internet symbol, and when a page opened, she typed in "F-a," the first two letters of Fallon, and the computer filled in the name of the last opened page: fairbanksdailynewsminer/business. When she clicked on the Website name, a September news story from the *Daily News-Miner's* business section appeared, with the headline, "Sheraton seeking site for proposed water-park hotel."

Corrine read slowly through the article about Starwood Hotel and Resorts, its ambitious plan to build a new hotel side-by-side with an indoor water park in Fairbanks. The corporation hoped to make a decision in time to start building in early spring.

A frown deepened across Corrine's face as she tried to figure out what the information meant to Angelo. It was a fantastical idea to attract tourism when that industry had been falling off for years. She asked herself, could the Sheraton be looking at the plot Angelo inherited from his Aunt Liza? I wished she could see the disappeared Eastwood folder I had seen on the computer desktop when Angelo was in the room.

Would Angelo's land be enough? she wondered. A 120-room hotel and a water park would need a lot of land, maybe double the size of the Eastwood property. The room turned colder, the chill creeping around her shoulders like the fingers of an unfriendly ghost. She spun her head around, the words, "Who's there?" stuck in her throat. She jerked the computer cord out of the wall and rushed out of the apartment, pulling the door shut behind her.

In the hall, her fear evaporated. She laughed at herself. "How silly and paranoid I am, Blue." I tried to push a gust of warm, comforting air toward her, but I failed. She moved on to the sixth and fifth floors, where all the apartments were vacated. Jasmina's apartment was the only one rented on the fourth floor.

Corrine saw the cracks in walls and along wooden floors multiply as she moved to the lower levels. In the second-floor apartment next to Lonnie's, she counted eighty-five on one wall. She was about to knock on Lonnie's door for a strictly business visit, but she pictured Angelo's mouth against his and she couldn't bring her poised knuckles down on the wooden barrier in front of her.

When she stepped off the elevator on the ground floor, the sign announcing that Istanbul Coffee was closed took her breath away, even though she'd been reading the paper often enough to already know the shop had been shuttered a couple of weeks ago when the pipes burst. She wondered if Jasmina was holed up in her apartment, angry, defeated, breaking things, weeping. Or, had she started up again somewhere else, invincibly offering coffee and her vivacious beauty, and maybe embarking on another self-improvement project, beadwork or Japanese cooking.

With hands cupped around her eyes, Corrine peered through the shop window. She could detect only dark shapes and shadows in the deserted interior, and a damp, sour smell escaped from under the door. A spray of chalky debris released from the ceiling and made her cough. She turned away and looked across the hall at the other darkened shop, Big Dipper Liquor.

Corrine expected Lonnie's store to be closed at this time of day, but a sign on the security gate that pulled down over the entrance was both familiar and unusual. She walked up to the sign and read, "Closed—For Now, Folks. See You Soon." A drawing of a leaping, iridescent salmon decorated an upper corner of the placard. Corrine recognized it as the notice that was posted only when Lonnie went on his annual fishing trip in July. It was nearly mid-November, and, even though their friendship had ended, she felt abandoned.

The askew front door swung inward with a dragging sound against the carpet. Corrine gasped and her heart quickened. She turned toward the sound apprehensively, expecting to see Angelo. Instead, a broad-shouldered man with thick silver hair and a handlebar mustache, wearing a black jacket and jeans, was stomping the snow from his boots just inside the entrance.

His tall frame blocked the faint glow from a streetlight and the glimmers of headlights on First Avenue filtering through the damaged glass of the entry. As he walked toward Corrine, she saw he carried a four-foot-long, tubular container under one arm. He almost walked into her in the dark hallway before abruptly stopping.

"Good morning," he said in a deep voice that vibrated through her. "I didn't mean to come up on you like that. I didn't see you."

The crisp, sea scent of the stranger teased Corrine's nose and she felt the flashlight hanging heavy from the end of her arm. Hesitantly she switched it on, conscious of how sloppily she was dressed, and ran her empty hand through the tangles of her loose hair. Then she set the flashlight sideways on the fire extinguisher enclosure that jutted out from the wall. The light stretched out toward the front door, allowing her and the man to see each other's faces without blinding either of them.

"Unfortunately, the coffee shop is closed," Corrine said.

"I'm not here for coffee," he said, "although I'm sorry to see that the place is closed. I make a point of stopping in whenever I'm up this way to hunt or fish."

Corrine glanced halfway back across her shoulder. "Of course, Lonnie's place is closed, but it's closed this time of day anyway."

The man let out a low laugh. "That's not what I'm after. When I drink my breakfast, it's a protein shake or a mango smoothie."

"Are you visiting someone in the building? Do you need help finding someone?"

"Actually, I know this building pretty well. I was hoping to speak to the owner and get a look around."

Corrine stiffened. "So, you're another one of the mayor's inspectors," she said, grabbing the flashlight and shining it in his face.

He shielded his eyes from the light beam. "No, nothing like that. I'm Anthony Aurelius." He extended his hand and Corrine warily let him shake hers. "Every time I come up here, I look at this grand old building, and I think it could be something more. I've heard it's fallen on hard times, and I thought maybe this is my opportunity to do something. I'm here to figure out if I can renovate it."

"Grand, old ... renovate? Why would you want to do that?"

"Well, I guess the practical answer would be money. But I have a personal stake in Big Blue as well."

"A personal stake. What do you mean?"

"Well, I spent seventy-two of the best hours of my life here in 1978. I was on my honeymoon with the girl of my dreams and the world with all its possibilities was spread out before me like a sky full of diamonds." A whimsical smile crossed the man's face. Corrine lowered the flashlight. "Do you happen to know where I can find the owner?"

Corrine offered her hand generously. "You've found her. Corinne Easter." She pulled her sweater closer around her baggy second layer of clothing. "You kind of caught me at a bad time. In my work clothes. I've been, uh, doing some cleanup in the empty apartments."

He ignored her apologies for her appearance, his genial expression unwavering. "Is it possible for me to look around?"

"Well," Corrine said hesitantly. "Some parts are not in such good shape."

"Those are the parts I would really like to see, so I can see what I would be working with, once I lay out my plan." He tapped the end of the metal tube. "And, of course, if you agree to it."

I felt Corrine aching to trust someone with good news. She gave him the tour that she had just taken, in reverse, from the second floor to the eleventh. Then they rode the elevator, standing across from each other on opposite sides, downstairs to look at the ruins of Istanbul Coffee.

"So you began a happy marriage right under this roof," she said as the elevator descended, and she pulled at her unkempt hair while trying to cover her embarrassing outfit with the slightly less humiliating sweater.

"I never said the marriage was happy. In fact, it was a big, messy catastrophe. It started out like a storybook, though. I fell in love with Alaska first, the hunting, the fishing, the magnificent wilderness, living off the land. And I couldn't help falling in love with the woman who saved my life from the most dangerous creature I've faced in Alaska."

Corrine forgot about the way she looked for a moment, intrigued by a potential rescue tale. "You were attacked by a grizzly?"

"No, it was king crab that got me."

"A crab, really?"

Anthony chuckled and nodded. "I love the food in Alaska, too. I guess you can tell that eating's important to me." He patted his substantial middle. "It was my first time up here, first time moose hunting, and I got lucky. I bagged a 16-pointer in the Fortymile, not bad for an outsider who didn't know Boone and Crockett from Jack and Jill. When I got back to town, I was celebrating at a bar with some buddies. The liquor was flowing and the food kept coming. I guess you could say I was over-celebrating, so much so that when a big, steaming plate of king crab legs was set down in front of me, I dug in, completely forgetting my allergy to seafood.

"Within three minutes, my eyeballs were golf balls, my lips were two pork chops, my throat shut off, and, although I don't remember this part, I fell off my bar stool and whacked my head on something, laid it open good." Anthony pulled the thick, white hair back from his forehead to reveal a zigzag scar on his right temple.

"Wow, you could have died?"

"Yes, but fortunately there happened to be a nurse in the house. She seemed to know exactly what was going on. I found out later that while the ambulance was on the way, she ran to her car and got a vial of epinephrine and a syringe that she kept in an emergency kit for her asthma. That shot in the thigh saved my life. And I learned from then on to always be prepared. Now, I carry an Epi-pen. I was hospitalized for a day after my head was stitched up, and that angel didn't leave my side the whole time. Before I left the hospital, I proposed, and three days later we were married."

"That does sound like a storybook. You know that would make a good story for Hattie McGee. She's doing a Sunday series on—"

"'Remembering Big Blue.' I read one of those stories, about the guy who owns the liquor store—started out as a teen-age store clerk and worked himself up from the bottom to the top. Now that's my kind of guy, a success story. My bride and I, on the other hand, we were a failure. We split up after three years."

"And since?"

"Since, I've been single. I guess those perfect seventy-two hours spoiled me for anything less. What about you? Any storybook romances?"

"Maybe one, or at least I thought it was at the time, but, no happily ever after for me either." She shifted her weight against the bar on the elevator's rear wall. By the numbers above the door she saw that they were passing between the fourth and third floor. "This is not a storybook world. I've tried to be content with what I have."

"That sounds a lot like lowering your expectations and that's something I don't do for love or money."

"You can't always have what you want."

"Maybe. I deal with investment and return and negotiation and value. Thing is, when you negotiate down, you have to be careful you're not lowering your value."

Corrine shrugged. She felt awkward and stimulated at the same time under Anthony's gaze. "You said you're a visitor to Alaska. Where do you live?" she asked, turning the conversation to a less personal direction.

"I'm based in Los Angeles, but I travel around the country looking for places I can redo. It's like flipping houses, but I work on a bigger scale than single-family homes." He slid his hand into the side pocket of his jacket, took out a business card, and handed it to her. She read "Aurelius, Inc." embossed in navy and gold.

"And you're successful?"

"So far, it's been great, by the millions great."

"You buy these places and then sell them?"

"Sometimes, not always. Sometimes I negotiate to buy an interest in a hotel or an office building before I renovate it."

"And that's what you want to do with Big Blue? Buy it and then maybe sell it?"

"Maybe."

"Suppose I don't want to sell."

"We'll talk," he said with a friendly smile.

"We're here, back on the first floor."

When Corrine unlocked the door to Istanbul Coffee, the cold air slammed into her. Scanning the room with the flashlight, she picked out the once elegant tables and chairs covered with a fine layer of grit. The floor was wet and sticky. A lump came up in her throat at the sight of the deadness in front of her. Anthony took the flashlight and trained it on the cracks in the bare walls.

"I'm going to get the construction spotlight out of my truck. Do you mind if I spend some time in here?"

"No, not at all." In the darkness, he couldn't see her wipe tears from her face. "Take as long as you want. I can come down and lock up later."

"I want to get some of my people into the building in the next few days, check for structural problems and figure out what's going on with the heat. I'll contact you first, of course. So far, I haven't seen anything I can't handle. Next step, you and I talk, then we talk to the city to see whose ear I need to bend to get this project started. I hear there's a meeting about the building tonight at City Hall."

"Tonight?"

"Seven o'clock, didn't you know? I'm going to be there to see where the city is in this abatement process." Anthony waved the metal tube in front of him. "I can show you my preliminary plans for the renovation, if you have some time."

"I don't have time today," she said and headed out to the hallway, with a furtive glance toward the front entrance for Angelo.

The light in Anthony's eyes dimmed with disappointment. "After today I have business to take care of between here and L.A. Can we meet two weeks from today?"

"That's the Tuesday before Thanksgiving."

"I think so. Is that a problem?"

"Not at all. We can meet in the ballroom."

"It's a date then," he said, beaming. "Do you really think the newspaper would be interested in my story?"

"You bet. I'll call Hattie and give her the number off your card, if you don't mind."

He nodded like a big, silver lead dog who knew exactly where he was headed.

Chapter Twenty-six

Angelo approached the Noble Street entrance as Corrine entered the penthouse and Anthony set up his light for a closer inspection of the coffee shop. As Anthony faced the western wall, his right foot pressed open a left-behind vein of positive vibrations that radiated out toward the front door. I forced the wave of energy through the overhang and a four-inch drift of snow which had accumulated there slid off and dropped onto Angelo's cashmere cap-covered head.

"What the fuck!" he yelled.

He continued to curse as he rubbed away the snow blinding his eyes, brushed the powder off his shoulders, and dug cold, wet lumps from under the collar of his jacket. When he tried to pull the door open, I held it shut until he broke the resistance with a strong jerk.

As soon as he stepped into the penthouse, shedding his soggy hat and dampened coat, he yelled out to Corrine, who was in the kitchen making herself a bowl of maple-flavored oatmeal. "What the hell is that inspector doing in the coffee shop?"

"That's Anthony Aurelius," Corrine said, stirring her porridge and blowing on it as she walked into the living room. "He's looking at renovating the building. He's going to be at the meeting tonight."

"Oh, yeah, the meeting, I told you about that, right?"

"I think I'll go."

"Really, darlin'? I'm going to make a clear, calculated presentation to the council and the mayor, updating them on the building, laying out for them just what it would take–and cost–to fix every single problem. They'll appreciate my transparency." I made all the overhead lights buzz and dim, and Angelo's shoulders twitched with irritation until the display subsided. "I don't think I'll need your help. In fact, your presence could be harmful."

"Harmful how?"

"We do want to get the mayor on our side."

"Well, yes, he is the one who's out to destroy Big Blue. That's all the more reason I should be there. I want to make sure he knows I'm going to stand and fight."

"Not a good idea, sweetheart. I know you're ready to come out swinging. But you, the owner of this building, the building that Henry Fornette blames for the death of his only son, confronting him in a public meeting, well, that's just going to make him dig in his heels. What this fight calls for is less fury than finesse. Of course, if you really think you should be there ..."

Corrine's face fell as she deferred to Angelo's assessment of the situation. "I suppose you're right. I want to do what's best for Big Blue. Do you think there will be other people there, speaking up for Blue?"

"Not really. I don't see why they would."

"Hattie's stories, don't you think there is public sentiment that we didn't have before?"

"Public sentiment is going to help about as much as those wackos with signs marching up and down the sidewalk. A good sideshow, but that's all it is, just a deflection. What's happened to your business sense, sugar babe? I gave you more credit than that."

"I suppose I do get a little emotional when it comes to Big Blue." I made the nearby table lamp flare with a knowing glow.

"Sometimes you worry me, my love, talking about this building like it's a person. You definitely can't be at that meeting while you're acting like some crazy cat lady talking to the walls."

"I'm not crazy. It's just Blue and I have been through so much together, I don't know what I would do without this place."

"Enough of this nonsense. Tell me about this Aurelius guy who's poking around downstairs," Angelo snorted. "Aurelius. That sounds like a made-up name."

"His card is right there." Corrine pointed with her chin to a business card on a side table.

Angelo picked up the card, sneered at it, and tossed it back down. "Renovating, you said? When did all this come about?" Angelo's fists were clenching.

"This morning. He took a look around and we had a talk," Corrine said as she stepped toward the couch, about to sit down with her hot cereal.

The bowl flew out of her hands as Angelo struck it. "You went behind my back?" His face flushed red, and purple veins stood out on his forehead. The fear he had put in her eyes made me want to hurl him across the room, but all I could manage was an extra exhale of warmth through the vents that raised the room temperature for a couple of minutes. Out of Corrine's sight, spirals of heat rose from the back of his neck.

Corrine squared her shoulders, willing her trembling hands still, determined to look directly into Angelo's eyes. "Big Blue is my building, Angelo," she said in a forced even voice.

The storm instantly dissipated from Angelo's face. His body relaxed, his hands hung loose. He smiled slowly, his mouth a crack, like one of the cracks on the coffee shop walls. "Of course it's your building, darlin'. I'm just a visitor. I've been thinking of leaving soon anyway. Aunt Liza's stuff is all taken care of."

"Leaving?" Corrine said, rubbing the bare spot on her left ring finger, with the kind of fear that comes when a person is watching for a monster and something worse jumps out. "But your land, don't you have plans for that?"

He glared at her warily. "Plans? What plans?"

"I-I mean, aren't you going to sell it or something?"

"Things are fine the way they are. I'll just keep the same property manager Aunt Liza had, keep collecting the rent. Really no reason for me to stay," he said as he located the bowl halfway across the room, oozing oatmeal onto the carpet.

He stooped to pick up the bowl and turned in Corrine's direction. "Except to help you out, my sweet. I have a sure-fire plan to convince the mayor to do some major repairs, get everything back up to standard." He set the bowl on a green lacquered table. "But you don't seem to need my help anymore. This building is coming down around your ears and I'm going to have the city looking at ways to help us put it back together, they just need a little more persuasion. I've even been using the rent from my property to subsidize the rents you've been losing, but, oh no, you don't want me getting involved."

"I didn't know, Angelo. I do need your help. I appreciate everything you're doing to fix Big Blue," she said, rushing to him, putting her arms around his waist. "Let's don't fight. I don't want you to leave." The lamp went dark as I felt her turn away from me and reach out for his deception.

He made her wait a couple of minutes into her hug before he reciprocated and circled his arms around her shoulders, bringing her cheek to his shoulder. "I'm not going anywhere, sweetheart. I just want to be kept in the loop. We're partners, right?"

Against his shoulder, she nodded. He impatiently broke the embrace. "Now, can you clean up this mess?" he said, pointing at the oatmeal spattered across the couch. She nodded again.

Chapter Twenty-seven

Jasmina rolled toward Leo as they lay naked in her bed. He studied a tiny paper crane held between his fingers. She reached out to touch his warm thigh, then slid her hand downward where it stopped at the nothingness below his knee. She moved her hand upward again, caressed his warm testicles and found his renewed erection as the origami bird fluttered to the floor.

"Ready to go again?" she asked, running her thumb from the tip of his dick slowly down to the base, then enclosing it in her gentle fingers.

"You keep me ready, baby," he said, pulling her up on top of him.

She straddled him, already wet again with desire, and slid him easily inside. She tilted her head back as she moved slowly up and down and in a circular motion at the same time. Although her eyes were shut, she could feel him watching her breasts bounce and the moisture oozed between her legs where he was rubbing his thumb with subtle pressure against the hood of her clit.

"Do you like that, babe?"

He made a point of repeating that question while they were fucking. She liked him asking it so much that sometimes she would say "yes" just because he asked. The first time he pinched the insides of her thighs, it had annoyed her. Then he asked, "Do you like that?" and she realized, yes, she did. It made her jump when he was inside her and that gave her an extra jolt of pleasure.

"What about what you like?" she asked, bending down to plant light kisses on his chest.

"Don't worry about me," he answered. "I get what I like. When you come like you never have before, that gives me a rush like you wouldn't believe, because I know I did that."

He brought her again to uncharted ecstasy and she forgot for a moment that he was a man with no legs. But shame leaked into the liquid pleasure that ran through her body as she thought that if she cared about him enough, she would never have to push his deformity out of her mind.

With satiated smiles, they slid reluctantly from opposite sides of the bed. He put on his prostheses as she pulled on jeans, not bothering with panties, and a fluffy sweater. The doorbell rang and she left to answer it as he went into the bathroom.

Angelo leaned casually against the door frame. "Good morning, darlin'," he said with a rakish smile. "Don't you look like a sexy ray of sunshine? You even smell like sex." He took a deep breath and his nostrils flared.

"Angelo? What are you doing here?"

"To get right down to it, I'd like to start up where we left off."

"Where we left off what?"

"Our unfinished business or, should I say unfinished pleasure, in your kitchen."

Jasmina stared at Angelo for a second and shook her head at his audacity. "How's Corrine?"

"She's fat and unhappy, the two things I can't stand in a woman." Angelo reached out and touched Jasmina's hip, letting his hand linger there. "But you've got just what I like."

Jasmina pushed Angelo's hand away. "Not this time, Angelo. I'm seeing someone."

"You're always seeing someone, Jasmina. You can put whoever it is this week on the back burner for me, right?" He grabbed her around the waist and pulled her to his chest. "A woman like you can't ever get enough."

"What the fuck, Angelo! I said no!" Jasmina shoved him into

the middle of the hallway.

"Bitch!" Angelo spit out as he stumbled backward, then regained his balance and composure. "You lost your business and now you're going to lose your apartment."

"What the fuck are you talking about? The notice to vacate is not for this part of the building. Are you saying Corrine is kicking me out?"

"The city is kicking you out. You and everybody else. The city is about to declare the building uninhabitable. By the end of the year, you're going to have to find someplace else to spread your legs for anyone who has a cock."

"Fuck you, Angelo. And fuck your limp-dick friend Henry Fornette, too."

"What's going on, babe?" a man's voice called behind Jasmina.

Angelo strained his neck to peer over Jasmina's shoulder at Leo in boxer shorts, his black, carbon-fiber legs exposed.

"Oh," Angelo said, leaning toward Jasmina so that only she heard him. "I see he's only half the man I am." He threw back his head and laughed as Jasmina slammed the door hard enough to shake the wall.

"Who was that?" Leo asked as she walked into his strong arms. "Hey, you're shaking."

"That was the landlord's son-of-a-bitch boyfriend coming to inform me that the fucking city is going to declare the building unfit for tenants." The raised strip of flesh on her cheek, the scar left from the coffee-shop fire, pulsed with rage.

"You can move in with me," he said. "We'll wake up together, go to bed together. We'll have Thanksgiving dinner together. We'll decorate the Christmas tree together. It'll be wonderful." He held her tighter. "Jasmina, I love you." Her body stiffened. "What is it, baby?"

"If you knew the things I've done, you wouldn't."

"I don't care what you've done."

"I need to get to work, baby," she said, pulling away, smiling up at him. "And you've got to leave for Seattle. "

"I'll drive you to the base before I go to the airport."

Her thoughts went back to the time he'd picked her up for their first dinner date, the day after they met at Istanbul Coffee, three weeks ago. He hadn't explained ahead of time, so she had to take it in all at once, the special hand controls in his sleek, black LeSabre because his sleek, black artificial legs could not operate the accelerator and brake. She had wanted to get out of the car, but she wanted to stay even more.

She had started loving him that night, before the wine and the halibut and the tiramisu and the laughter and the touching of fingertips across the table. Even before he told her about playing football in Sandy Beach, South Carolina, about losing his wife of twelve years to cancer, about running from his grief to four tours in the Mideast, about losing his legs in a firefight in the mountains of Afghanistan in 2005. Even before the good-night kiss in the hallway against the wall next to her apartment door, the kiss that promised all the time in the world for more.

How did I let this get so serious, she thought, when I know I can't stick with it? She looked at the dozens of folded paper cranes scattered across the nightstand and suspended on thin strings in the window. Another fleeting project that she would leave behind for the next and the next, exercises that wouldn't change her deep down inside where it counted.

As Leo gathered up his keys and change, she watched him like he was a character in a movie, too good to really be in her life. She forced herself to ask, "When your wife had cancer, that changed the way you were with each other, didn't it?"

He was startled by the question for a moment before he answered, "Drastically. She was such a beautiful, vibrant woman. We had a joyful, active life. The cancer took that away. Every day was sadder and lonelier, and neither of us knew how to stop that any more than we could stop her dying."

"But you stuck with her until the end, right?"

"Yes, of course."

She looked away from him and asked, "Did you ever think of

not doing that?"

Leo stared at her, without words for a few seconds. "Leave her to suffer and die alone? Never. What kind of person does that?"

Me, she said inside her head. If she fooled herself into thinking they had a future together, there would come an inevitable and terrible day when he would see that underneath her beautiful shell was a cowardly creature who would turn her back on him, like she had done to her husband, at the first sign of hard times. He deserved someone he could count on forever.

"I can take a taxi," she said. "I don't want you to miss your flight and disappoint all those kids at the children's hospital. They're looking forward to seeing a real-life superhero."

She kissed him lightly on the mouth for what she knew was the last time. Of course, she'd have to give up the coffee kiosk. He'd be there every day if she didn't, asking her why, begging her to change her mind. Maybe she would have to make a deal with Henry Fornette after all.

As the door shut behind Leo, Jasmina plucked a stray paper bird off the rumpled bed. She pulled the wings outward until the tiny creation was undone, just a plain piece of paper again in a matter of seconds.

Chapter Twenty-eight

Anthony had unrolled his building design plans and tacked them down on a large sheet of plywood supported by two sawhorses when Corrine walked into the ballroom. She wore a lightweight, ankle-length dress. Although it had once fit loosely, it was now just roomy enough to hide most of the bulges around her middle. A pale blue shawl was draped around her shoulders just below her unbound hair, which caught the lamplight with some of its former luster. The foundation she hadn't worn in months wasn't blended along her jaw and cheeks as expertly as it once had been, but her rose-pink lipstick brightened her pale face and set off her blue eyes.

The sight of her drew a pleased smile across Anthony's face. Through his eyes I again saw my beautiful Corrine, with some flaws within that I hadn't seen before Angelo came along.

"I'm glad you could find time to meet with me," Anthony said. "I'd like for Angelo to be here, too, give him a different perspective. Is he coming later?"

"He has another important meeting tonight with the mayor and the city council. He thinks this will be the deciding discussion about how the city can help us make all the needed repairs."

Anthony looked confused. "Repairs? I thought the meeting tonight was with the Sheraton people, about whether they're going to put up or pull out."

"The Sheraton people?" She thought of the news story she'd

read on the computer in Miss Liza's old apartment. "Why would Angelo ... There must be more than one thing on the agenda. One thing doesn't have to be related to the other."

"Let's worry about that later. Do you want to come around here and take a look?"

Corrine moved to Anthony's side and studied the drawings of the first floor. "What's happened to this room, to the ballroom?"

Anthony traced his fingers along the lines that defined the room on the drawing. "That's the indoor swimming pool. I considered adding a hot tub, too, but there'll be Jacuzzis in the individual units."

"Oh, I see," Corrine said with a nod that contrasted with her look of non-comprehension. She peeled back a design sheet to look at plans for the second and third floors. "There are only three units on these floors. I have six now."

Anthony again pointed as he explained, "Upscale condos require more space and you see I've put in courtyards with full west-facing windows. There'll be thirty-one units altogether, counting your penthouse, which should stay virtually unchanged."

Corrine stepped back from the makeshift table. "Anthony, this is beautiful, but it's so ambitious. I can't afford to make over the building like this. What's this going to cost?"

"I'd say twelve million is a reasonable estimate."

"Twelve million?" Corrine nearly choked on the words.

"Right, but you're looking at a twenty-million-dollar property when it's done. And I think the city would like the sound of that, tax wise, especially when you take into account that it would probably cost three million if the city has to tear it down."

"Who's talking about tearing it down? Angelo's going to get the city to subsidize some repairs and it would be great if you could update it a little to attract the tenants back, but this, this is a total makeover." She backed away from the table like it was a hot stove.

"Corrine, let's look at reality here. I've seen a lot of buildings that needed a lot of work. I don't know what Angelo's expertise is in this area or what he told you about the last council meeting. Perhaps he's been trying to spare your feelings. Look, this is my life's work, and I'm telling you unless Big Blue has a total makeover, the city is bent on tearing it down. Some plaster and paint and Sunday features in the paper aren't going to save anything. I know you can see that, Corrine, just look around you."

Corrine's eyes circled the walls of the ballroom and gazed up at the ceiling as though she could see through all the floors and up into every damaged apartment. A weight descended onto her shoulders and I felt my walls sag under the burden of her stress. "Angelo won't let that happen. He knows how dear Big Blue is to me. If the city … if they won't work with us … well, I don't see the city backing a twelve-million-dollar fantasy."

"I build fantasies into realities, that's what I do."

Corrine laughed mockingly. "The biggest fantasy would be me getting my hands on twelve million dollars. Do you have a plan for making that a reality?"

"Yes, actually I do. I have an accounting firm that specializes in pursuing subsidies and it's already checked into some that we think will work for this project: There's a loophole we can work for a loan guarantee from the Bureau of Indian Affairs because of the location, a historic property credit from the National Park Service, a New Market Tax Credit becomes available through the Treasury Department in February. And I'd be willing to put up some of my own money for a small interest in the property."

"I know it's just a property to you and to the city, but it's not just a property to me, Anthony. I love Big Blue."

I knew Mr. Holbrook had moved out of 804 along with his Etta James collection a month ago, but I swore I heard the violin strains of "At Last."

Tears sprang into Corrine's eyes, but before her face collapsed into a contorted, weeping mask, Anthony walked over to her, put his arms around her, and guided her head gently into his shoulder.

"I can see how you feel about Big Blue. I told you I have a soft spot for this place myself. Next week, I get my crack at the city council, to present my plans in detail. How about once we find out how tonight's meeting with the city goes, you, Angelo, and I sit down and talk about how we can work together to give this old building a new life? Do you think we could do that?"

Corrine looked up at him with an emerging smile. "We can absolutely do that." He relaxed his embrace and she stepped back, folded her arms and gave him a firm nod.

"Oh, I almost forgot to show this to you." He pulled a page of newspaper folded in quarters from the inside pocket of his denim jacket. He uncreased the newspaper and held up a feature story and photo of himself standing outside my front entrance and brandishing his metal tube of building plans. Corrine recognized the photo from Hattie's recent story but not the layout. "The *Los Angeles Times* picked up the piece Hattie McGee did on me. They played it as a local angle."

"L.A. builder finds his Last Frontier." Corrine clapped her hands as she read the headline. "You didn't reveal which apartment you and your bride stayed in during the happiest days of your life. Did you forget which one it was?"

"I'll never forget that. It was what is now 706."

Corrine didn't know whether to laugh or cry at his answer. She remembered the oasis of fresh air in the apartment when she had toured the deteriorating building. "It's seen better days," she said and thanked Anthony for sharing his building plan. As she headed for the elevator, she heard him rolling up his pictures of the future.

She was seated on the green sofa, still in the breezy dress and shawl, sipping a glass of red wine when Angelo stomped in, slamming the door behind him. "How did the meeting go?" she asked, her voice trembling as she watched his dark expression.

"Disastrous," he barked, as he fell into a chair, "that's how it went. Totally disastrous."

"The city didn't see things our way?" She picked up a second glass of wine from a side table and offered it to him. He refused it with a slash of his hand.

"Our way? No. The city is no help. The mayor's a fucking idiot."

"But you tried, Angelo."

"Damn right I tried. I tried until I talked a blue hole in the floor. If we can't be ready by March, they said. By March! And whose fucking fault is that? No one but that foot-dragging dickhead, Henry Fornette. They're not putting up, they're pulling out, and there's nothing I can do about it."

"Pulling out? You mean the Sheraton people?"

"What do you know about the Sheraton people?"

"I-I just heard they were on the agenda. I thought maybe you were talking to them, too."

"Why would I be talking to the Sheraton people?"

"About your land. About how they may want to build on your land."

"What the fuck are you talking about?" Angelo leapt to his feet and stood over Corrine with his fists clenched at his sides. "They're not building on any land, at least not in Fairbanks. And I told you I don't have any plans for that land except to keep things the way they are. How do you even know about meeting with the Sheraton people? Who have you been talking to?"

"Anthony came by with some renovation plans—"

Angelo's hand struck her jaw hard enough to jerk her head sideways. Blood trickled down her chin from where her lower lip was split. I shook the room with rage, banging the frames of pictures and mirrors against the walls, rattling the windows to the verge of shattering.

"Stop it!" he yelled up to the ceiling, jabbing the air with both fists. "Sto-o-op i-i-i-it!" He raised his hand again and waited for my outburst to subside. Corrine covered her face with her hands and cowered against the corner of the couch. "You stupid bitch, I told you not to go behind my back."

I sent a bolt of heat through the cord of a glass-shaded lamp on the side table and up through the light bulb inside, bursting the glass, sending shards into Angelo's raised hand.

"Fuck!" he cried out and fell back into the chair. Corrine cautiously lowered the shield of her palms. The side of her face was bright red with the imprint of Angelo's hand. She tried to hold back the sound of her sobs.

He glared at her, his breath puffing out in quick, angry bursts. "Renovation plans, what a joke," he spit out like venom. "The city won't give us a dime for renovation, for anything." He narrowed his eyes. "I'll make them pay one way or another. They'll pay that three million, not me. And you can bet that piece of shit Henry Fornette will pay. All he had to do was convince them to take action. It's his fault!"

Angelo stomped his feet on the floor and beat the arms of the chair with his fists like a spoiled child. Tears seeped out of the corners of his eyes. "He ruined it! He ruined everything!"

Corrine reached out her hand to him to calm his wrath. "I don't understand what you're talking about, but it's not over yet, Angelo. Anthony has a plan."

"Anthony, Anthony. If I hear that name I again, I swear I'll ..." Angelo started to push up out of the chair, gritted his teeth, and glared at Corrine.

She retreated farther into the side of the couch and pushed her palms outward in front of her. "Wait, just listen, Angelo. Anthony is going to present his renovation plan to the council next week. He says the tax revenue will be too appealing to turn down. The city will have to stop its abatement process. Anthony wants to talk, to meet with both of us."

"With both of us?" Angelo sat down again. "What do you know about these big renovation plans?"

Corrine relaxed and her eyes lit up. "They're really something. He plans to turn Big Blue into thirty luxury condos with courtyards and a swimming pool."

"Condos. Courtyards. Swimming pool. And how much does he need to transform this, this catastrophe?"

"He says twelve million but—"

Angelo laughed until more tears rolled out of his eyes. "Twelve million. Is that all?" He laughed some more, wiping the tears off his cheeks, before he sputtered to a stop. "Oh, darlin', I'm sorry, you were saying?"

"There are subsidies I can apply for and he'll chip in some, maybe the city, too. After all, he's going to convince them that Big Blue will be worth almost twice that once the renovations are done."

Angelo sneered. "I suppose you want me to keep chipping in to bail you out."

"No, Angelo, I never asked you to begin with."

"You say Anthony is making his 'Save Big Blue' presentation to the council next week?"

"Yes."

"Okay, sure, let's meet with him." I saw rigid, black plates lining up in his mind, like weapons being organized for an attack. "We'll have him over for dinner Friday. Come here, babe." Corrine didn't move.

"It's okay," he coaxed. "Don't be afraid." She brushed her hand against her swelling jaw. "You know I didn't mean to do that. It's just that when you go behind my back like that, I feel abandoned all over again, like I was when I was cut out of my mother's life and Aunt Liza's life."

"I didn't go behind your back, Angelo," she said through her faded sobs, "I just didn't have a chance to tell you."

"Of course you didn't. You're right. Now, come here, please." He stretched out his arm to her.

Corrine rose warily from the couch, walked over to Angelo, and sat down as he opened his lap. He placed her arms around his neck. "So we'll have Anthony over the day after Thanksgiving?" she asked, her voice still quivering.

"Yeah. I'll cook some of my famous shrimp and crab etouffee."

Corrine pulled her arms back with alarm. "No, not that. Anthony doesn't eat seafood."

Angelo smiled and kissed Corrine's bruised cheek. "Oh, a

picky eater, huh? Well maybe I'll give him a call and discuss the menu with him. I saw his card around here somewhere."

He kissed her again on the cheek, then the mouth. He pulled her dress down to her waist. She stiffened and tried to pull away. He kissed her bare breasts, then the curve of her neck. "I'm sorry, my love, I'm so sorry," he whispered with each kiss.

The tendons in her neck and shoulders slackened, her head fell back, and she moaned in answer to his attentions. He laid her down on the floor. She bent her knees and let her legs fall open. As he lowered himself between her thighs, she guided him inside her.

He brushed her hair gently from her purpled cheek, licked the dried blood from her mouth, and whispered, "I'll never hurt you again, sweetheart. I promise. Can you forgive me?"

She lifted her hips up to meet his slow, deep thrust.

I burst the light bulbs in all the rooms, one by one, but Corrine was oblivious with passion and misguided mercy.

Chapter Twenty-nine

Lonnie headed for his liquor store to open shop as soon as he parked his Jeep, although his shoulders sagged with exhaustion from the drive home down the Richardson, and from something else that I couldn't identify. A man leaned against the security gate. Lonnie smelled the booze on him from ten feet away. As Lonnie moved closer, he recognized the muscled physique and chiseled face of the Wounded Warrior from the September 11 newspaper photo with the mayor. He was still handsome even while slumped against the wall, not only drunk, but also crying.

"I need a bottle," the man blubbered as he wrung some type-written pages in his hands.

Lonnie unlocked and lifted the metal gate. It rolled upward with a screech and a bang. "Looks like you've had one already, man."

"I've been down at The Mecca, but they won't sell me anymore."

"No surprise there," Lonnie said, shaking his head. "They don't want to get sued again for a drunk driver killing someone. You didn't drive here, did you?"

"I puked in a cab, so I don't think so."

"You don't think ...? Okay, come inside and we'll figure this out." He put his arm around the man and led him into the store, stopping to let him lean against his side when he stumbled. Lonnie pulled a folding chair out from behind the counter, set it up, and motioned for the visitor to sit.

"You gonna gimme a bottle?" the man pleaded, less vigorously than before.

Lonnie ignored the pitiful entreaty, pulled out another chair and sat down knee to knee with the drunken man. "I'm Lonnie and you're ..."

"Leo."

"I'm guessing you're not really a drinking man, Leo. Am I right?"

Leo twisted the loose papers, bowed his head, and nodded, looking ashamed. "I don't' know how many times I've told my young troops, 'When you try to solve a problem with alcohol, you create another.' Now I'm ... " His voice trailed off into sobs.

"Why don't you tell me why you're doing this to yourself, Leo?"

"I can't live without her."

Lonnie shook his head. "A woman. I should've known." He put his hand on Leo's knee and felt the prosthesis below the bone. "Hey, man, seems you've had to deal with a lot in your life and you've come through it. How long have you known this woman?"

"A month."

"One month, and you're sure you can't live without her?"

"If you knew Jasmina, you wouldn't be asking me that."

"Jasmina, hmmm."

"We were going to spend Thanksgiving together and she just stopped answering my calls. She's blocked my number. Two nights ago I banged on her door for half an hour, but she wouldn't open it. I thought that snake Henry Fornette was with her, so I went to his office yesterday and asked him face to face. He told me he was at a council meeting Tuesday night. I didn't believe his lying ass, so I made him give me a copy of the minutes." He waved the papers he held at Lonnie. "He was at the meeting like he said. Why won't she talk to me? If she would just give me an answer ..."

"I'm going to give you a ride home and you can tell me all about this Jasmina on the way there."

Lonnie pulled the metal gate back down, locked up the store, and helped Leo outside and into the front passenger side of his Jeep. The Army officer slumped against the window.

"Where do you live?" Lonnie started up the engine.

"Fort Wainwright."

"I'm not familiar with the base." Lonnie slipped the vehicle into reverse. "Can you give me directions once we get there?"

"Just ask the guy at the gate where the base commander's house is."

Lonnie backed up and pointed the Jeep toward Noble Street. "Commander, would you take out your military ID now so I can have it ready? Military checkpoints with armed guards tend to make me a little nervous, especially when I might be asked to explain why I'm transporting an intoxicated, Caucasian colonel." Leo fumbled in his pocket and handed his ID to Lonnie.

Lonnie looked at the laminated card with the sober image of his passenger. "Colonel Gregory Leonides," he read. "I'm in the presence of royalty, royally messed up, that is. Brother, what we do for love." He shook his head.

Forty minutes later, Lonnie pulled the Jeep back into the parking lot alone. As he exited the vehicle, he noticed the crumpled pages Leo had left behind on the seat. He swept up the minutes from the city council meeting. Halfway back to my front door he remembered to retrieve his travel bag from the back of his vehicle, spied the photos of Miss Liza and the hastily thrown-in papers from 706, and gathered those up as well.

It was after eleven p.m., hardly worth opening the store again. After all, it was Thanksgiving, most people were home with their families. Besides, he had a mission on the fourth floor.

He headed up to his apartment first, dropped his bag between the living room and kitchen, stacked the photos on the kitchen counter, and was about to toss Leo's papers into the trash can under the sink when I pushed the window open. A chilly breeze rushed into the room, grabbed the papers and photos from Lonnie's hand, and scattered them across the floor.

Lonnie crawled and scooted across the tile, pursuing the papers as they tried to escape his grasp under the power of the sustained breeze. The typed name "Angelo Fallon" caught his eye as he trapped a page under his hand. When he took a closer look at the council meeting minutes he realized the discussion involved Angelo and was all about plans for my future.

"Fuck me sideways," he said, and repeated the phrase as he read through the minutes. Remembering his fourth-floor mission, he set the papers atop the photos on the counter. "Tomorrow," he said. "This shit gets settled tomorrow, even if I have to kick some ass."

I banged the window shut to signal that I would gladly take some of that action.

He took a bottle of wine from his bag, uncorked it, retrieved two wide-globed wine glasses from a cupboard, and headed to Jasmina's apartment.

"It's Lonnie! Open up!" he shouted through the door after banging on it for nearly five minutes.

Jasmina opened the door a few inches and leaned her head against the edge. Lonnie's appreciative look showed that even with her face puffy from crying, no makeup, her hair in disarray, and some crusty stuff in the corner of one eye, Jasmina still looked gorgeous.

"What the fuck, Lonnie?" she greeted him.

"How can such a beautiful woman have such an ugly mouth?"

"Fuck you, Lonnie. You get me out of bed at midnight to criticize my language? Are you drunk?"

"Naw, Jasmina, let me in."

"Go away, Lonnie. It's been a long night." She started to close the door, but Lonnie grabbed it, wedging his hand between the door edge and the jamb. The glasses he held upside down by their stems with his other hand clinked against the wine bottle.

"Please, Jasmina, let me come in and sit down. Have a Thanksgiving drink with me. Like you said, it's been a long night."

Jasmina surrendered to Lonnie's pleading eyes and opened the door just enough to let him brush past her. "Wow," he said, taking in the room.

The back wall was painted a rich red, but the rest of the room and all the furnishings were an elegant mix of white and gold. Cornices over the windows and entrances to other rooms replaced squared corners with Mediterranean arches bordered in sprays of painted-on gold leaves. "In all these years, I've never been in your apartment. This is like a palace."

"So you're here to talk about interior decorating? Oh, that's right, you're gay." Jasmina glared at him with arms crossed, the swell of her breasts displayed through the gap of her rose-colored, satin robe.

Lonnie set the wine and goblets on a glass-topped table in front of the couch and lowered himself onto a brocade cushion. "I'm here to drink a toast with you," he said as he filled each glass a third-full with the dark, red wine. "This is a very nice Cabernet. It needs to breathe a little. Come sit with me."

Jasmina sat as far away from Lonnie as she could on the other end of the couch. "A toast to what?"

"To William Good."

"William Good? I've heard that name before."

"Yummy Good?"

"Oh, yeah." Jasmina slapped her thigh as she curled her legs under her. "William Good is the CEO of Yummy Good Doughnuts." She frowned. "And exactly why would we be toasting him?"

"William died yesterday."

"I haven't been keeping up with the news. I've read he was kind of a recluse, but still why are we - - "

"His family has kept his death from the media so far. He died in Alaska."

"In Alaska? He wouldn't even open a shop up here. I had to order Yummy Good from the Lower 48 for my once-a-month specials. How do you know so much about him?"

"You know about my July fishing trips?"

Jasmina snickered. "Yeah, your fishing trips. Oooh, big secret. We all know what you're doing with your line and sinker, Lonnie. You have a young stud in a cabin somewhere down the Richardson Highway."

"On Paxson Lake, to be exact. And it wasn't some young stud, although William was about ten years younger than me."

"William Good is your lover?"

"Was my lover."

Jasmina's face softened. "I'm sorry. But how ... was it AIDS?"

"Again, the gay stereotype. William lived in fear of that, how it would affect his business empire if he was outed. He married three times to keep up the pretense, even had a child with wife number one thirty years ago."

"I'm sorry, Lonnie, I didn't mean ... how did he die?"

"It was cancer, in his brain. It took him very quickly. I got a call a couple of days ago. His ex-wives and his son wanted to let me know he was about to leave us, that he had chosen to die at the house on Paxson Lake, that I needed to get there immediately. I was alone with him when he took his last breath, according to his final wishes, not his wives, not even his son, just me. Then I left right after, like he wanted, no lingering goodbyes. He didn't want me at his memorial service. His body will be cremated and his ashes taken back to Connecticut."

"He must have loved you, Lonnie." Jasmina scooted across the couch, closer to him.

"Yes, he loved me. And I loved him."

"You had a chance to tell him that one last time, right?"

"Yes, as he was dying, I gave him all my love. But while he was alive? While he was alive, all I was willing to give him was one fishing trip a year. He wanted me to stay at the house in Paxson for the summers when he was there. He begged me to do that for the last seven years. He said if I would stay with him, he wouldn't care if the whole world knew about him, that he would come out for me, that maybe someday when the laws changed we would get married."

"Why didn't you do it, Lonnie? William Good is one of the richest men in America. Fuck, your life would be ... wow."

"I told myself I had my own business to run, that I like my low-key life. But the truth is, Jasmina, I was afraid that I was the one who would be found out. Not my gayness. Shit, I'm sixty-five, what the hell do I care about what people think about that? I was afraid, terrified actually, that if I was with him more than just that one fishing trip a year, that he would find out who I really am, that he would find out that I'm not worthy of being loved."

"Not you, Lonnie. You never gave it a chance."

"No, I didn't. And all I can do now is this." Lonnie picked up both glasses and handed one to Jasmina. "Here's to you, William, you were the best of lovers, in every way." Lonnie clinked his glass against Jasmina's and took a long, slow drink.

Jasmina took a sip and licked her lips. "This is wonderful. William had very good taste in wine as well as men."

Lonnie shrugged off the compliment and savored another drink, letting it roll over his tongue. "1996 Screaming Eagle Cabernet Sauvignon, about two thousand dollars."

"Wow, but I guess that was pennies to him. He was worth billions, right?"

"Don't I know it. CEO annual bonuses over a million for the past ten years. Hmmm, he always said he got his real annual bonus in July." Lonnie laughed. "And he put his money where his mouth is. He ... it takes my breath away to say it ... left me ten million dollars."

"Ten?" Jasmina put her hand over her heart. "Million?" She breathed out in short huffs. "Dollars?"

"Yeah, I can't quite wrap my mind around it. A couple of days ago I was a small-time, liquor-store owner, and today I'm a multi-millionaire."

"So I guess we're toasting your good fortune, too." She held up her glass to clink against Lonnie's a second time.

"My good fortune was to be loved by William Good. My bad

fortune is that I never loved him well enough, and now it's too late."

Jasmina reached out and touched Lonnie's leg. "I know it sounds like a bad TV line, Lonnie, but I'm so sorry for your loss."

"I'm actually not here to talk about my loss. I'm here to talk about yours."

"My loss?"

"Yes, because there's still time to change that, because maybe you don't have to wait until you're sixty-five to not be an idiot."

"What are you talking about, Lonnie? The only thing I've lost is my shop, and that's all Corrine's fault."

"We'll get to Corrine later. I'm not talking about losing your shop."

"What then, Lonnie?"

"I gave a man a ride home tonight, a drunken man, a very heartbroken man. A man who is in love with you down to his soul and back again."

"Leo," she breathed out the name.

"Leo. Now my question is: What the hell are you doing, girl? How many shots do you think you're going to get at real love that you think you can let this one pass you by? From where I sit, your score in the love game is a big, fat zero."

"I'm not good enough for him, Lonnie," she said, setting her wine glass down, averting her eyes. "He deserves better."

"He deserves, he deserves. You're a genius, Jasmina, you can figure out for someone else what they deserve. It's really about what you deserve, isn't it?"

"I don't know what you mean, Lonnie."

"You think you don't deserve Leo. Just like I thought I didn't deserve William. People like us, people who have done bad things like us, we can't have anyone good to love us. People like us have sins to atone for, people like us deprive ourselves to pay our penance. Year after year we deprive ourselves of all the sweet, wonderful love that is offered to us with sincere, outstretched, pleading arms. Is that what you think, Jasmina, is that what you think?"

Jasmina nodded and tears spilled down her face.

Lonnie put down his glass and took one of her hands in his. "Well, think about this, sweetie. We're not just depriving ourselves of love, we're depriving them of love. We're breaking their hearts, we're killing their souls. Do you want that blood on your hands, too? Do you, Jasmina, because, I can tell you, it's really hard to wash off."

Jasmina shook her head. With a trembling hand, she set down her wine glass and it overturned on the table, spilling the spare contents. She looked at Lonnie apologetically. He stood the glass upright and offered her his unfinished glass of wine. She held up her palm in refusal. "I shouldn't be drinking."

"It's just a little."

"I shouldn't be drinking at all." She took a deep breath and exhaled. "I'm pregnant."

Lonnie's eyes widened. The corners of his mouth twitched in the involuntary beginning of a grin. "Leo's?"

Jasmina nodded. "Oh, Lonnie, what the fuck am I going to do?" Lonnie set down his glass and opened his arms to let Jasmina collapse against him, her shoulders heaving with sobs.

He stroked the back of her head. "Do you love him, honey?"

Jasmina sat up and wiped the tears and snot from her face with the back of her hand. "Yes, like I've never loved anyone."

"Well, then, what you're going to do is call him and tell him. I'm sure he can take it from there."

"You're right, Lonnie. I'm going to call him right now."

Lonnie grabbed her shoulders. "Whoa, girl. Let that man sleep for about the next fourteen hours. He was in bad shape when I left him. I doubt he'll remember how he got home. If you call him now, he won't remember that either. Trust me on this. I know about the effects of alcohol."

He chucked her tenderly under the chin. Jasmina responded with a weak smile. "Do you want me to get you something else besides wine to drink? I could make some coffee if you point me in the right direction."

"No, thanks, Lonnie. I'm fine now."

"How far along are you?"

"Three weeks." She smiled and touched her belly. "You know what's funny? After I saw the stick turn blue, the first thing I wanted to do was run upstairs and tell Corrine. I was halfway out the door when I remembered, we're not friends anymore." Tears welled up in her eyes again.

"Corrine and you are still friends, sweetie. The two of you are just lost, like you and I were, and you have to find a way back to each other."

"What were you and I angry at each other about anyway, Lonnie? I don't remember."

"Me neither. Why don't we go see Corrine tomorrow?"

"You'll come with me?"

"Of course. I have a lot of things I need to talk to Corrine about." He patted her leg, stood up, and stretched. "Now, you should get some rest, little mama." She giggled and reached her hand out so that he could pull her to her feet. "Want me to tuck you in?"

"I'd like that."

She rested her head on his shoulder as he put his arm around her and they walked toward the bedroom. I felt the north side of me warming with an invisible balm. The heat was working again.

Chapter Thirty

Corrine vigorously stirred fluffy white mounds in a crockery mixing bowl with a wire whip. Suddenly she felt hands at her waist tugging her backward. The bowl tipped and a glob of coconut and whipped cream splatted onto her wrist.

"What are you doing, precious?" Angelo's voice vibrated into her ear as he relaxed his grasp on her hips and kissed her cheek.

"Finishing up the frosting for my coconut cake. Which you almost ruined."

"You're up awful early and already baked a cake?" He stole a fingerful of the frosting from the bowl.

"I had to get up early to get into my kitchen without you interfering."

"Oh, interfering, am I?" He pushed the front of his body against the back of hers.

"Angelo, come on, let me finish. This cake is one of my specialties and I want it to be perfect for tonight." She slipped away from him, mounded the frosting on one of the three cake layers that sat on separate plates on the center island, picked up a narrow spatula, and began spreading the frothy topping.

"All right, you finish up, darlin', and then get out of the way of the master chef. I'm going to prepare a dinner for tonight that will so impress Anthony Aurelius that I'll have him eating out of my hand, pardon the pun, when it comes to fixing up this building. And I don't need you in my domain looking over my shoulder while I'm stirring and seasoning."

"Your domain, but my kitchen, buster."

"Oh, are we having a little power struggle?" He leaned on the island and reached for another taste of frosting but she tapped his hand away.

"Well, you don't expect me to just sit in the other room all day and stay out of your way?"

"Of course not, my love. I have a terrific idea. It's Black Friday. How about you go shopping for something beautiful to wear tonight? When's the last time you got something for yourself?"

Corrine lifted the crowning cake layer onto the other two stacked sections. "I've hardly been out for months. And I can't remember when I've bought a new dress."

"I told you it was terrific idea. You can take the Caddy and go down to the mall or the stores on Johansen, wherever you want."

Corrine froze for a second with the frosting-covered spatula in her hand. "I'd rather shop downtown. There are some nice places just down the street that I can walk to."

"I don't think that's such a good idea. It's really slick out there. You should drive even if it's just a few blocks."

She swirled the creamy frosting around the sides of the cake. "The parking will be terrible. I'm not going to drive. I'll wear my Yaktrax."

"Your what?"

"Crampons. They're like putting chains on your tires, only they go on your shoes. I'll be perfectly safe." She garnished the top of the cake with a handful of shredded coconut.

"Well, I'm not so sure."

"You want me out of your domain, so I will oblige." Placing a glass cover over the cake, she gave the plate underneath a little twirl. "A masterpiece, if I do say so myself." She playfully wagged her finger at him. "Don't you dare sneak even a fraction of a smidgen of that frosting. I'll see you in a few hours." After she pecked him on the cheek, she sailed out of the kitchen with a wave of her hand.

Wearing her ice grippers, Corrine clomped north up Cushman, staring in amazement at a couple of young women prancing in high heels down sidewalks glazed by another round of freezing rain. She passed historic City Hall and the Federal Building and nodded at the Art Deco style structures as if greeting old friends she hadn't seen in far too long.

The unseasonable warmth of the snow-stingy winter made for a comfortable six-block walk to two boutiques on opposite sides of the street. One & Only had been around for years and Jewel's Fantasies had cropped up in the last few months.

Corrine reveled in her freedom for close to four hours. Even after Angelo called her on her cell to say Anthony was already on his way, she lingered an extra half hour over a grande mocha at a coffee house across from what used to be the Penney's building.

As she waited for the elevator on my ground floor, she hugged a black and pink shopping bag. A red dress was folded inside the bag along with gold jewelry wrapped in pink tissue paper. She smiled at the realization that she had remembered to accessorize. She thought about the red, open-toe pumps hidden away in the back of her closet, the ones with the dangerous-looking rows of gold spikes that ran up and down the heels. Never in a million years had she thought she would ever wear those outlandish shoes, a birthday gift from Jasmina two years ago. But now she felt almost like she had when she and Angelo were first together.

Angelo had been so sweet and gentle since the day he ... She touched the tender, yellow-purple mark on her face and pushed aside the memory of his angry hand. She imagined instead how the red heels would look with the long, bell-sleeved dress that had floated seductively when she moved back and forth in front of the dressing room mirror.

The new dress was a size twelve, not the eight she would have worn six months ago. That store's clothes must run small, she decided, holding her package like a prize as she stood in front of the elevator, anxious to show it off to Angelo. She didn't hear Lonnie and Jasmina as they came up behind her, and she jumped at the sound of Lonnie's voice.

"Corrine, we need to talk to you."

She whirled around and stared at them as though they were strangers whom she had to size up to see if they meant her harm. "I don't have anything to talk to you two about," she said, injecting a chill into each word.

The sight of Corrine's bruised cheek made Lonnie hesitate before he spoke again. "Please, Corrine. We've known each other a long time. Can't we please come inside my store and talk for a few minutes?"

"No, leave me alone." The elevator door opened and Corrine stepped inside.

Lonnie held his hand against the rubber edge of one of the doors, blocking it from closing.

"Please," Jasmina added.

"I said leave me alone," Corrine said, agitated. She pushed the "close door" button. As the doors slid toward each other, Lonnie stepped into the elevator, grabbed Jasmina's hand, and pulled her in behind him before the doors shut.

Corrine glared at Lonnie and Jasmina as the elevator glided upward two floors. "Corrine—" Lonnie began again before she interrupted him.

"I won't listen to you, you sluts."

As the elevator passed the fourth floor, I made it shudder. The passengers looked at the walls and ceiling. As the elevator rose past the fifth floor I slowed it down. At the seventh floor, it was barely crawling upward. "What the fuck," Jasmina said.

"It's a little slow," Lonnie said. Both women glared at him for stating the obvious like he was offering some kind of comfort.

Corrine backed into a rear corner and clutched her bag. Between the eighth and ninth floor I stopped the elevator with a swift, short jerk. The ceiling light went dead. The three passengers didn't say a word. Corrine punched the useless emergency button twenty times, each time more frenzied than the last, before she gave up and sank to the floor, covering the top of her head with her hands and letting the bag fall into her lap.

Lonnie and Jasmina sat down across from her.

"You'll listen to us now, Corrine," Lonnie said.

Corrine pulled out her cell phone and attempted to call Angelo, but the phone didn't work inside the dark box. She left the screen on for light. "I don't have time for this. We asked Anthony Aurelius over for dinner. I'm late. He's already upstairs. Angelo's going to talk to him about fixing up Big Blue." Corrine futilely slapped the bottom of the closed doors.

"The last thing Angelo wants is to fix up Big Blue," Lonnie said.

"You don't know what you're talking about," Corrine shot back.

"Did he do that to your face, honey?" Jasmina asked.

Corrine's hand flew up to her cheek to cover the discolored skin. "Angelo's helping me to save Big Blue."

"The only one Angelo has been helping is himself, to a sweet deal with the city once he got Big Blue torn down so the Sheraton could build a new hotel and water park," Lonnie countered. "The Sheraton needs both lots, not just the one he owns next door. Angelo's only problem is that he couldn't guarantee the Sheraton people that he could demolish Big Blue soon enough."

"What ... that ...that doesn't make any sense," Corrine stammered. "Why would he be talking to Anthony if he doesn't want to save Big Blue? How did you come up with that crazy story?"

"It's all in the minutes of this week's council meeting, which I was going to show you down in the store. I don't know what Angelo's game plan is now that the Sheraton decided to build in Canada. Unless he's just out for revenge on one of us."

"Revenge for what?" Corrine shook her head in confusion.

"Yeah, revenge for what?" Jasmina echoed. "You didn't fill me in on any of this."

"For the sins of your past, Jasmina, or for the sins of Corrine's past, or for the sins of my past."

"But Angelo didn't even know us until six months ago," Jasmina said. "Why would he want to do anything to us?"

"Because he's a Frayer."

"A what?" Corrine shouted.

"A Frayer," Lonnie and Jasmina said simultaneously, and Lonnie continued, "It's from a French word that means 'unravel.' Frayers are a clan from the backwoods of Louisiana. They have special powers to wreak havoc, like what's been happening to Big Blue ever since Angelo moved in. People who want revenge pay them well to unravel the lives of those they want to even the score with."

"What's that got to do with Angelo?" Corrine said with a scowl and a dismissive wave of her hand. "Big Blue is just getting old. What score? I don't believe you. I wouldn't trust you, Lonnie Jackson, as far as I could throw Big Blue."

"Would you trust me if I told you what score? Would you trust me if I told you something I did that I'm so ashamed of that I've never told anybody?"

Corrine crossed her arms and turned her head to the wall, trying to will herself not to hear anymore.

"When I was sixteen, seventeen," Lonnie began, "I worked after school as a clerk, stock boy, broom pusher, at Leibowitz Drug in Cleveland. A boy was lucky to get a job back then in my neighborhood, other than stealing or selling weed for the older guys. Miss Leibowitz paid me good and she was kind to me. She never raised her voice to me even when I counted the change wrong or knocked something over. If I was late getting to work because I had to stay after school, she would say, 'Ah, boychick, your education is your future. This little store can wait.' She'd even send me home with her homemade chicken soup sometimes because she knew my daddy wasn't working and we didn't always have food in the house.

"She was kind of nosy, though. She'd ask me if I had a girlfriend, and she would give me this sly wink. I knew even then that I was gay, but we didn't use that word back in the day. I think that wink was Miss Leibowitz's way of telling me she knew, but she wasn't going to judge."

Corrine relaxed her arms. She was looking at Lonnie, drawn into his story, waiting for what would happen next.

He continued, "Like I said, one of the ways of making money in that neighborhood was stealing. There was a dude named T.J. He didn't know too much about anything outside the block, but what he did know was how to crack a safe—he was self-taught—and how to pull information out of people without them even noticing. He knew where I worked and it only took a couple of times shooting the bull with him before he knew what hours I worked, when I was alone before closing time, and all about Miss Leibowitz's safe, where it was located, and when it held a large amount of cash.

"He also figured out, or at least had strong suspicions about which way I swung, and we both knew that kind of thing didn't play well in the 'hood. He used that as leverage to get me to leave the store unlocked one night after I finished my shift so he could get in and get back to that safe. It all went down without a hitch. T.J. was lifting nine hundred dollars while I was on my way home.

"But that night, Miss Leibowitz, for some reason, came back to the store. She surprised the thief and he whacked her in the head. When I heard the police were looking to question me about a robbery and attempted murder, I booked. I took my saved-up earnings for the last two months, hopped a freight train, and eventually made it up here by hitchhiking and working odd jobs."

"What happened to Miss Leibowitz?" Corrine asked.

"I kept in touch with my folks and some of the neighborhood dudes for a while. They told me she was never right in the head after that. That woman survived a Nazi death camp, but the robbery and the hit in the head did her in. She stayed in her house, didn't talk to anybody, just sat and stared at the TV all day long. She wouldn't even get up to go to the bathroom unless her grandson, who was staying with her, took her. She was dead two years later.

"When one of my boys told me her grandson was asking about where I was, I cut my ties with anyone back home, except my mama. We exchanged Christmas cards every year until she died three years ago. In the last one she sent, she wrote that T.J. got himself shot dead and Miss Leibowitz's grandson had retired from the post office.

"I never stop thinking about how kind that old woman was to me and how I repaid that kindness by robbing her of her life. I can see how someone, maybe her grandson, would want revenge for that. I don't see how I can be forgiven for what I've done."

"I forgive you, Lonnie," Jasmina said, stroking the side of Lonnie's face. "I never was a good Bible student when I was a girl. I would sneak out of class to watch American movies, that's how I learned to speak the cursing type of English. But the one verse I remember is this: 'Let he who is without sin cast the first stone.' I have my own sins to confess."

"Being promiscuous is not the worst thing in the world," Corrine interjected. "You're young and beautiful. I probably would be the same way if I looked like you."

Jasmina smiled and shook her head. "If only that was all I've done, but I'm going to tell you something much worse that I've never told anyone."

Lonnie put his arm around Jasmina's shoulders as she began. "I was married to the handsomest, most romantic, kind-hearted man in the world. He was a lieutenant in the U.S. Army stationed in Turkey. I met him at a museum while I was on a school field trip. It was an instant attraction for both of us. We couldn't keep our hands off each other. A cousin of a woman my mother knew from the grocery store saw us having sex in his car. It only took a couple of days for the news to reach my mother's ear. I had dishonored my family. My parents kicked me out of the house. But, it was okay, I thought, who needs them? I have the man of my dreams.

"We got married on the base. I was Mrs. Michael Jones. I was going to live in a nice house in Seattle, Washington, U.S.A. Michael was promoted to captain. We had a second wedding, a big one with his parents, his grandparents, his sisters, his cousins, in Seattle. I wore the most beautiful dress. Our wedding photo looked like a magazine cover, the perfect couple.

"Then Michael was deployed to Afghanistan. I waited for my hero to come home in fourteen months. But he came home in six months, with half his face burned off, his skin all raw and shriveled up, a lump the size of a baseball on the side of his shaved head. When I first saw him, I was in shock. I was thinking, 'Who is this monster? Where is my beautiful husband? Where is the man of my dreams?' But I'd said 'for better or for worse' twice. So I was supposed to love him, right?

"I tried to love him. I tried for six months. But I couldn't love this thing that I had to wake up and look at every morning. I wasn't like all those brave people in the commercials about the wounded warriors. I was repulsed by the sight of him. I couldn't keep that smile on my face and I couldn't hide that I wanted to turn away. I turned away every time he came near me. And even when I wasn't looking at him, I saw his eyes pleading with me, 'Please love me, Jasmina,' and I told him I can't."

Jasmina was sobbing and pulling the neck of her shirt up to wipe her nose and eyes. "And he said ..." She swallowed hard. " ... he said, 'It's okay, baby. It's a difficult adjustment. You just need time.' And I knew that I was stuck on the cover image of the romance novels I read when I was a teenager, and I wasn't going to adjust, that it wasn't in me to adjust, no matter how much time I had. And he said, 'I'm sorry, baby, I'm so sorry.' This good, good man who didn't do anything wrong was apologizing to me. He was apologizing for going to war and getting his face blown off and making me feel bad.

"That's when I knew I couldn't let him stay with a woman who doesn't deserve him, but I couldn't leave him, and he wouldn't leave me. So I had to make him leave. I had to do something so terrible that he would hate me enough to walk out on me. I set him up to find me in our bed with another man. That did it. That drove him away from me, but not the way I planned.

"After he shouted, 'Get the fuck out, you whore!' about a dozen times, he got one of his guns, put it under his chin, and pulled the trigger. I guess he was so upset from what he had seen he couldn't hold the gun straight. The bullet entered his upper jaw and came out above his ear. He was in the hospital for a while, his mouth wired shut. That gave me plenty of time to go back to our house, pack my things, and leave for the airport. I was going to leave my car at the airport and fly away to the most remote place in America I could think of, Alaska.

"But before I left him forever, I went by the hospital. I parked the car as close to the entrance as I could. I was sitting there, gripping the wheel, trying to get the courage to at least go up to the floor where he was and tell him, I don't know what. I'm sorry? He's better off without me? I heard something hit my windshield and this big crack burst across it right in front of my face. Then something hit it again. I saw through the cracks the face of a crazy woman pounding on my windshield with a concrete brick. She was shouting, 'I'll kill you! I'll kill you for what you did to my brother!' I recognized one of Michael's sisters.

"I think she probably would have killed me if I hadn't sped out of that parking lot. I was shaking all the way to the airport, and I didn't stop shaking until the plane was in the sky. I don't think I was ever going to get up the nerve to go into that hospital. If I had, I think Michael would have forgiven me. But I deserved to sit in that car and have my head smashed in with a brick. I didn't deserve to be forgiven."

Corrine wiped away the tears she'd been crying while listening to Jasmina. "I forgive you, Jasmina. I forgive you because I can't cast stones either. You didn't kill your husband. What I've never told anyone since I came to Alaska is that I killed mine."

"No," Jasmina said with a gasp. "You couldn't do that, Corrine, not you."

Chapter Thirty-one

The light in the elevator buzzed and blinked as I lost my concentration. I had wanted Lonnie and Jasmina to talk to Corrine without her being able to walk away. I hadn't bargained on the pain this was causing her, but none of us could turn back.

"Tell us what happened, honey," Lonnie urged Corrine.

She took a trembling breath and began. "I grew up in Dime, Texas. Not much going on there, but we did have a Dairy Queen. That's where I was working when I was barely nineteen. I didn't have much ambition past making Dilly Bars and chili cheese dogs. But what I did have was a body that wouldn't quit, hair down to my waist, and my big, blue eyes. I was one foxy chick. In those days, Jasmina, I could have given you a run for your money."

Jasmina smiled and reached forward to give Corrine a playful pat on the leg.

"I wasn't looking for my Prince Charming to come waltzing into DQ, but one day there he was, Price Cunningham. I don't know how much you know about American TV shows, Jasmina, but I know Lonnie remembers 'Dallas.' It was about a rich Texas family, the Ewings. The Cunninghams were the Ewings in real life. You couldn't walk across Texas without bumping into one of their oil wells.

"So Price Cunningham glided into DQ, with those sparks in his blue eyes, and his sights set on me, little Corey Mae Plunkett. Before the end of the day, we were sharing a chocolate double-dipped cone and a whole lot more in the back seat of his red Camaro.

"I thought, 'I've been with Price Cunningham, and if nothing else exciting ever happens to me, that's a story I can tell the rest of my life.' But Price wasn't done. He kept coming back for months, hanging around for hours at a time. Once, he bought every item on the menu, just so the boss wouldn't give me a hard time about taking an extra long break and visiting with him.

"Then he asked me to marry him. I was in shock. Of course, I said yes. No surprise, his family hated me, someone of my low station marrying into the Cunningham dynasty. When I was on his arm at high-class functions, people whispered and snickered behind my back. The gossip columnists nicknamed me the 'Dairy Queen.'

"Price never left my side when we were in public, and the status of 'wife' made me feel safe. Of course the vacations in Hawaii and the Bahamas, the clothes, the jewelry, the house in The Woodlands, my Mustang convertible, also made the ridicule bearable. But even with his love and all the extras, there was one thing missing.

"We had talked before we got married about having a family someday. I really wanted babies. That's the one real regret I have in my life, and, Jasmina, I hope that you take note."

Jasmina smiled, looked over at Lonnie, and behind her hand mouthed the words, "I'm telling Leo tomorrow night."

Corrine went on. "After we got married, every time I brought up the baby subject, he would avoid talking about it. We had been married two years when I confronted him about it one night. My mama would tell me when I was a little girl, 'Corey Mae, when you have chocolate cake, don't ask for chocolate pie.' I didn't follow her advice. I couldn't be content with what I had even though I was living a life that most women only dream about.

"I told him I wanted a baby. He said, 'Not yet,' for the thousandth time and I kept at him to tell me why. Finally, he said, 'I like your gorgeous body the way it is and I don't want anything to change that.' I couldn't believe that was his reason. I started laughing. I said, 'I'll get back in shape.'

"He flew off the handle. 'No, you won't,' he said. 'It won't be the same. My mother was a beautiful woman, then she had four kids, and now she's shot. It's no wonder my dad is chasing his secretary around the desk and jumping on everything else that wiggles and jiggles.'

"It was my turn to go off. I told him he was the most horribly selfish person I had ever known. I told him I couldn't live with someone who was so self-centered. I stormed out of the house and got in my car. I just wanted to get out of there, get away from him as fast as I could. I put my Mustang in reverse and jammed on the accelerator."

Corrine paused, bit her lower lip, took in a breath. "I didn't know that he had run out the front door after me. I didn't see him behind the car. I didn't even know what that awful sound was when the car ran over him. The car was all the way on the other side of him before I saw him lying there. The cops were there in minutes. I don't even know who called them.

"His family wanted me charged with murder, but I ended up being tried for manslaughter and got off with a hung jury. I didn't really get off. There was no place I could go from Houston to Dallas where I wasn't hounded by threatening phone calls, my car and house vandalized. I was refused service at stores, restaurants, called names. 'Murderer' was one of the kinder things I was called.

"I had a right to the fortune Price left behind, but his family contested the will and their lawyers said they could tie it up for at least ten years. I took the money I could get my hands on out of the bank accounts and bought a plane ticket to Alaska where I heard they were hiring cooks in the pipeline camps. I was always a good cook, and, before Price, I had never minded hard work and long hours.

"For years I kept looking over my shoulder, waiting for one of the Cunninghams to drag me back to Texas and get their brand of justice. I felt safer when I married Jack, but I think it was being married that made me feel protected, not the man I was with. By the time Jack died, I figured I should be too old to be scared anymore, but I've never felt safe when I'm alone. And there's not a day that goes by that I don't think, 'Corey Mae, if only you hadn't asked for chocolate pie, Price would still be alive.' I killed the man I loved and I can't forgive myself for that."

Lonnie got up and sat down beside Corrine. He laid her head on his shoulder. "I forgive you, sweetie, I forgive you."

Corrine looked up at the dark elevator ceiling. "We must have been stuck in here an hour already."

"Someone will come looking for the elevator. Someone must be wondering about why you haven't made it home," Lonnie answered.

Jasmina scooted over to Lonnie and Corrine and the three of them huddled with arms around each other. "I don't care if we're stuck in here all night as long as I don't ever lose my friends again," Corrine said.

Tears spilled down her cheeks and flowed out of Jasmina's and Lonnie's eyes. And I felt water flowing freely through all the turned-on taps in the apartments where the faucets had only sputtered and trickled for a couple of months.

"You're not going to lose us," Lonnie said. "And we're going to make sure you don't lose Big Blue."

"I still can't believe what you said about Angelo."

"Corrine." Jasmina's tone commanded her attention. "Would you rather believe a man who hits you?"

"It was only once, and he didn't mean it."

"It's only once if you don't see him again. You told me that, Corrine, and I never forgot it."

Corrine bit her lip and looked down, unable to argue with Jasmina and her own words. I jerked the elevator, the light in the ceiling flickered, and the elevator resumed its rise to what was waiting on the twelfth floor.

Chapter Thirty-two

Corrine's heart was pounding as she opened the penthouse door and entered while Lonnie and Jasmina waited outside. She heard male laughter, loud chuckles joined by a deep roar. The mellow sounds of Miles Davis's trumpet floated above the human noise. Angelo and Anthony stood with their backs to the door, looking out through the rear window, drawing small circles in the air with their whiskey glasses to punctuate their discussion. Angelo turned around at the sound of the door closing.

Corrine took a few tentative steps toward him and knew that he had already detected her wariness. "What happened, babe?" he said, meeting her halfway across the room and planting a kiss on her cheek. "I was about to send out a search party for you."

She looked over Angelo's shoulder and greeted their dinner guest. "Hello, Anthony. Thank you for coming. I hope I haven't kept you waiting too long."

"Well, better late than never, right, sweetheart?" Angelo said with a grin.

Anthony raised his glass toward Corrine. "Thanks for inviting me."

"So, what happened?" Angelo said, studying Corrine's face with suspicion.

"I was stuck in the elevator," Corrine said. "I tried calling you, but my phone didn't work."

"Oh, my poor darlin'." Angelo caressed her bruised face and

she winced. "That elevator is a hazard, like so many things in this old building that Anthony and I have been talking about. Now, I think we're almost ready to put the talk on hold to get to the main event, the dinner we've promised Anthony to lure him over here."

"Of course. Let me just put this up," Corrine said, lifting the pink and black bag.

"Hold on," Angelo said. "Since we've waited all this time for you to come back from your big shopping adventure, why don't you show us the goods? I'll get the food on the table while you change–okay, baby doll?"

"Sure," Corrine said as she walked toward the bedroom. "Oh, Angelo, would you please set five places at the table? I invited a couple more guests. I hope you don't mind, sweetheart. You always cook so much extra."

Angelo's mouth fell open, but before he could respond to Corrine, she closed the bedroom door. Angelo shot Anthony an embarrassed smile. "That woman, always full of surprises."

"That's the best kind," Anthony said, finishing the last swallow of his drink. "You're a lucky man."

"That I am. Pour yourself another one, I'll be right back." Angelo headed into the kitchen, the first of three trips to bring out bowls, plates, silverware, warm bread, salad, and a tureen of something hot and spicy.

Corrine emerged from the bedroom in the new red dress, set off with a gold cuff bracelet and hoop earrings, and scarlet pumps with gold spikes up and down the heels. "Well, I'm not sure about these crazy shoes, but what do you think?"

"You look fabulous," Anthony said.

Angelo looked annoyed that Anthony had usurped his chance to make the first comment on Corrine's look. He followed up with a half-hearted whistle as the doorbell chimed. Corrine moved toward the door, but Angelo cut off her path. "Our extra guests must be here. You and Anthony go ahead and sit down at the table."

Angelo swung the door open and froze as he saw Lonnie and

Jasmina standing in front of him. "Lonnie, Jasmina," he said with a nervous laugh when his power of speech returned. He maintained his stance, blocking their entrance.

"Come on in, guys!" Corrine shouted from the dining room.

"Yeah, come in," Angelo hissed, still not moving.

"Thanks for having us," Jasmina called back in the direction of the dining room.

Lonnie was recovering his breath from running down and then up the stairs, not trusting the elevator. What he went down to retrieve from his store bulged in the inside pocket of his jacket. He pasted on a grin and extended his hand for Angelo to shake.

Angelo gripped Lonnie's hand for a second before dropping it and wiping his palm against his pants leg. "Nice to have you," Angelo said, his voice like cold syrup. "Take your coat?"

"No thanks," Lonnie said, straightening the front of his jacket.

Angelo stood aside a few inches and as Lonnie and Jasmina squeezed past, he whispered, "Nice to have all the people in this building whom I've already had, if you know what I mean."

Jasmina glared at Angelo and clenched her fist. Lonnie put his hand on her back and ushered her toward the dining room. Corrine and Anthony stood across from each other behind two of the six chairs that surrounded a table that looked like a huge, iridescent slab of abalone. Corrine introduced Anthony to Lonnie as Anthony and Jasmina became reacquainted, as fellow guests rather than as customer and coffee shop proprietor. Angelo took a seat at the head of the table with Corrine and Anthony at either side. Jasmina and Lonnie slid into the remaining seats.

Angelo filled bowls from the tureen directly in front of him and passed them down to each guest. "This smells great," Lonnie said, looking at his bowl of thick red broth and chunks of meat peppered with spices. "What is this?"

"My own creation, Cajun chili. Dig in." Angelo's eyes traveled around the table and came to rest on Anthony who finished his second whiskey before picking up a spoon.

Lonnie took his first mouthful of the spicy stew. "What is this meat?"

Angelo chuckled. "Don't tell me you've never had gator, man."

"This is tasty," Lonnie said as his dinner companions nodded in agreement after their first sample. "But there's some other kind of meat in here, too. It tastes like, mmm, can't quite ... m-m-m, tastes like shrimp."

Corrine's spoon fell from her fingers as she watched Anthony across the table. Within a matter of seconds his right eye swelled almost completely shut. His lips, nose, and ears ballooned into grotesque masses. A sandpaper-like rash spread across his cheeks, chin, and neck. He clutched his throat with both hands, making a croaking sound as he pushed back from the table.

"What have you done?!" Corrine yelled at Angelo as she leapt up from the table. Angelo sat calmly, resting his elbows on the table, his hands under his chin with fingers interlaced. "Lonnie, help me get Anthony to the couch."

As Lonnie guided the larger man into the living room, Corrine dug through the pockets of Anthony's pants and his tweed jacket, muttering, "He told me he's always prepared." Her search yielded a pack of gum, two quarters, a mechanical pencil, a mini notebook, and a moose hide wallet.

As Lonnie maneuvered the choking man, whose fingers had become sausages, onto the edge of the sofa, Corrine raced to the coat rack by the door and plunged her hands into the pockets of Anthony's long leather coat–and pulled out an EpiPen pack and a bottle of liquid Benadryl. Pushing Lonnie to the side, she unwrapped the epinephrine injector, drew her arm back, took aim, and stabbed Anthony in the thigh. He jerked back, his mouth agape, and she poured some of the Benadryl over his tongue, then stroked his throat to help it go down.

Sweat poured down Anthony's face as his breathing eased. Corrine knelt beside him, counting his exhalations with her own. Jasmina joined them and swabbed Anthony's forehead with a wet dish towel. Lonnie paced beside the couch, mumbling, "Jesus, man, Jesus."

After several minutes, Anthony's rash faded. The swelling around his eyes were bruise-like crescents, and his lips, ears, nose, and fingers shrunk to a more normal size. "Is he going to be okay?" Lonnie asked Corrine, recognizing her as the closest thing to an expert. "What happened?"

"He has a severe allergy to seafood. Let's get him to the bedroom where he can have room to lie down. Anthony, can you stand up, can you walk?"

Anthony nodded and Lonnie assisted him to the bedroom. Corrine positioned two pillows against the headboard so that Anthony could recline in a half-seated position. "I think we should take him to the hospital," Lonnie said, nervously scratching the back of his head.

"No," Anthony said, clearing his scratchy throat, "I'll be all right. Let me lie here for a while. My heart is racing, but it should calm down in a bit. The Benadryl will make me really sleepy."

"I'm going to check on Jasmina," Lonnie said.

Anthony closed his eyes, breathed out slowly. "Corrine?" She squatted down by the bed and leaned her ear in to hear him. "You better be careful."

"What's wrong?" She grasped his hand.

He squeezed her hand back and managed a weak smile. "I had to marry the last woman who saved my life."

She smiled and patted his arm. "I don't think that will be necessary. You should rest. We'll check on you in a while." Anthony closed his eyes, already sinking into sleep.

Corrine marched into the dining room where Angelo remained seated and relaxed. Lonnie and Jasmina stood in the living room, unsure about what to do next. "You tried to kill him!" Corrine screamed at Angelo. "You said you would talk to him about the menu. He must have told you about his allergy. Why did you do it?! Why?!" Corrine launched her body at Angelo, planted her fists in his chest, and knocked him off his chair.

Angelo scrambled to his feet, shook out his shirtsleeves, stiffened his posture to project confidence but pulled a chair between himself and Corrine. Lonnie and Jasmina rushed to Corrine's side.

"The jig is up, sweetheart," he said, coolly straightening his cuffs. "He was going to unravel everything I have in place."

"You're the Frayer!" Lonnie shouted, jabbing a finger in Angelo's direction. "You were hired to unravel our lives."

"It looks like someone has been doing his research," Angelo said. "But you only have it part right. Yes, I was paid an obscene sum by a wealthy family in Texas to make sure one of you was frayed, unraveled like an old, dried-up piece of twine." He winked at Corrine. "I never ask why. I take the money up front, and they don't owe me any explanations.

"But I had my own incentive to uncover your unsavory secrets so that I could break you down and separate you from Corrine. I had to isolate my little sugar pie and get her under control so that I could do some real damage to the building without her getting wise and coming to the rescue."

"You're trying to tear Big Blue down, not save it," Corrine banged her fist on the table as she hurled the accusation.

"Not trying, darlin'," Angelo said with a nasty grin, "I will tear this building down."

Corrine recoiled from the threat, feeling again his hand striking her face. "Why, Angelo? The Sheraton people pulled out. Why do you need Big Blue torn down when they're not going to build here anyway? Because the Cunninghams want me ruined? Is that it?"

"Oh, poor, sweet, afraid-to-be-alone Corrine. Yes, the Cunninghams did want you crushed. The hotel deal was a bonus. I used Henry Fornette's vengeance against the building that killed his son–with a little bit of my help, of course–to extract an extra payoff. That was the business side. But, the Cunninghams and Henry had no idea that I planned all along to bring the building down as my personal project."

"Why, Angelo?" Corrine asked. "What do you, someone from Louisiana who had never set foot inside until Miss Liza died, have against Big Blue?"

"Ah, my dear Aunt Liza." Angelo walked around the table. The others matched his steps to keep him in front of them, the four making a slow circle around the room.

Lonnie pulled the mutilated photos of Liza Beechwood from his inside jacket pocket and tossed them on the table. "This Aunt Liza who was so dear to you?"

"Yes," Angelo said as he gathered up the photos and held them to his chest with mock affection. "Aunt Liza who gave me so many happy boyhood memories," he lilted, then snarled, "and ripped them away by deserting me to live in this rat-hole building with her new family.

"What do you think it was like for me, a sensitive little boy neglected by his mother, shunned by his father, never caressed, never kissed, never sung to, never hearing a sweet word. It was like having no home. All I ever wanted was up here, inside these putrid walls.

"I hated Aunt Liza for abandoning me. I wish I had killed her myself. I could have, you know. I've known I was a Frayer since I was seventeen. She wasn't so gifted. She would have been no match for me." He strode to an open window and tossed the photos out.

Returning to the head of the table, Angelo narrowed his eyes. His jaw tightened. "I'll still kill this building where she chose to spend her last days with you. I was hers, not the three of you. Sunny and Bear and Lil' Bit, you're the ones who'll be without a home now, when this building is gone."

"We're going to save Big Blue," Corrine countered, her chin raised like a defiant warrior's.

Angelo tossed his head back and laughed. "The city will have everyone kicked out of here before the new year. The abatement process is going forward."

"Anthony has a plan to renovate it. And I'm totally behind his plan. We'll convince the city to get behind it, too."

"The city isn't going to back some fantasy. You misguided dreamers can't pull it off, and you know it. This building is going to be designated unfit for habitation in one month, condemned in four months, and reduced to dust in six. You can't stop it or even slow it down. Face it. I won. Now, Lonnie and Jasmina, why don't you go on home, while you still have a place to stay; and, Corrine, maybe you could call a cab for our friend in the bedroom before you clean up this table. I've lost my appetite."

Corrine took a step forward, ready to jump on Angelo again. Lonnie put out an arm to hold her back.

"We're not done with you, Angelo," Lonnie said, stiffening into a fighting stance, his legs apart and his hands raised to his waist.

"That's right," Jasmina said. "You're not getting away with this."

Angelo wagged his finger at them. "Don't you be sore losers, now. The game is over. The three of you made it a lot of fun though. I didn't really expect that. All that pent-up desire, and I just stroked it and sucked it and squeezed it any way I wanted to.

"Corrine, you really were quite interesting in the beginning, the way you responded to my dick inside you. If I closed my eyes, I could swear I was fucking a woman half your age. Too bad you let yourself go the way you did.

"Jasmina, fantasizing about you going down on me actually got me hotter than the real thing. I guess I expected more from someone with your experience although I've never seen such an exquisite body.

"Of course, both of you take second place to Lonnie. It's not your fault, ladies. It's just anatomy. In general, a man's mouth and tongue are bigger than a woman's so we can give better head, you know, cover more surface at one time. And the other orifice we use, well, it's tighter than any pussy. But, Lonnie, man, I have to say, even with all your good qualities, your old-school inhibitions tend to get in the way."

Lonnie let Angelo's words roll off him. "You're wrong, Angelo. We are going to find a way to stop what you're doing to Big Blue, and in the meantime we're going to slow down the damage.

Things started going bad when you moved in and things are going to start getting better when you leave. You're going to get out of here right now."

"You're man enough to make me leave? I don't think so." His dick stiffened against his leg with this confident pronouncement that he was still in control.

Lonnie pulled the pistol that he normally kept in his cash register out of his jacket pocket, and pointed it at Angelo's chest.

Angelo's eyes widened and he took a step backward. "Now, hold on, man." Sweat beaded on his forehead and heat waves rose off the back of his head. His hard-on wilted. "When's the last time you used one of those? That thing could go off."

"You're the loser, Angelo," Lonnie said, his gun hand and voice steady as steel. "I read about how you Frayers give yourselves clever, little nicknames like Satan wannabes. Angelo Fallon. You're nothing but a pathetic Fallen Angel. Now you're going to fall your ass right out of this building. You can walk downstairs and out the door, get in your Caddy, and keep driving until you cross the Louisiana state line. Or, I can march you back to that window and toss you twelve stories down on the asphalt and splatter your brains worse than Harper Fornette's. Your choice, motherfucker."

The faint smell of smoke emanated from Angelo's body. His face colored deep red and his body trembled. "You don't tell me to leave! I'm a Frayer!" Threads of spit sprayed from his mouth. But I saw pale, cold fingers of fear snaking through his mind, erasing the bright flames of confidence. "I'll destroy you! I'll destroy this fucking building! I'll destroy all of you!"

Lonnie raised the gun six inches and evenly measured out his words. "Third choice. I put a bullet through your head."

Jasmina grabbed a utensil from the table. "I put this knife through your heart."

Corrine reached behind her and picked up from a side table a weighty, green jade lighter made in the shape of a Buddha. "I smash this into your skull."

Angelo and the other three glared at each other in fuming silence. I separated a chunk of plaster from the ceiling just above Angelo's head and let it fall, striking his forehead. He stepped backward and rubbed his head. I followed with a larger piece of the ceiling, this time glancing it off his shoulder. He backed up into the living room.

Panic bounced around in his head like an erratic ping-pong ball. A foreign, bitter taste coated his tongue. Even while denying it, he knew the taste was defeat. Corrine, Lonnie, and Jasmina, holding their weapons, advanced toward him with every step he took in reverse.

As Angelo scanned the ceiling, looking for more threatening plaster, he sidestepped toward the fireplace. I let a gust of air through the flue, making the fire flare and spit sparks at his ankle, where they burned through his thin sock. He grabbed above his foot and stumbled back, tripped over the leg of a side table, and landed on his butt.

He was crab walking across the white carpet toward the door when the tinkle of swaying crystal birds in the chandelier above him drew his eyes upward. I hated to damage such a beautiful fixture, but I couldn't help myself. I broke the chandelier loose, and, even though Angelo tried to roll out of the way, it plunged down on his head.

Dazed, Angelo scrambled to his feet and ran toward the door with his three adversaries closing in. He snatched his coat off the rack and found his car keys in the pocket. Throwing the coat over his shoulder, he snagged his earring and a trickle of blood tattooed the side of his neck. With a terrorized look back at his foes, he grabbed the door handle. I held the door closed for a few seconds and then allowed him to pull it open a few inches before I forced it shut again. He panted and made little animal cries as he yanked the door handle again and again. The ping-pong ball in his head became an urgent hammer.

Finally, I released the door as he was pulling it, and it sprung back against his right cheekbone. He yelped and tore out through the door, but not before Corrine let her red high heel fly with pin-point accuracy, delivering a vicious blow to the back of his head. Even in her fury, she couldn't help tempering rage with kindness—the jade Buddha lighter might have killed him.

Angelo threw open the stairwell door with such force he banged his knuckles against the wall. He ran down the stairs two at a time, and slipped a couple of times, screeching as he hit his tailbone on the stair edges. When he reached the ground floor, breathless, he stumbled down the hallway toward the front door. While he tried to avoid the rain of glass I sent down from fractured light fixtures, he tripped over the carpet edge. I de-layed his final exit by jamming the front door until he kicked it in desperation with both feet.

When Angelo was finally outside, he glanced up at the over-hang, remembering the load of snow I had previously dumped on his head. This time there was no snow, just a three-foot icicle that I broke free as his head was craned upward. It stabbed his left cheek and he squealed in pain.

My long-malfunctioning motion lights blazed in triumph as Angelo slipped and slid along the icy sidewalk to his baby-blue Cadillac. The pinhole eyes of Miss Liza stared up at him from the photos scattered around the car like parade debris. His sweaty fingers fumbled with his keys before he finally opened the door. A shower of gravel sent down from my roof pinged off the Caddy, digging little craters in the hood as he lunged into the driver's seat.

Angelo was about to turn the key in the ignition when a globe of green jade flew down from the sky. Its trajectory would have sent it crashing into the asphalt in front of the Caddy, but I flipped open a lower-level window so that the object caromed off it . The Buddha lighter smashed through the windshield, glanced off the dashboard, and landed where I sent it, between Angelo's legs, ter-rifying inches from his once-powerful cock. I sensed the heat rushing behind his rib cage, surrounding his heart and lungs, vi-brating against the inside of his mouth.

Twelve stories directly above, Corrine leaned out a window and dusted off her hands, not so kind after all. She watched for the car to lurch out of the parking lot, anticipated the sound of tires struggling for traction on icy asphalt. She heard Lonnie and Jasmina walk up behind her, and felt a hand from each touch down on her shoulders.

A red-orange ball of fire burst inside the Caddy. Within seconds, flames shot out of both the front windows and engulfed the roof. When a fire engine screamed into the parking lot minutes later, dodging curious onlookers in the street, the car was already a gutted, smoking hulk. A twisted, black figure, with teeth exposed in a grotesque grin, leaned forward against the steering wheel.

Chapter Thirty-three

Police officers, two male and one female, arrived at the penthouse shortly after assessing the scene in the parking lot. The interval was long enough for Corrine to retrieve her shoe from outside the door, for Jasmina to right an overturned dining room chair, and for Lonnie to transfer a left-behind photo of Miss Liza to the kitchen trash. In a pass through the living room, Corrine spied the black jade lighter on a table, reminding her of its green twin that she tossed out the window, but there was neither time nor opportunity to discreetly search for and recover it. Wherever it landed, Corrine surmised, it was likely destroyed or distorted beyond recognition in the fire.

When the scene she watched from the penthouse window replayed in her memory, the only sound she heard was the sudden roar of the blaze, no call for help, no warning, then smoke-covered silence, before the sirens split the air. Had she seen his hands on the steering wheel, jerking at the door, a twitch of panic or fear? She didn't know.

Lonnie and Jasmina assured her that those things would have been impossible to see from twelve stories above. They unnecessarily advised her not to tell the police about the conflict in the dining room. Her contact with law enforcement in Texas had already prepared her to withhold information.

One of the officers questioned Corrine for an hour and a half while she sat in a living room chair, her knees drawn up to her chest under the long red dress, her arms encircling her legs in a defensive posture. Lonnie looked out of the dining room at her, protectively, from his seat at the abalone table where the female officer talked with him. Jasmina watched Corrine, unable to hear what she was saying from where she sat on the bed in Corrine's bedroom, facing the third officer.

Lonnie calmly walked the female officer through the recent events–a social-business dinner to discuss renovation plans–while the cold remains of the dinner congealed in abandoned bowls. "Haven't you heard about all the problems with Big Blue?" he asked the officer, while the pistol in his jacket pocket pressed against his ribs. Lonnie went on to point out the evidence of the deterioration: a chunk of ceiling fallen to the dining room floor, the wreckage of a crystal chandelier in the living room, and that was just the damage that night.

Jasmina explained to her interrogator Anthony's dramatic allergic reaction to the food and the chaotic rush of everyone else to respond. The police declined to disturb the still passed-out Anthony, who was obviously in no condition to have witnessed anything.

There was no need for Corrine, Lonnie, or Jasmina to embellish or detract from their accounts of standing and watching from a window twelve floors away as the car caught fire. The officers assured them that the incident was under investigation.

Two mornings later Corrine handed out disposable cups of hot coffee and freshly baked banana cookies to the Bluers pacing the sidewalk across from my front entrance. Their number had dwindled to three and their signs were tattered from the recent assaults of unseasonable rain and wind. They nodded their appreciation to Corrine. The air had turned colder overnight and smelled of impending snow.

Corrine glanced toward my southern wall and walked haltingly toward the side parking lot. A black outline of the Caddy on the pavement was the only evidence of Angelo's fiery death.

Using the tips of her gloved fingers, she rubbed the chill from her cheeks as she met Anthony, who was watching her charity to the Bluers from just inside the front door.

"It's the first day of December and it looks like winter is finally coming. I should have told them to go home and stay warm," she said, referring to the protesters.

"We won't need them after Tuesday," Anthony said. "When I talk to the council, I'm going to insist on another inspection. Now that the water and heat problems have resolved themselves, the city can't designate Big Blue unfit for habitation. We've had quite a turn of events."

"Yes," Corrine said, "two days ago, Big Blue and you were both fighting for your lives, and now that threat is gone. Still, no one deserves to die that way, not even Angelo."

"You must know that's out of your hands. You didn't have anything to do with how he lived or how he died."

"I can't help thinking about that horrible fire. A living person reduced to ashes, just like that."

"Let's look to the future. Tonight I'm going to show off my building plans to you again and to your friends since I didn't have a chance to do that the other night. It's kind of like what Mark Twain said: the news of Big Blue's death is greatly exaggerated."

"Well, there's still the twelve-million-dollar problem and that's not exaggerated."

"If you can organize a get-together at your place after all that you've been through in the last couple of days, I know you can find a way."

"I couldn't let another day go by without celebrating the good things, Big Blue's future and Jasmina's baby. I can't believe she woke me up at five yesterday morning to tell me–and then her and Leo's announcement when Lonnie and I ran into them in the hallway. That was my first time meeting him, while they're against the wall in the middle of ... well. And, maybe the best reason of all to celebrate is I have my old friends back."

"And also a new one?" Anthony winked at her.

"Of course."

"Let's go up and get the party started, shall we?"

"Maybe we should take the stairs. The last time I was in the elevator ..."

"Come on," Anthony said, putting out his hand for her to take. "I'm feeling bullet-proof today."

They stepped into the elevator as Lonnie held the door open from the inside. A six-foot Douglas fir encased in orange webbing leaned against the wall behind him. "Thanks for getting the tree, Lonnie," Corrine said and kissed him on the cheek.

"No problem," he said as he pushed the button for the penthouse, and the elevator glided smoothly upward. "Can't have a tree-trimming party without one." Lonnie shifted the dark purple box he held in the crook of his arm. "And if you've got the egg nog, honey, I've got the Crown."

"You didn't have to bring the whiskey, too, Lonnie," Corrine said, "You've done so many favors for me lately."

"You're helping me out, sweetie. This is just one less bottle I'll have to liquidate."

"Liquidate? What are you talking about?"

"It's time for me to get out of the liquor store business."

"Why now, Lonnie? Anthony can get Big Dipper Liquor back to the way it used to be."

"That's right. My crews are going to start on your place and Jasmina's coffee shop as soon as we get out from under this abatement mess," Anthony said. "Your business will be going full speed again in no time."

"I'll leave that to someone else." Lonnie's lips spread into a slow, peaceful smile. "Life is short and I want to spend the rest of my time making music."

Jasmina and Leo were waiting at the penthouse door toting bags and a covered basket that emitted a sweet, buttery aroma.

"Don't tell me you walked up twelve floors in your condition, Jasmina," Corrine said with an admonishing frown.

"No, the man of my dreams just carried me up the whole way."

Jasmina and Leo burst into laughter and then said in unison, "Just kidding."

"But I would have if you'd asked me to, baby," Leo said, his eyes dancing as he looked down at Jasmina and then kissed her lightly on the mouth.

"Oh, baby, that is the sweetest," Jasmina gushed.

"Okay, it's getting a little gooey here," said Lonnie as Corrine opened the penthouse door and ushered everyone in. "I know you lovebirds are planning to tie the knot on Christmas Eve, so maybe you should cool it until the honeymoon and give the rest of us a break."

Two hours later, the bare tree was transformed with glittery gold and blue globes, feathery doves caught in its branches, and swirls of twinkling white lights. Jasmina, who did most of the decorating, was on her knees in front of the toilet throwing up egg nog. Leo rubbed her back and dabbed her face with a wet washcloth.

"And this is the swimming pool," Anthony explained to Lonnie, as he pointed to the building plans he'd laid out on Corrine's dining room table, after Leo's baklava and Corrine's coconut cake had been devoured. "There won't be another building in Alaska like Big Blue. I'll get my advertising people in gear and Corrine will have these units sold before they're even finished. At five hundred thousand per unit, ten percent down to hold them, only ten pre-sold will bring in half a million."

"This is a hell of a plan," Lonnie said, taking a sip of Crown Royal without the egg nog and not minding that his brandy would have gone down better.

Corrine leaned against the back of the chair where Lonnie was seated. "Yeah, and, let's say I can pre-sell ten units, I'll only have eleven-and-half million to go."

"You're working on those grants, right?" Anthony asked. "And you're going to get that new tax credit."

Corrine pulled out a chair next to Lonnie's, sat down, and looked down at a scattering of pastry crumbs on the table. "It's not going to work, Anthony," she said in a wobbly voice. "It's an incredible plan, and I have all the confidence in the world that you can make Big Blue over grander than ever, but I just don't have the financial backup. Angelo was right, it's just a fantasy."

Lonnie pushed his chair back and pulled Corrine to her feet, holding her shoulders to make her face him. "Angelo's not right. He's not in control anymore. Do you hear me, girl? You're calling the shots now. You have to do this, for Big Blue and for you."

She looked away from him, her shoulders slumped in defeat. "How, Lonnie?"

"Just so happens, I have ten million dollars. I figure I can spare nine and a half. That'll leave me enough to maintain comfortably. I don't need the rest. I wouldn't know how to live high on the hog if I tried."

"Lonnie, how do you have ten million dollars?"

"I came into an unexpected inheritance recently."

"Come on, Lonnie, you're joking, right?"

"He's not," Jasmina said as she walked into the room, leaning on Leo's arm, her face pale but animated. "He really does have ten million dollars."

Corrine's eyes bounced from Jasmina to Lonnie to Jasmina and back to Lonnie. Her mouth hung open as she absorbed the news about her friend's fortune. "But, Lonnie, even if you have the money, and even if you're not drunk and you really know what you're offering, and even if I were to accept your offer, I don't see how I could ever pay you back."

"Give me one of Anthony's new condos, eleventh floor, the one with the best view, and we'll call it even."

"But that's five hundred thousand dollars for ten million."

"Sounds fair to me. Deal?" Lonnie put out his hand.

Corrine moved her hand hesitantly toward his, then shook it. "Deal." She put her arms around his neck and gently kissed his lips. "Lonnie, this is the second time in three days that you've saved my life. If it wasn't for you, Angelo would still be - -"

"Well, he's not."

Chimes sounded and Leo left the room to answer the door.

Corrine walked to a south-facing window and looked down at the parking lot where she last saw the Caddy parked with Angelo inside.

She shivered. "What do you think happened in that car, Lonnie? I don't understand it."

Lonnie thought about what he had read about the Frayers, how they might spontaneously catch fire, and the time he had seen what looked like smoke coming off Angelo's body in Corrine's penthouse. "He was a Frayer. I'd say it was his own power killed him."

"Corrine," Leo said in a party's-over tone as he re-entered the room. "Some police detectives are here to ask you some questions."

Chapter Thirty-four

The older detective, in crumpled brown pants and jacket, introduced himself as Hodges and his younger partner, dressed in a crisp black suit, as Villanova. Corrine offered them a seat on the pale green couch and sat to the side of them in the lavender chair.

Lonnie pulled up the ottoman and took a seat a couple of feet from Corrine. Jasmina and Leo stood guard to one side of the couch while Anthony did the same at the other side. Although surrounded and outnumbered, the detectives were not intimidated and seemed to have no interest in separating witnesses to dissect individual stories.

"What was your relationship with Mr. Fallon, Ms. Easter?" Hodges began.

"We were friends."

"According to some of your residents, he was living with you, he was your lover. Is that so?" the older detective asked as if he was inquiring what she had for breakfast.

"Well, yes," Corrine answered, coloring with embarrassment. "We did have a ... a relationship." Smiles of recognition passed between Jasmina and Villanova. "You see, I broke my leg last summer and he was kind enough to take care of me."

"Were you and Mr. Fallon having any disagreements at the time of his demise?" Hodges continued as he picked up the black jade Buddha from a nearby table and tossed it from hand to hand.

"Disagreements? Well, like any couple does, but nothing that we weren't resolving."

"I understand that Mr. Fallon was trying to have this building torn down, the building you've owned for many, many years. Did you agree with that?"

"Well, no, I mean, he wasn't, I mean ..."

"He wasn't trying to have this building torn down?"

"We were going to renovate it. We were making plans. That's why we invited Anthony, Mr. Aurelius, to dinner, to discuss the renovation plans."

"That's right," Anthony interjected. "There may have been a demolition plan at one time but that was dependent on a business deal that fell through. We were, we are, doing a major renovation."

Hodges continued to toss the lighter back and forth between his hands. Corrine nervously followed the motion.

"What does Corrine and Angelo and disagreements have to do with what happened?" Lonnie threw in, stiffening his posture. "There was some kind of mechanical malfunction, the car caught fire, and Angelo burned to death, end of story."

"Except it's the other way around," Hodges said, delighting in revealing unexpected news.

"The other way around?" Corrine asked with confusion wrinkling her forehead.

"According to the investigation, Mr. Fallon caught fire and then the car burned."

Corrine gasped. "But how ..." In her mind she saw the green lighter falling in slow motion toward the parking lot.

"How did Mr. Fallon take the news when the business deal Mr. Aurelius mentioned fell through?" Hodges took back control of the inquiry.

"He was rather distraught would be a good way to describe it," Corrine answered, regaining her composure.

"We found some photos at the scene. Do you—" The younger detective flashed a wink at Jasmina. "Detective Villanova, are we keeping you from something here?"

The younger man grinned sheepishly. "No, just me and the young lady, we dated at one time."

"We're here to do a job. Pay attention," Hodges barked. "Do you need me to ask her to leave the room, or should I have you removed from the case?"

"No, sir, we're fine. I'm fine. Paying attention, Hodge." Leo moved closer to Jasmina and put his arm around her waist.

"As I was saying," Hodges went on, with a sideways glare at his partner, "we found some photos at the scene, several photos of the same woman." He pulled out his cell, brought up a picture of one of the photos found in the parking lot, and showed it to Corrine. "This woman. Do you know if she meant something to Mr. Fallon?"

"That was Angelo's great-aunt, Liza Beechwood. She lived here for many years. When she died last spring, Angelo came up from Louisiana to settle her affairs. That's why he was here."

"Why him? Why a great-nephew from Louisiana?"

"They were close from the time he was a child. He told me she was like a mother to him."

"How did he take her passing?"

"He was really upset."

"Did he express any of those feelings recently?"

"He was talking about Miss Liza at the dinner right before he left."

"That's right," Jasmina added. "He was very distressed about Miss Liza and he was talking about her death. Lonnie heard him, too." Lonnie nodded.

"Would you say he was dwelling on her death?" Hodges inquired, taking in the added input from Jasmina and Lonnie.

"I see where you're headed," Lonnie interrupted, visibly excited. "You think he committed suicide. You think he set himself on fire."

"We don't want to jump to any conclusions," the younger detective chimed in, letting his senior partner know he was back on task. "The investigation is ongoing."

Hodges looked over at Villanova with an irritated grimace for breaking the rhythm of his questions. He set the black Buddha down with a clang on the table in front of Corrine. "Do you have more than one lighter like this one?"

"Yes." Corrine replied cautiously. "There's another one in the bedroom made of white jade. Do you want to see it?" She adjusted her legs to rise from the chair, but the detective motioned for her to stay seated.

"You're not a smoker, are you, Ms. Easter? I mean you keep this place smelling very fresh, no tell-tale reek caught in the curtains or the upholstery."

"I'm not, but my late husband smoked cigars and a friend of his had those Buddha lighters made so he could have one in every room, not just because he smoked. He thought the Buddha was lucky. My husband was a gambler."

"Had one in every room?" Corrine nodded. "So there was one in the dining room also?" Corrine nodded with less conviction. Hodges picked up the black jade sculpture and held it out in front of him. "Ms. Easter, do you know how a lighter very much like this one wound up in Mr. Fallon's car?"

"No, I ... I don't," Corrine stammered, shooting a glance at Lonnie. "Is that what he used to ... maybe he took it with him when he left?"

"Why would he do that, Ms. Easter?"

"I don't know."

"Was Mr. Fallon a smoker?"

"I ... I don't know." Her uneasy voice caused Lonnie to lean toward her and Jasmina to take a step closer.

"You shared a bed with the man and you don't know if he smoked?"

"He told me he sometimes smoked pot but he didn't do that in here. Like you said, I like to keep the place smelling fresh." Corrine relaxed her shoulders and smiled slightly, pleased with her response.

"You're a widow, right Ms. Easter?"

"Yes, Jack's been gone almost twenty-five years."

"And how did your husband die?"

"Heart failure, he was quite a bit older than me."

"And what about the husband before that, how did he die?"

The color drained from Corrine's face and her mouth went dry. "It was an accident, a terrible accident," she said, her voice shaking out of control.

"An accident? Not quite, Ms. Easter. You were charged with manslaughter, isn't that correct?"

Lonnie jumped to his feet. "She was acquitted!"

"Not exactly," Hodges said calmly. "My understanding is the jury couldn't reach a verdict."

"This is fucking ridiculous!" Jasmina shouted. "You're accusing Corrine like she's a serial killer. She was standing on the fucking twelfth floor with us, looking out the window when it happened. We told the police that the first fucking time."

"Villanova, you want to calm your girlfriend down?" Hodges said, not responding with so much as a flinch to Jasmina's verbal attack.

The younger detective started to stand, but Leo put out his palm in a "stop" motion and gently rubbed Jasmina's back with his other hand. "I can take care of my fiancée, detective. Pregnant women can be very emotional." Villanova sank back onto the couch as Jasmina and Leo gave each other a bird kiss on the lips.

"No one's accusing Ms. Easter," Hodges said. He returned the lighter to the table and stood, motioning for Villanova to do the same. "Thank you for your time, Ms. Easter. We'll notify you one way or the other as to how the investigation turns out." He acknowledged the rest of the people in the room with a nod and pulled out his cell phone. "I'm going to call in an officer from downstairs to take possession of Mr. Fallon's personal belongings. Those may give us a clue to his state of mind before his death. If you would cooperate by showing the officer where those things are, Ms. Easter?"

"Certainly, detective." Corrine rose and walked the two men to the door.

Villanova gave Jasmina a parting smile. The detectives exited the penthouse and entered the elevator.

"They're hiding something," Hodges said as the doors slid shut.

"Yeah, but the only way it's murder from inside the car from twelve floors up is if one of them threw in a Molotov cocktail," Villanova said to his partner.

"And that won't fly because there was no accelerant found."

"You think someone tossed that lighter from the twelfth floor through the windshield, from the shatter patterns found on the glass fragments, right? But, if the lighter set Mr. Fallon on fire, it didn't flick on by itself. He's the only one who could have done it."

"Yep, I can't figure any other way, kid."

"Hey, Hodge, what do you make of the coroner saying his organs were toasted from the inside out?"

"I don't see how that could happen, unless the guy drank something flammable and then, well, how would he—whew, that's too far out for me to even think about."

"But, like you said, no accelerant found, ingested or not."

"Willie's been known to take a nip now and then. Maybe his judgment was clouded by that bottle of gin he keeps under the autopsy table."

"Yeah, maybe. The only other explanation is he spontaneously combusted."

Hodges chuckled as the elevator door opened on the ground floor. "Yeah, right. This is Fairbanks, kid, not the Twilight Zone."

Chapter Thirty-five

Anthony's workers hauled soggy flooring, crumbling dry wall, ruined fixtures, and other debris out of the wreckage of Istanbul Coffee. He hadn't waited for the city to stop the abatement process. A building inspector would be out within a week, but the day after the council meeting Anthony set up a renovation staging area in the ballroom, or, I guess I should say, the swimming pool room.

A crew Anthony called The Mold Busters, armed with high-tech chemicals, was cleaning apartments on the other floors. Plasterers launched the first attack on the hundreds of superficial cracks that marred the walls that would not be knocked down. Timetables and charts showing division of tasks and work sites for electricians, plumbers, carpenters, and laborers were posted on the ballroom walls, along with detailed drawings of each room and photos of its present condition.

"You should have seen the mayor," Anthony told Lonnie when they passed in the hall as Lonnie headed outside with a ladder in tow. "He was still fighting to bring Big Blue down, but everybody else was on the other side. When he couldn't think of any logical arguments to make, he started raving about how his life was ruined by some creature, like the Swamp Thing. I think he called it a Frayer. I've never seen a person's face turn that particular shade of purple. I thought he was going to burst into flames."

"I've heard that's possible," Lonnie said without cracking a smile.

Lonnie hung a ten-foot banner across the outside front of the store. It proclaimed in red letters, "Liquidation! Everything must go! Save! Save! Save!" On the sidewalk, the "Save Big Blue" marchers were replaced by a man in a parka carrying a tall yellow sign that repeated the words on Lonnie's banner, plus "Big Dipper Liquor" and its address. Lonnie had hired three other people to advertise with similar signs on the busiest corners in town, Cushman and Seventh, Airport Way and the Steese Highway, and College Road and the Johansen Expressway.

He also brought in a second cash register and hired an extra clerk for as many days as it would take to empty the store. Two temporary employees stood by to cart out boxes of liquor and cases of beer for the bulk buyers who needed assistance. By mid-afternoon, a steady stream of customers flowed down the hallway and in and out of the store; and as the harmonies of The Temptations and The Dells filled Big Dipper Liquor, its shelves gave up their wares.

Two thirtyish men in suits and pastel shirts with gelled hair circled the interior of the shop. One of them scratched in a notebook while the other wielded a tape measure. Lonnie walked up to them with a smile and his hand outstretched. "The next generation, I presume."

The couple introduced themselves as Jon and Jay. "Feel free to look around," Lonnie said, "and if you have any questions—" The vibration of the cell phone in his back pocket interrupted him.

"Corrine, what's wrong?" he said into the phone.

He stepped out into the hall to get away from the hubbub in the store. Seconds later he ordered the temporary clerk, "Hold down the fort. I'll be right back." In a few minutes he was at the penthouse door, entreating Corrine to release the deadbolt and the extra lock she'd had Anthony put on the door the day after the tree-trimming.

When Lonnie entered her place, Corrine stood frozen. He guided her back into the room, all the while asking her, "What is it?"

She turned and pointed to the bedroom. "In there," she said.

Lonnie approached the bedroom warily, wondering if he should have again brought his gun with him. He pushed the half-closed door open all the way. "What, Corrine?" he asked. "I don't see anything or anyone. Come here, tell me what has gotten you so upset."

She tiptoed up behind him and hid against his back. "There," she whispered against his ear. "In the corner of the closet." Lonnie stepped into the room and looked where Corrine had directed him. He recognized Angelo's black, contoured saxophone case. "I forgot it was back there when the police picked up his things. It's like he's still here, like his spirit won't leave."

Lonnie grasped both of her hands and pulled her into the room. "Honey, he's not here. He's gone, forever. It's just a horn, a hunk of brass, not a spirit. I'll take it to Hoyt's Music. I'm sure someone who can appreciate a good, second-hand instrument will be happy to buy it." Lonnie leaned the horn against the wall outside the room.

Corrine sat down on the bed. "The police think I had something to do with it."

"But you didn't. And, the detectives sounded like they're leaning toward suicide."

"I dropped that lighter out of the window. What if they figure that out?"

"It still doesn't mean you killed him. You didn't ignite the lighter."

"I saw the lighter smash the windshield. What if it knocked Angelo out and that's why he didn't escape?"

"You mean escape setting himself on fire—which you couldn't have known he would do, which he couldn't have done in the first place if he was knocked out? That doesn't make any sense."

"I know I sound crazy, but ever since that visit from the detectives, I'm afraid to open the door or to answer my phone. It's like I'm expecting Angelo to come back."

"The only way Angelo Fallon's coming back is if you keep letting him inside your head."

The door chimes rang and Corrine jumped at the sound. "Who could that be?" She bit the corner of a fingernail.

Lonnie opened the door and Jasmina walked in with Leo pulling a large, flat box with a picture on the side of a laughing baby inside a colorful contraption.

"Look what we found!" Jasmina's excited voice drew Corrine out of the bedroom. "It's a baby gym! Having a kid is so much fun. We get to shop for toys that are more fun than any toys we had when we were kids." Corrine forced a smile and Jasmina immediately noticed the effort. "Hey, sweetie, what's wrong?"

"My nerves are a little on edge."

"She found Angelo's saxophone. The police didn't take it," Lonnie explained.

"Hey, don't worry about me," Corrine said with a nervous laugh. "Bring that box over here, Leo. I want to take a look at your toy." Corrine's cell phone buzzed from atop a glass table and she again gnawed at her fingernail. "Can you answer that for me, Lonnie?"

Jasmina put her arms gently around Corrine and patted her back. They heard Lonnie say, "Yes, Detective Hodges, she's right here."

With a shaking hand, Corrine took the phone from Lonnie. As she listened and nodded, everyone else in the room held their breath. "Thank you, detective," she said with finality, set the phone down, and collapsed onto the couch with her eyes shut and hand pressed against her heart.

"Well?" said Lonnie.

"Corrine?" said Jasmina.

"What's the verdict?" said Leo, then "Sorry, I mean, what did the detective say?"

Corrine sighed heavily and opened her eyes that were bright with tears. "The police think Angelo's death is a suicide, but the coroner won't officially call it that. He's ruling it accidental. The case is closed."

"Yes!" Lonnie and Jasmina shouted out at the same time, then both hugged Corrine and wiped the tears off her cheeks.

Jasmina pulled a white paper bag out of her sizable purse. "We also brought cookies and Hawaiian coffee. I'm going to make the coffee. We all deserve some time to relax."

A few minutes later they were gathered around the dining room table sipping coffee and munching on white chocolate macadamia nut cookies. No one spoke for several minutes.

"I know this sounds weird," Corrine said, "but until Detective Hodges told me the case was closed, it was like Angelo was still in control of my life. Now, no more looking over my shoulder. I can finally believe that it's over."

"He can't harm you or anyone else anymore," Jasmina said.

"Angelo Fallon is gone for good," Lonnie said.

The light fixture overhead surged with brilliance. The people seated at the table looked up in surprise, but I couldn't help adding my own punctuation to the moment.

Corrine stood up as if in a daze and moved toward the kitchen. Lonnie and Jasmina threw concerned glances at each other, then looked back at Corrine. "Where are you going, sweetie?" Lonnie asked. He and Jasmina followed her into the kitchen and watched her walk toward the back door that led to the roof.

"I have to go out," Corrine said, not turning around.

"Out where?" Jasmina asked. "Don't you want to put your coat on first?"

"I won't be outside long."

"But where?" Lonnie asked.

"I'm going to start at the top and walk through Big Blue and breathe in every sensational dust particle, hear every fantastic squeak in the floors, feel every rough edge and every smooth hollow, appreciate every incredible hinge and nail and each grain of grit that's held this place upright for sixty years. Funny, I've been around for sixty years, and I'm still standing, too. Big Blue and me, we make a great couple, don't you think?" She glanced back at Lonnie and Jasmina, but didn't wait for an answer.

I swung the back door open and Corrine took the exit to my roof. Her tennis-shoed feet left tracks in the shallow snow as she walked to the center. Her toes would feel the cold soon. The weak afternoon light was fading to muddy darkness. She turned in a slow circle, looking out over the city.

Blue and green Christmas lights dripped down the sides of the Marriott's top floors. A figure with a headlamp and skis strapped to the back of a bulky parka paused on the Cushman Street Bridge with a canine companion. The ice on the Chena River wasn't thick enough yet for skijoring. The figure and the dog moved on south, past a huddle of homeless people on the corner at First Avenue.

The open windows at Immaculate Conception Church released the sweet strains of a choir rehearsal. A group of workers atop the courthouse scurried around with flashlights, like children playing tag. Then a burst of hundreds of white lights revealed a Christmas tree topped with a blinking star in the center of the courthouse roof.

Two men tussled outside a Second Avenue bar under a neon sign with two of its five letters burnt out, making an "Oasis" an "_as_s." A snow shovel scraped the sidewalk in front of a shop on Third, and the metallic screeches bounced off the side of a building.

Brake lights made a string of red beads along the Steese Highway and Airport Way as traffic crawled from work to home. Here and there, a pulsating white light signaled a school bus bringing its precious cargo through. The perfume of birch wood burning in wood stoves and fireplaces drifted across downtown from the bordering neighborhoods.

"We made it through again, Blue," Corrine said, and I heard her thoughts continue: Just like last time. Jack was thinking about selling you to the city to pay his gambling debts. But I knew the city would tear you down if it got its hands on you, just to be rid of all the unsavory activity that went on here. You would have been gone and I would have had no place to call home. I told him I wouldn't sign as co-owner, that he would have to find some other way to get the money.

"I did it for us, Blue."

I can't tell you, Corrine, but Jack was thinking of another way, the insurance policy he had on you. Maybe he wouldn't have gone through with it, but I couldn't take a chance, as shady as he was. I saw pictures run through his mind of the two of you on the roof, drinking wine at sunset, a romantic setting. But we know Jack wasn't romantic and in his thoughts you were near the roof edge, your back to him, looking into the blushing sky.

That morning when you were out volunteering at the food bank and he was still in bed, I ejected all the bottles at once from the bathroom cabinet. They bounced against the mirror and clattered over the sink and floor.

The commotion jerked him out of his sleep and sent his fragile heart flip-flopping. He managed to crawl to the bathroom, tried to retrieve one of his nitroglycerin tablets to put under his tongue. The pill bottles were jumbled all over the floor. It was impossible to find the right one in the dark, and I made sure the light didn't work even though he made a valiant effort to reach the switch.

I did it for us, Corrine.

Corrine shivered in the damp, cold air–or maybe from a stray piece of the chilling memory that had just run through me—and pulled her knee-length sweater tighter around herself. It was almost time to go inside. With her toe, she drew a wide arc in the snow, a smile I showed to the sky, because we were together again.

After

Summer solstice 2014 is a big day for me. The temperatures are more normal this year, and no one is complaining except the newcomers from Texas and southern California lured up by better job prospects. It looks like fire season will be off to a calm start due to the recent heavy rains. This year the talk on the sidewalks and in the shops is about the rising Chena River and the Salcha and Goodpaster to the east that have already overflowed their banks.

Around town, the charismatic visitor from Louisiana is all but forgotten. The single-fatality car fire faded away long ago as a topic of conversation, even before the normal summer buzz about weather and fishing and who will sign up for next winter's Yukon Quest dog sled race.

Corrine brings the last tray of homemade snacks up to the rooftop party. There aren't any residents to attend this year, since I won't be ready for general occupancy until August. She's invited her closest friends and Anthony's work crews instead.

Jasmina is sunken into a lawn chair, her knees spread apart to accommodate her eight-month pregnant belly as Leo stands behind her, rubbing her shoulders. Lately, Jasmina refers to herself as Moby Dick, although she says she'll be back in her belly-dancing costume for this year's Golden Days Parade. I think she's never been so beautiful. I only see her when she's working at the refurbished Istanbul Coffee since she and Leo bought a house with a big yard off the Old Steese Highway.

The deluge of customers and Jasmina's swollen feet have necessitated the hiring of two young baristas, both named Heather, who work part-time during the week and full-time on weekends. She's set the grand opening of her second store for September.

A group of activists calling themselves "We Deserve Better" are pushing Leo to run for mayor. Henry Fornette was charged with misusing city funds for personal real estate deals and, after paying restitution, he was sent packing back to Louisiana.

Lonnie's fingers fly over his keyboard as the guests involuntarily rock to "That's the Way I Like It," the nineties hit by KC and the Sunshine Band. Lonnie spends most of his time in the music studio in his eleventh-floor condo when he's not on tour throughout Alaska, western Canada, and the Pacific Northwest with trumpeter Mack the Knife.

Mack is also one of Lonnie's lovers. The other is Darius Brown, a young drummer. The two men know about each other, but neither requires Lonnie to make a choice, and Lonnie's not ready to settle down even though he's retired from his business. Big Dipper Liquor is now Blue Vineyard, a hip wine bar owned by partners Jon and Jay.

Corrine, with sixteen pounds shed at the gym and flexibility restored through physical therapy and her renewed commitment to power yoga, weaves among her guests in a flowing teal dress. Her platinum hair glows under the evening sun and her blue eyes are dancing.

"Did you try the fish tacos? How about the mushrooms? You need a refill on that gin and tonic? How about a mimosa?" she sings out. "Anthony, do you need anything?"

"All I need is you by my side, angel," he answers, putting his arm around her waist.

The plaintive, sweet sound of a saxophone drifts up to the roof from a street musician cradling his second-hand instrument.

"No other place I'd rather be," she says, pressing her body into his side. In the past two months, Corrine has come to admire Anthony's talents between the sheets even more than his business vision. Still, though rejuvenated, she's not ready for a man to move in with her again.

All the condo units have been pre-sold, although Anthony's entire project won't be completed until the end of October. None of the remaining tenants could afford to buy, but Corrine waived their rent for the last few months and gave them time to relocate. Most were happy to leave the construction noise behind.

It's been quite a change for me, walls knocked out, new floors laid, rewiring, re-plumbing, new windows installed, fresh coats of paint. My outside is different, too. Only my first floor is blue, a deep, royal shade, and the other eleven are pale gold. Folks will continue to call me Big Blue, though. Tradition dies hard in this town.

I don't mind going through another makeover, as long as Corrine stays with me. She's the best thing that's happened to me in more than sixty years. I would shout that across the Alaska Range, if walls could talk.

CPSIA information can be obtained
at www.ICGtesting.com
Printed in the USA
FSOW02n1720130218
44287FS